BLOODLUST BLUES

BOOKS BY LUANNE BENNETT

THE FITHEACH TRILOGY

The Amulet Thief

The Blood Thief

The Destiny Thief

THE KATIE BISHOP SERIES

Crossroads of Bones

Blackthorn Grove

Shifter's Moon

Dark Nightingale

Bayou Kings

Conjure Queen

Dirt Witch

Daddy Darkest

HOUSE OF WINTERBORNE SERIES

Dark Legacy

Savage Sons

King's Reckoning

THE CHRONICLES OF JESSE AMES

Red Widow

Gods & Savages

Open Season

BLOODLUST BLUES

LUANNE BENNETT

SECOND SKY

Published by Second Sky in 2024

An imprint of Storyfire Ltd.
Carmelite House
50 Victoria Embankment
London EC4Y 0DZ
United Kingdom

www.secondskybooks.com

The authorised representative in the EEA is Hachette Ireland
8 Castlecourt Centre
Dublin 15 D15 XTP3
Ireland
(email: info@hbgi.ie)

ISBN: 978-1-83525-241-3
eBook ISBN: 978-1-83525-240-6

For those lost along the way.

ONE

I don't usually look up when someone walks into my bar, but something sparked my interest this time. A tickle in my throat. The hairs on the back of my neck standing erect. All those little things I'd learned to never ignore.

Tall and skinny with an unshaven face, a stranger entered and stopped, his eyes shifting around the room. And when I say stranger, I mean *stranger*. I knew everyone in Crimson, including most people's private business—what they did for a living, if they had a heavy hand with their spouse or children, who they were sleeping with. Tending bar gave folks around here the misguided idea that I was their therapist, so all their dirty little secrets made their way into my ears whether I wanted to hear them or not. But I'd never seen this guy before.

It was Thursday night, so it was slower than usual at the White Stag, simply known as the Stag to the locals. Slow enough for me to be tending bar solo. Most people were broke by now and waiting to get paid the next day so they could come in here and blow it all again. But since a high percentage of our customers are vampires, I usually cut them off before they get stupid. They like their alcohol, but they can be mean drunks, and no one wants an inebriated vampire running around town.

"Hey, Charley!"

Charley, short for Charlotte, was my preferred name. The only people who called me by my birth name were telemarketers and the IRS.

I pulled my eyes away from the stranger and looked at the customer bellowing my name from the other end of the bar. "I'm not deaf."

He slid his empty glass toward me. "Give me a refill."

I poured him another draft with my eyes fixed on the guy who was still standing near the door. He didn't sit well with me. I guess you could call it intuition. Slinging drinks at the Stag since I was old enough to legally do so qualified me to read people, and I was usually pretty damn accurate in my assessment of them. Or maybe I'd gotten it from my mother. She could sense trouble from a mile away, and she'd send it right back out the door before it had time to fester.

I inherited the bar from my mother when she died two years ago. She got in her car and left for work one day and never came home. They found her Chevy at the bottom of the river the next morning. The police report said her blood alcohol level was nearly twice the legal limit, but her death had always been suspicious to those who knew her well. In the twenty-eight years I've been on this earth, I could count on one hand how many times I'd seen Delia Underwood drink more than a single glass of wine, and even that was rare. For someone who owned a bar, she was cheerfully sober ninety-nine percent of the time, so drinking in her car on the way to work was utter horseshit.

And then there was her natural resistance to mind-altering substances. My mother was a witch, and not one of those palm-reading fakes. A real one.

When I glanced at the order window, my line cook, Dog,

who also doubled as the Stag's bouncer, was watching me staring at the guy by the door. The man's eyes darted around the room continuously, and his right hand kept dipping into his jacket pocket.

There was a question in Dog's eyes, but I shook my head for him to stay put in the kitchen. No need to start a ruckus with the guy. Yet.

The stranger finally moved when the front door opened and another customer nearly collided with him. He walked up to the bar and nudged between two regulars, quickly looking away when I caught him eyeing me. By the way he kept licking the corner of his mouth and rubbing his left hand against the bar, I could tell he was nervous. But he wasn't flashing a set of fangs, which a nervous vampire would be doing, so that was a plus. He was human. If he decided to do something stupid, like rob the place, he'd be sorely disappointed with the receipts from a slow Thursday night. But I had a feeling he wasn't here for the cash in the register.

"What can I get you?" I said as I walked up to him and steadied my eyes on his. He stared back at me without saying a word, and I noticed a bead of sweat getting ready to drip down the side of his face. "This isn't a bus stop, so buy a drink or there's the exit." I nodded to the front door.

Hearing my warning, the two customers sitting on either side of him grabbed their drinks and got up, making room for the shit that was about to hit the fan. I was definitely my mother's daughter, and everyone in the place knew it.

His jaw clenched as he reached into his pocket again but hesitated to pull his hand back out. "Where is it?" It was barely a whisper.

I glanced at Dog through the order window again before looking back at the guy. He was in a full sweat now, and he was starting to shake.

"Honey, you're going to have to be a little more specific than that."

He'd found his voice again, and now a gun was pointed at my face. "The blood!"

I figured that's what he was after. I was just hoping I was wrong.

Throwing my hands in the air, I backed up toward the shelf of liquor behind me. I could have grabbed one of the bottles and tried to slam it into his head, but I wasn't faster than a bullet.

"It's in the back room," I whispered, trying not to broadcast it.

He leaned over the bar and pressed the muzzle to my forehead, his hand shaking badly. "Then *fucking* go get it!"

"Okay, take it easy," I said, stepping back. "No offense, but you don't look so good." He looked like he was ready to collapse from whatever drugs he was on. Probably opioids. If I stalled, he just might.

I needed to get him into the back room with me, not only so Dog and I could foil his poorly thought-out robbery, but also to prevent the entire town from finding out by morning about our little side hustle back there. The vampire blood co-op.

"You do realize there's a door to the alley back there?" He just stared at me blankly. Did I have to spell it out for him? "What makes you think I won't take off through the alley?"

He muttered a few curse words and glanced at the handful of customers who'd corralled themselves into the back of the room only big enough to accommodate a few tables and chairs. "What about them?"

This guy was just plain stupid.

"Well, if we hurry, you can be out the back door before the cops show up." Crimson had a police force of three, so I wasn't holding my breath on them arriving anytime soon.

He waved his gun at me to take the lead. "Move!"

I hurried toward the hallway that led past the kitchen and down to the back room. The truth was, there was no blood back there. Unlike the idiot pointing a gun at my back, I wasn't stupid. The sale of vampire blood was illegal. Our next delivery wasn't scheduled until tomorrow night, and to stay one step ahead of the police, my partner never showed up with it until an hour before the members of the co-op were lining up in the alley to take delivery. No evidence, no crime.

A second after I walked through the door, Dog shoved me out of the way and snatched the gun out of the guy's hand. Piece of cake due to Dog's impressive size. There wasn't a man, woman, or child in Crimson stupid enough to take him on.

The guy lost his balance and hit the wall, letting out a sharp gasp when he saw his piece in Dog's hand. "You son of a—"

Dog waved the gun in front of the idiot's face. "Is that any way to talk to a man holding a loaded gun?"

"It ain't loaded," the guy said.

Dog opened the cylinder to take a look. "Well, will you look at that?" He chuckled. "It's empty."

I wanted to give the guy a piece of my mind right in the groin, but time was ticking. "What do we do with him now?" I said to Dog. "He knows about the co-op." Which brought up a more important question. "*How* do you know about the co-op?" It was like Fight Club. The first rule of the co-op was: you do not talk about the co-op.

Dog let out a steady breath. "I guess we need to kill him."

I played along. "Unless he talks." I cocked my head and gave him a pointed look. "Who told you about it?"

When he stood there pressed to the wall with his mouth zipped up tight, Dog headed for the desk next to the back door. "I think I've got some bullets around here somewhere."

The guy suddenly reached into his boot and pulled out a knife, charging at me while Dog had his back to us. I jumped out of the way and hit the floor, kicking him in the chest with the heel of my boot when he grabbed at me. He flew back against the wall, but the drugs must have given him a burst of adrenaline, as he came at me again.

Dog turned, shifting into a massive gray wolf. He was on top of the man a moment later, tearing at his arm until the knife flipped out of his hand and slid across the floor. I climbed to my feet and ran toward it. By the time I grabbed it and straightened up, Dog had already shifted back and was standing naked over the guy, watching him take a breath and then go still. I was pretty sure he was dead.

"Jesus, Dog. I didn't think you were serious about killing him."

He stared down at the lifeless junkie. "I wasn't. I broke his arm at best. Then he went limp right under me. I think he had a heart attack."

By the look in the guy's eyes and the way he had been shaking back in the bar, it didn't surprise me. "We need to get him out of here before the cops show up."

Dog grabbed his clothes off the floor and went into the kitchen to get his phone. When he came back, he was dressed and finishing up a call. He grabbed the guy and slung him over his shoulder like he weighed nothing, but Dog was a six-foot-five wolf shifter built like a linebacker. He was also the leader of the local pack, hence his name, which was short for Top Dog. His mundane name was Tommy Holt, but he answered to Dog unless he was sitting in front of a judge.

Clearly overqualified to flip burgers, Dog had nearly bitten my head off when I'd offered him an assistant manager job. He made it abundantly clear he had no interest in any form of management whatsoever. He just wanted to come to work, make a buck, and go home at the end of the day without taking his job with him. I could respect that. There were days when I wanted to leave it all behind myself. Like right now.

He headed for the back door. "The cops just pulled up. I'll get rid of this shitbag while you deal with them."

Before I could say anything, Dog slipped through the back door into the alley, and Rick Carter was calling my name from the bar area.

I straightened my shirt and hair and went back up front. "How's it going, Officer Carter?"

Rick Carter was standing by the bar with his gun drawn. He placed it back in its holster as he surveyed the room. Then he brought his eyes back around to mine. "What happened, Charley? We got a handful of calls saying the Stag was being held up."

And it only took you twenty minutes to get here. I kept the comment to myself, grateful for Crimson PD's turtle-like speed. Other than occasional disputes between vampires and humans or vandalism calls, we didn't have a lot of serious crime around here. Nothing major. This was probably the most excitement Rick Carter had seen in years.

"It was nothing. Just some lowlife addict with a gun, but Dog managed to chase him out. Everything's fine now, so there's no need to take a report." I let out a chuckle for effect. "The gun wasn't even loaded."

Carter narrowed his eyes. "Oh yeah? How do you know that?"

"Because he dropped it on his way out." Anticipating his next request, I told him to wait a second and went back to get it. If he followed me, I'd have a hell of a time explaining the blood on the floor from where Dog had nearly chewed the guy's arm off. I handed it to him as I walked back out.

"Damn it, Charley. Your prints are all over it now." He pulled a handkerchief from his pocket before taking it from me.

"Sorry. Dog touched it too. I guess we weren't thinking."

He looked around the bar. "And where exactly is Dog?"

"He went out to make sure the guy wasn't still hanging around town."

Carter still had a skeptical look on his face. "Did he look familiar?"

"I never saw him before. I'm sure he's long gone by now." Six feet under to be exact.

Carter scribbled something on his notepad and stuffed it back in his pocket. "All right. If I have any more questions, I'll stop by tomorrow. You need to lock the front door after I leave."

"Will do." I smiled and waited for him to walk out before he got curious and decided to take a look around like a normal cop would. But this was Crimson. Normal was optional.

He had one foot out the door when he turned around. "What's this about blood?"

"Blood?" I needed to think fast. "What do you mean?"

"One of the witnesses heard the man mention blood. In fact, he said the suspect demanded it from you." His eyes narrowed again.

"Like I said, he looked like an addict." Crimson had seen its share of drugs creep into the community over the past decade, and vampire blood had become the drug of choice for both good and bad reasons. "Money, drink, drugs. He was looking for anything he could get his hands on. That's all."

After a moment of awkward silence, I moved the conversation along. "It's getting late, and I'd like to straighten up and get out of here. So if you don't mind..."

He nodded and continued out the door. "You have a good night, Charley. Be safe."

"You too."

I took his advice and locked the door behind him. Then I went into the back to clean up any evidence on the floor, wondering where that body would end up tonight.

Now we were talking *bodies*?

Our endeavor had just gone from community service to

something deadly. Something that came with the threat of finding a gun pointed at my face. A powder keg that could unbalance the tightrope of tolerance this town had been walking, if certain humans got wind of what we were doing. The one thing I knew with absolute certainty was that we were all in for a dangerous ride.

TWO

After the events at the bar last night, I spent half the afternoon obsessing over who could have opened their mouth about the co-op, when I should have been cleaning my house. The other half was spent worrying about the blood deliveries tonight. I'd probably look at every stranger who walked into the Stag as a possible threat for the foreseeable future.

Something hit the floor in the kitchen. When I went to see what it was, I spotted a box of cereal on the floor, and my eyes landed on top of the refrigerator. I pointed my finger at Rex. "Don't. You. Dare."

He turned his glossy black eyes to mine and cocked his head. The second I took a step toward him, he flapped his wings, knocking over the mason jar next to him. It rolled, thankfully stopping at the edge of the refrigerator. But the coins inside cascaded out and hit the floor in a spray of copper and silver. Rex cawed and flew down, grabbing a shiny quarter with his beak before heading for the open window.

"You *better* get out of here!" I watched him fly up into a tree. Then I grabbed a broom and started sweeping up the coins. Never a dull moment living with a crow.

Rex—short for T-Rex—had a loud mouth and a single white feather in the middle of his right wing. He adopted me when both his parents were killed by some moron with a gun. The three of them used to perch up in that same tree he'd just flown into, and he'd squawk at Mom and Dad for hours. I intervened before the guy had a chance to shoot a third round into Rex.

Outside of hunting season, crows were protected under the Migratory Bird Treaty Act. Believe me, I would have delivered the bastard to the county sheriff myself if he hadn't taken off when I ran toward his truck. Just another redneck driving around looking for target practice. After that, I took care of Rex until he was self-sufficient, feeding him a mixture of hard-boiled eggs, dog food, and cereal. Now he refused to leave. I guess he preferred me over other crows.

I decided to leave the mess on the floor and walked out the door because I was late getting to the Stag. After climbing into my old pickup, I stuck my head out the window and looked up at Rex in the tree overhead. "Stay out of trouble."

The quarter dropped, bouncing off the hood as he took off from the tree limb and sailed over the garage.

I lived about ten minutes outside of town in the farmhouse I grew up in. The one my mother left me. It was built in 1915 and had a lot of charm. It also had a roof that was a hard wind away from a major leak and noisy old plumbing. But it sat on two acres of land, giving me privacy. Nothing worse than staring into your neighbor's house every time you looked out your window.

My closest neighbor, Mr. Craven, often entertained at all hours of the night, which was typical for a vampire. Occasionally, I saw him working in his garden early in the morning or at dusk.

Contrary to what most people thought, not all vampires combusted the second a tiny bit of sunlight hit their skin. It was no different than humans getting a sunburn versus a tan. They were all different, although basking in strong sunlight wasn't advised for any of them.

There were two types of vampires in Crimson: the kind that could go about their business by adjusting their schedules around the sun's peak rays, and those who were more sensitive and lived in the shadows, only coming out of their homes at night. Either way, the sun could serve as a cautionary tale. Take the Wilsons down the road, for example. Janice Wilson got herself into a predicament a couple of years ago in town. She fell asleep in her car after drinking herself into oblivion. They found her the next morning, half-dead and withered, with the sun nearly burning a hole straight through her face. She survived, but to this day she was scarred from the ordeal. Half her face was gone.

Vampires really shouldn't drink, but they sure like their alcohol.

I passed the colorful sign on the state road that said WELCOME TO CRIMSON. Anyone who continued into town was entering a place where the worlds met. A place where you could get a hamburger cooked by a shifter or a beer served to you by a witch. You could even get your hair cut by a vampire. Crimson, Georgia, was home to all kinds of supernatural types, and they were the norm around here. Of course, there were humans too. My father was human. Family life wasn't his thing, it seems. So, with my mother's blessing, he left town before I was born, then he never bothered to come back. It was probably for the best.

A human actually founded the town in 1892, but it quickly became a mecca for witches. Next had come the vampires, which now made up the highest percentage of the population after humans. For the most part, people were civil to each other, but we had a few bigots in town who preferred to avoid anyone of the supernatural persuasion.

It was Friday evening, the start of a busy weekend at the Stag. Within the hour, the citizens of Crimson would be lined up in the back alley to pick up their pre-orders of vampire blood, and I'd make sure every last one of them got what they needed whether it was legal or not.

It was six p.m. by the time I got there. I usually tried to get in earlier when Lucy was working because I knew without even walking inside that the bar probably hadn't been properly prepped for one of our busiest nights of the week.

I pulled into my parking space directly in front of the large stag head over the bar's front door. My mother had the head commissioned by a wood carver years ago when she opened the place. Originally painted white, it was now covered with layers of colorful graffiti. It's become a rite of passage for the students of Crimson High, an annual tradition. Every year, a graduating senior makes his way up there to leave a mark for the class.

The front door flew open before I could reach for the handle, and out stumbled Bill Meadows, one of my regulars, nearly taking me down with him when he lost his balance and careered toward the street.

"Whoa!" I stepped aside and tried to grab his arm, but he slipped through my fingers and crashed into the hood of my truck. Lucky for him it didn't leave a dent.

Dog came through the door with Lucy right behind him. She had her hands planted on her hips and a growl in her voice. "You ever say that to me again, I'll knock your teeth out!"

Well, okay. We were starting off the evening with a bang.

I glanced at Bill, who was rubbing his shoulder, and then at my employees. "Will someone tell me what's going on?"

Lucy's eyes were shooting daggers. "I bent down to pick up a bin of glasses, and that idiot was hanging over the bar getting an eyeful of my ass!" She tugged at her short skirt to pull it down an inch. "Then he told me he wanted to lick it!" You didn't want to piss Lucy off. She was small but mean and came from one of Crimson's more notorious families. The Wyatts. The kind of folks you didn't want to mess with. The males in the family were wolves, but the family legacy somehow skipped the females. Still, she'd probably learned how to beat the crap out of someone by the age of three, with her brothers nipping at her all the time.

I picked up Bill's baseball cap that had flown off his head and landed next to my feet. "Go home, Bill."

"Come on, Charley." He snatched his hat back. "It's not like I grabbed her. And she was asking for it, wearing that napkin disguised as a skirt."

Man, the restraint I had to practice sometimes to keep myself from getting arrested.

Dog flashed his amber eyes at Bill and took a step toward him, his long black braid swaying like a snake against his back.

I nodded to the metal spatula gripped tightly in his hand. "What are you planning to do with that? Flip him to death?"

A low growl came from Dog's throat, followed by a menacing grin. "I just might."

Dog's impressive size was enough to scare anyone, and that's all he was trying to do. For Bill's sake more than Lucy's.

Turning back to my foolish customer, I gave him something to pray on. "You better hope she doesn't tell her brothers about this." They'd bust him up just for looking at her wrong. Good thing he didn't touch her. Then he'd be dead.

Bill put his hat back on his head, glaring at the three of us with defiance in his eyes. He wasn't a bad guy, and he'd been a customer for a long time. Divorced for several years, he lived back home with his mother now and kept his nose clean. Although he was a bit of a cheapskate who sometimes needed to be reminded to pay his tab.

Lucy glared back at him with a smirk. "Yeah, you better run home to your mama."

"That's enough," I said. "It's over." I motioned for Lucy to go back inside so I could have a word with Dog.

"You don't need to know," he said before I could ask what he'd done with the body. "No one's ever going to have to look at his sorry face again."

"I feel so much better now." I actually did. If you wanted to get rid of a body, the pack was your best option.

"What happened with Carter?" he asked.

I shrugged. "The usual. Nothing."

"Good. Let's forget this ever happened."

I followed him inside and looked around the place. As expected, none of the prep work had been done. The peanut bowls on the bar were empty and the floor was a mess. "Can you pretend to actually work here and grab a mop?" I said to Lucy when she walked behind the bar. If she didn't mix a mean drink and show up on time most days, I'd start looking for a new bartender.

The Stag was small, but I preferred to think of it as intimate. The back wall looked like a New York City subway car, with graffiti and signatures covering every inch of it. Like that stag head above the entrance. My mother had started the tradition by inviting customers to put their names on the wall, making the bar a living register of just about everyone who'd ever set foot in the place.

First and foremost, the White Stag was a bar. We offered a limited menu of casual food like burgers and fries, but there were no waitstaff. If you weren't sitting at the bar, you seated yourself and picked up your order when your name was called.

When Lucy grabbed a dry mop and started sluggishly moving it across the floor, I took it from her. "I'll do it myself. Can you at least wipe down the bar? All this should have been done already." I would have done most of it myself before leaving last night, but I was busy fending off a clusterfuck of a robbery and too tired to deal with cleaning anything but all that blood in the back room.

The Stag had three bartenders—Lucy, Beau, and me. Beau was late. As usual.

When the front door opened, I turned around expecting to see Beau walk in. But it wasn't him. It was someone with a delivery that really shouldn't have been coming through the front door. "Get that bag out of here." I nodded to the hallway and handed the mop back to Lucy. "I'll be back in a few minutes. Have Beau finish mopping when he gets here."

Dog glanced at the vampire through the order window and shook his head. Everyone knew the rules about deliveries, but apparently this guy hadn't gotten the memo. But since he had no business walking in here with a bag of vampire blood in the first place, his lack of etiquette was no surprise.

When we reached the back room, I nearly chewed his head off. "Are you trying to get us shut down?" I ran my hands over my face before grabbing the conspicuous bag from him. Was it a mesh laundry bag? A plastic container of blood was clearly visible through it for the entire world to see. "Well?"

He shrugged. "Well, what?"

"Never mind." I knew the guy, but he wasn't a member of the co-op. I examined the deli container filled with crimson liquid. "What's your name again?"

"Kenny."

"Well, *Kenny*, where'd you get this, and who told you to bring it in here?" Suddenly the whole damn world seemed to know about us, and I needed to find out who was running their mouth.

He looked half-bewildered, like walking down the street with it was normal. "It's mine. I heard you pay cash for blood."

"From who?"

"Just talk down in Little Crimson."

Little Crimson was an area just outside of town known for

its high vampire population. It wasn't that humans weren't welcome there. They just preferred not to reside next door to others who lived their lives mostly after dark. Too much noise and goings-on in the middle of the night wasn't for everyone, unless you *were* a vampire or an extreme night owl. It was a culture clash more than anything that segregated the residents of Little Crimson from *Big Crimson*, which was how vampires referred to the rest of the town.

But that didn't give every vampire in Crimson an invitation to drop by with a bag of blood whenever they were short on cash. You had to be a member of the co-op to "donate." We had a strict vetting process.

We weren't drug dealers. We provided a public service. Like most places in the country, there were a lot of people in town—both humans and otherwise—who had fallen on hard times. Many of them were forced to go without health insurance. And there were others who couldn't get relief from conventional medicine.

My friend Patrick had suggested it. Vampire blood was good for everything from weight loss to arthritis, and those suffering from cancer and other major illnesses needed relief from debilitating pain. But what locked in my decision to open the co-op was the memory of watching Patrick suffer. He'd gotten hooked on prescription painkillers from a shoulder injury. The drugs nearly killed him. When nothing else worked to clean him up, he found a vampire to turn him. It cured his addiction. Short of turning every suffering person in town, vampire blood therapy was the next best thing.

So, the co-op was born. The humans in Crimson got affordable, non-addictive relief for what ailed them, and the vampires got a little extra income to help keep the lights on. I took a small cut to cover my expenses, but I didn't do it for the money. The bar brought in enough to afford me a decent living. Everyone was happy, and we were fulfilling a real need in the community.

Our only concern was the risk of being raided by the Crimson PD. Well, *raided* was an exaggeration. With only three officers, including the chief, it wasn't very hard to operate right under their noses. But if word kept getting out, it could land us in jail. Vampire blood is classified as a Schedule 1 drug. A move initiated by the pharmaceutical industry a few years back when it started to cut into their profits on a national level. We stayed one step ahead of the authorities by only keeping enough on hand to fulfill orders at any given time, usually once a week, and we changed our delivery dates often just in case. In order to sell or purchase blood, you had to be a member of the co-op, and that required a thorough vetting process, which was a problem for the vampire standing in front of me right now.

"Have you even been tested?" I asked Kenny. Members were only allowed to donate twice a month, and it required being tested for certain blood-borne pathogens within twenty-four hours. Vampires might not suffer from the diseases they contracted while feeding, but humans sure did. If you wanted to be a part of the co-op, you had to be squeaky clean. Conveniently, one of our members was a local doctor who served as our official tester. He also referred many of his own patients to us.

"I'm clean."

"Good. Stop by Monday night and fill out the proper paperwork. If you check out, we might be able to do business together." I grabbed a paper bag from the desk and stuck the container in it before handing it back to him. "Now, get this out of here, and don't ever walk through my front door with blood again. Understand?"

He glanced at the bag. "What am I supposed to do with it?"

"Pour it down your kitchen sink for all I care. You're not selling it here until you've been screened."

I glanced at the time and started to get nervous. Co-op

members would be lining up soon, and our supply hadn't gotten here yet.

"It's time for you to leave." I opened the door to the alley to show him out. Patrick finally arrived as Kenny was walking down the steps. "You're late," I said as he walked inside.

He ignored me and glanced back at the door. "What the hell was Kenny doing here?"

"Trying to sell me a deli container full of blood."

He dropped his chin to look at me over his unnecessary sunglasses. "Seriously?"

I'd called him that afternoon to tell him about the incident last night, so Kenny showing up was just another confirmation that we needed to tighten up around here. "Do I look like I'm joking? You need to find out who Kenny's been talking to."

"I'm on it."

He was wearing a bright orange shirt that nobody else in town would have been caught dead in, and his curly black hair was coiffed into a smooth wave on top of his head. "You're going to blind the members with that shirt, and you might want to go easy on the product next time."

He smoothed the sides of his hair. "Baby, I look good. Why don't you take the night off and come out with me."

"I can't just leave, Patrick. Someday you'll grow up and learn about a thing called *responsibilities*."

"Suit yourself." He set the briefcase on the desk and opened it. It contained multiple rows of plastic vials taped to the sides to prevent them from getting jumbled around inside. Enough blood for each customer who had pre-ordered. He removed the tape but kept them inside the case. There were a hundred and six vials at a cost of ninety-five dollars each. A bargain considering it only took a few drops to ease suffering, so a vial went a long way. On the street, they would have gone for three hundred each. Down in Atlanta, close to a thousand.

Mabel Gentry walked up and knocked on the doorframe.

"I'm a few minutes early, but I was hoping I could get my blood now." Her right hand was shaking, and she kept shifting her weight from one foot to the other. Mabel was in her fifties and she'd never had children, but she looked much older. Her husband had died three years back and left her with a small pension, which was something. She was fighting to get her disability, but that could take years. At least the house was paid off.

"Of course. Come inside." I pulled up a chair so she could sit down.

Her fingers were knobbly and stiff from rheumatoid arthritis, making it painful for me to watch as she struggled to unsnap her wallet. She handed me a fifty, two twenties, and then started to reach for a bunch of change on the side.

"You know what?" I said to her. "We're running a special this week. Seventy-five dollars a vial."

Patrick gave me a funny look, but I shook my head discreetly.

"Really?" There was a brief light in her eyes. "That's a nice surprise."

I gave her one of the twenties back and told her we were good. After handing her a vial, I walked her to the door. "I'll see you in a few weeks, Mabel. You get home safe."

Patrick was still giving me that look when I turned around. "You're a real bleeding heart, Charley, but you ain't gonna be feeling so generous when folks start expecting that every week. We need to pay for that product. And we're already a lot cheaper than what she'd be paying for a month's supply of her pills down at the pharmacy."

I went over to the desk and pulled twenty-five dollars from the drawer and tossed it into the briefcase. "The woman probably doesn't have food in her house. But don't worry, I get it. I can't afford to make it a habit."

"Girl, you can't save the whole world."

After staring at him for a moment and holding my tongue, I decided to go see if Beau had shown up yet. He was a good worker, but he was always a few minutes late. "Can you take care of this tonight without me? I need to find my missing bartender before the rush starts."

"Yeah, I've got it. Go take care of your business." Patrick reached into his pocket and pulled out a small glass jar, keeping it at the ready as he walked over to the door and looked out. Those blood vials were made of plastic for a reason. If the cops ever rounded the corner in the alley and tried to catch us in the act, Patrick had a handy little acid bomb that would turn the evidence into a pile of sizzling goo before they ever made it inside. And there was a button under the bar up front that would activate a red light in the back room if the cops ever came charging in through the Stag's front door. We all protected the co-op, and my employees knew when to use that button. But on top of the police, now we had to worry about lowlifes trying to rob us. Our side hustle was getting riskier by the day, and I had a feeling our duct-taped security system would need to be upgraded before long.

When I walked back up front, Lucy was nowhere to be seen, but Beau was stocking up on clean glasses behind the bar and the floor was slightly wet from a fresh mopping. If I could combine the two, I'd have the perfect employee.

I noticed a distinct hint of highlights in his brown hair, and it looked freshly cut and styled. "So that's why you're late," I said. "Had to get yourself pretty for the weekend. Where's Lucy?"

"I'm eating my dinner," Lucy said from behind me.

She'd come out from the kitchen with half a sandwich in one hand and a bottle of beer in the other.

"You know you're not allowed to drink on the clock."

Her brow formed into an irritated twist. "This ain't drinking." Turning the bottle up to finish it, she walked behind the bar and tossed it in the trash before grabbing a rag to actually do some work. "It ain't drinking until I've knocked back at least a six-pack."

"I should fire you."

She stopped wiping down the bar and put her hands on her hips, pinning me with a stare. "Don't do me any favors."

She was a handful, but Crimson didn't exactly have a large pool of job applicants looking for bartender work. And the ones who did want the job came with just as much baggage as Lucy Wyatt. Besides, I'd known her since grade school. She was rough around the edges, but she was also honest and loyal. Someone could drop a fifty on the floor and she'd go out of her way to find out who it belonged to. And God help anyone who walked in here and badmouthed me behind my back. I could live with her bad habits, as long as she didn't cross a certain line.

Beau was a different bird entirely. A Southern boy through and through. A former football jock without a mean bone in his body. Other than his chronic tardiness, he was easy. Although he did spend an awful lot of time staring at himself in the mirror that ran along the back wall behind the bar, like he was doing right now.

"Are you finished looking at yourself?" I said to him.

Dog came out from the kitchen and set a tub of freshly cleaned glasses behind the bar. "Don't look at yourself too hard," he warned Beau. "It's disrespectful to the spirits in the mirror. They'll gouge your eyes out while you're sleeping."

Beau chuckled and shifted his eyes to Dog. "You're kidding, right?"

"I don't know," I said. "If anyone knows about spirits, it's Dog." Being our resident expert on skinwalkers and other Native American lore, it was hard not to wonder to what degree he was messing with Beau. And mirror scrying was an ancient form of magic in many cultures and practices.

Beau looked over his shoulder at me as his smile returned.

"You want me to look good for the ladies tonight, don't you?" Then he turned back around to fuss with his hair again.

Curious about those spirits, I looked back at the long mirror just as a car outside came into view in the reflection. It was driving past the bar, but the angle wasn't right. Instead of seeing a side view of the vehicle, I was staring at its front end. At its headlights. It had swerved, and it was careering straight toward the Stag.

THREE

I turned and froze, fixing my eyes on the car coming straight toward the building. Everything seemed to move in slow motion. Even the sound in my ears lowered to a whisper. And then a surge of energy raced through my veins, radiating from every pore in my body as a blinding light appeared in front of me. Outside, in front of the bar.

The car flipped, clipping the tail end of my truck before ricocheting back out into the street.

Beau was yelling at me somewhere in the room, and the next thing I knew, he was on top of me as I hit the floor.

I pushed him off me and climbed to my feet, my heart racing as I looked around the room to make sure I wasn't seeing things. The bar hadn't been touched, and the car was upside down in the middle of the street.

"Call 911!" I yelled to anyone listening before running toward the door. Beau and Dog were right behind me when I ran out into the street to check on the driver. A woman I'd never seen before was trapped inside the car, suspended upside down by her seatbelt. She was barely breathing and bleeding profusely from a large gash on her forehead.

"Is she alive?" Beau asked.

"Barely." A crowd was starting to gather. "Patrick's in the back. Go tell him to close up shop before the cops get here." I grabbed his arm when he turned to run back inside. "Get one of those vials while you're back there and bring it to me."

He stood there looking at me like my words hadn't registered.

"Now!"

That did the trick.

With the nearest hospital one town over, it would take at least ten or fifteen minutes for an ambulance to arrive. But the woman was running out of time, and Crimson PD would be showing up at any moment.

The woman's breathing suddenly stopped. "She's going to die if we don't get her out of the car and get some vampire blood into her," I said to Dog. When I struggled to release her seatbelt, Dog pushed me aside and yanked it free, pulling the woman through the window.

Beau came running back out a moment later and handed me the vial. "Patrick cleared out."

I held it to the woman's mouth, making sure no one saw it. The blood coated her lips and started to drip down her chin as sirens sounded in the distance. "Come on, lady, swallow." It wasn't wise to take such a large dose all at once, the results were... unpredictable. But the alternative was worse. She was a dead woman if I didn't get some of it down her throat.

With a violent lurch, the woman suddenly gasped, choking down the vampire blood as her eyelids flipped open.

"You're okay," I told her. "You were in a car accident, but the ambulance is on the way."

She rolled her head toward me. A second later, her fingers were wrapped around the collar of my shirt, yanking me down to her face. Her skin began to flush bright red, and there was wildness in her eyes as if she was pleading with me to help her.

It was the blood. The high dose was doing a number on her head.

Her grip tightened, and my shirt started to dig into my neck. "Let go of me!"

A grunt came from her mouth as her eyes grew wider. The harder I tried to pull away, the tighter she gripped, the blood making her strong as an ox. I was starting to panic as my breathing suffered.

The veins in her neck bulged, and her mouth gaped like a baby bird. "Help... me!"

Dog pried her hands away from my shirt and pinned her to the ground. "Are you okay?" he asked me.

"I am now."

The police finally arrived and took over.

Dog looked me square in the eye. "What the hell just happened?"

"I don't know, but we're coming up on a full moon." It had been a strange week, and my adrenaline was coursing painfully through my veins.

Tom Murphy, Crimson's other officer, was walking our way with a notepad in his hand. I couldn't think straight, let alone give a statement. "Can you stick around and talk to Murphy? I need to walk it off."

"Is it happening to you again?"

"You didn't see the light?" It had looked like half a dozen flares going off in the street to my eyes.

"Light?" He cocked his head. "No. I just saw that car flip."

I'd been having weird spells, for lack of a better way to describe them. Adrenaline rushes that would have me buzzing like a live wire. It was normal to have a reaction like that when a car nearly took out your bar and everyone in it, but this time it was different. Much more intense.

Before Murphy could corner me, I slipped into the crowd

that had gathered and walked down the sidewalk. It felt like a swarm of bees was swimming through my veins and making me want to puke. Wouldn't that be a lovely sight?

After making it to the end of the town square, I crossed the street and started to walk back up the other side. I spotted Candy on the block up ahead. She was sitting in one of the wicker chairs she'd placed in front of her shop, watching the spectacle in front of the Stag.

I reached her shop and sat down in the chair next to hers, my haywire adrenaline suddenly settling. "What a night, and it's only seven o'clock."

An ambulance flew past us as she took a drag of her cigarette and blew the smoke out slowly into the evening air. "I guess so."

"When are you going to quit that?" I would have mentioned for the tenth time how bad it was for her, but a witch didn't have to worry about lung disease any more than a vampire needed to fear hepatitis, so she'd just ignore me.

After taking another drag, she studied the cigarette between her fingers. "You're right." Then she snuffed it out with her shoe and tossed it into the trash can on the sidewalk.

If only it were that easy for the rest of the population.

She nodded toward the flashing lights. "Is that your doing?"

"The accident? Some woman lost control of her car and nearly drove it straight into the Stag."

"I guess that would have really ruined your night." She uncrossed her legs and stood up, winking at me. "Why don't you come inside so we can have us a visit. I haven't seen you in a while."

I was just here yesterday.

Candy was my mother's best friend and the biggest believer that Delia Underwood's death wasn't an accident. Like my mother, she was a real witch. A bona fide, card-carrying spell queen. Not one of those tarot-reading charlatans looking for a town full of suckers to hang a shingle and run a racket. Although she does offer tarot readings to people who come through Crimson on their way up to the hiking trails in the mountains. No one complains about the tourists, though. The extra traffic brings in a nice chunk of revenue for the town.

I was just a teenager when Candy arrived in Crimson, fourteen years ago. I'd never seen anything like her. She was larger than life, with her long red ponytail and knee-high boots with five-inch heels. She wore thick black eyeliner that made her eyes turn up at the outer edges like a cat's, and she had a tattoo of the goddess Hecate in the hollow of her neck. It must have hurt like hell to have it applied. I had to get to know this creature. My mother was just as fascinated, but the rest of Crimson's witches were less than welcoming. To them she was just a washed-up stripper from Atlanta who'd planned poorly for retirement and needed some rinky-dink town to go off and die in. They were wrong. She *was* an ex-stripper, but she had more magic in her fake eyelashes than most of them had in their power finger.

Walking through the veil of hot-pink beads strung across the entryway, I followed her inside. Hecate's Cauldron was an interesting place. As many times as I'd been in her shop over the years, there was always something new to catch my eye. The display case along the left wall housed the most fascinating items, and there was an oversized hourglass on top of it counting down the sand grains inside.

I noticed a strange object in the case. "Is that a—?"

"Mummified penis? Go on. You can say it. It's not going to jump out at you." She leaned her hip against the case and grinned. "Does wonders in a potency spell."

"I bet it does." She kept staring at me. "What?"

"I was just thinking about your mama. You have a good eye

like she did." She glanced at the phallic object. "Most people would have just seen a shriveled-up piece of beef jerky in that case. But not you."

It did kind of look like that.

She sighed heavily. "Every time I look at you, it makes me miss her even more."

At fifty-seven, Candy could still work a pole as agilely as a woman half her age. In fact, she had one installed in the corner of the shop shortly after opening for business, to remind folks that she was proud of who she was. It also made the human women in town keep a close eye on their men. But there wasn't a man in Crimson worthy of a glance from her. Candy didn't have much of a taste for humans anyway. She preferred her men with a bite, and there were plenty of wolves and vampires in town to satisfy her needs.

A banging sound came from somewhere in the shop, and I could hear a muffled voice beyond the walls. "What's that noise?" I listened for it again.

Her eyes darted to the door at the other end of the room. "Must be rats."

"Rats, my ass. Who's in there?"

Candy had a little side hustle of her own going on. Therapy work, as she called it. We didn't talk about it, but it was nothing illegal. At least I didn't think it was.

A wide smile spread across her face as she winked at me. "Don't you worry about that." She glanced at the hourglass on the display case. "My session is about up, honey, so you need to be on your way." She shooed me toward the door, locking it behind me as she pulled down the shade. Why she bothered was beyond me because I could still see inside through the front window.

After watching Candy disappear through that door in the back of her shop, I crossed the street and went back down the sidewalk toward the commotion, hoping Tom Murphy was finished taking Dog's statement and long gone. I tried to avoid the man as much as possible.

The ambulance passed me as I was walking up to Dog. He was standing in front of the bar watching a tow truck hitch up the woman's car. "You don't just swerve out of control and flip your car doing fifteen miles per hour unless you're on your phone or doing something else distracting."

Dog grunted. "Unless she was speeding."

God help anyone who violated the strictly enforced speed limit around the square.

I spotted Tom Murphy heading our way. He was looking right at me, so I couldn't escape.

Dog followed my gaze and pointed his thumb over his shoulder. "I need to prep the kitchen, so you're on your own this time."

"Thanks." I stuck my hands in my pockets and got ready for an unpleasant conversation. Murphy gave me a headache.

"Are you avoiding me, Charley?" Murphy asked when he caught up to me.

"Why would I do that?"

"Sure looks like you are." He stared at me for a few uncomfortable seconds. "I heard you had some trouble last night, and then this comes along."

Carter must have given him an earful. "Last night was nothing we couldn't handle. It wasn't even worth Officer Carter's time."

He dropped it and glanced over my shoulder toward Hecate's Cauldron. "I saw you coming out of Candy's place."

And so it begins.

"Can we move this along? I've got a bar to run."

Murphy dated my mother for a while when I was a teenager. He was controlling and made her miserable. Though I'd never witnessed it, I suspected he'd put his hands on her once or twice. It was Candy who finally convinced her to dump him. How a guy like Tom Murphy ever got his hooks into a witch like Delia Underwood was a mystery to both of us. He'd resented Candy ever since. That was a long time ago, even if he acted like it was yesterday. The man was delusional and thought he had some warped parental right to tell me what to do.

When he stood there staring at me, I lost my patience. "I'm twenty-eight years old, Tom. You need to stay out of my business."

He glanced back at the car being towed away. "That right there is police business, and I have a few questions for you."

I looked at the time. "You've got five minutes."

"You can start by telling me what happened."

"I looked out the front window and saw a car barreling toward the Stag. A second later, it stopped dead and flipped. Then it slid sideways out into the street. That's it."

He eyed me closely. "Don't you think that's a little odd?"

"This is Crimson, Tom. Everything around here is odd. By the way, I'm going to need that woman's insurance information." I nodded to my truck. "She clipped me pretty good when her car flipped." It was an old pickup, but that dent in the side was getting fixed.

"It'll be on the accident report." He scribbled something down. "The victim gave us a different account of what happened."

That's all I needed. A *he said, she said* with the insurance companies. But I had witnesses. "You're telling me the woman who just got taken away in an ambulance was lucid enough to give a statement?"

"Lucid? No, not exactly. She was rambling like she was high as a kite."

That's because she was.

I deadpanned him. "I rest my case. Maybe you should test

her for amphetamines. That would explain her trying to drive her car into my bar." Vampire blood was undetectable, so I didn't have to worry about that.

"Mm-hmm." He squinted at me for a moment before letting out a steady breath. "Helen Stovall. She lives just over the state line in South Carolina. Said she was compelled to get into her car and drive, but after she got on the road, she has no memory of how she got to Crimson."

"It sounds like she needs a shrink." I was getting antsier by the minute. I had customers to serve, and I needed to call Patrick to see about getting our *other* customers taken care of. For all I knew, they were already lined up in the alley wondering what was going on. "Why are you telling me all this?"

He got an uncomfortable look on his face. "Because she said that voice in her head told her to drive straight into your bar."

"Like I said, she needs a shrink."

"Maybe, but stranger things have happened in this town. I just thought I'd let you know before you read it on the accident report."

"I appreciate that. Can I go now?"

He stuffed his notepad in his pocket and nodded. "I'll have the official report ready by morning. You can stop by the station and pick up a copy."

This entire week had been one I preferred to be done with, ending with a woman trying to drive her car straight through my bar—on purpose. Not to mention what had happened to that car. Something had stopped it, and that light had come from me. I could feel it in my bones. Maybe it was time to seriously consider what Candy was always telling me—that I was just like my mother.

After ending the conversation with Murphy, I went back into the Stag and watched through the window to make sure he didn't decide to follow me inside. Satisfied that he was gone, I headed for the back room to call Patrick. I stuck my head out into the alley and found it empty, but I could feel eyes on me. The unmistakable sensation of someone, or something, watching me.

I walked down the steps and scanned the narrow corridor, paying particular attention to the large dumpster on the right. "Is anyone out here?"

Something brushed against my legs, and I nearly jumped out of my skin. It was a cat, and a sorry-looking one at that. An orange tabby that looked like it hadn't had a good meal in a while. One of its eyes was half shut.

"Who are you?" I half expected it to answer me, and in Crimson that was entirely possible.

When I bent down and tried to pick it up, it scurried away. A few seconds later, it was back at my feet. When I tried to pick it up again, it let me. "It's okay..." I lifted its tail. "...boy." Not knowing what else to do, I carried him inside.

Dog looked at him when I walked into the kitchen. "What's that?"

"What does it look like? Got any hamburger meat? Or french fries? What do cats eat?" I'd always had dogs growing up.

He went into the walk-in pantry and came back out with a can of tuna. "He'll like this." As he opened it, he got a good look at the cat. "That thing needs a bath. He's got fleas."

"How do you know?"

"I can smell them." Dog had a hell of a nose, but then he was a wolf. I was surprised he didn't try to eat the poor thing.

Lucy stuck her head through the order window and spotted him in my arms. "Is that a cat?"

"Yep. Found him out back. Now I just have to figure out what to do with him."

She grinned. "I'll take him. Richie's kids have been bugging him for a pet."

Her brother was a nightmare, and his kids were a chip off the old block. Life at the Wyatt compound would be a cruel fate. There wasn't a chance in hell she was getting her hands on this cat.

"Sorry," I said. "He's taken. Meet the White Stag's resident rodent hunter."

FOUR

By nine o'clock, the Stag was packed. You couldn't get a seat at the bar, and the tables had all filled up.

Lucy had disappeared again, taking her time in the ladies' room, so I rolled up my sleeves and stepped behind the bar. I felt the unshakable urge to shut the place down early, due to the crazy events of the day. But a closed bar meant no income and a lot of pissed-off customers. Never once in the Stag's history had it ever closed early, and the only time we'd closed entirely on a regular business day was when my mother died. It was her bar, after all.

The stag head out front had been draped in a black veil for three days while the town mourned the passing of Delia Underwood. But not everyone was sad to see her go, especially the preacher over at the Baptist church. The lettering on the church sign was changed the day of her memorial service. It said GOD CORRECTS HIS MISTAKES. Although they did lose some of their congregation after that despicable stunt.

"Charley! Can I get a beer?"

I snapped out of it and headed for the tap. "You want light

or dark?" We served beer on tap two ways—Stag light and Stag dark, made by a brewery two towns over, just for us.

"What do I always have?"

Mike had been a customer long enough for me to know his preference for dark, but I always asked anyway. I set the glass down in front of him and started to walk to the other end of the bar.

"Hey!" he called out before I could disappear.

And I was so close to a clean getaway.

I braced myself before turning around. "What is it, Mike?"

A goofy grin appeared on his face. I hated to always shoot him down when he asked me out, but I'd hate it even more if I had to spend the evening with him. Mike wasn't my type. There wasn't a man in Crimson that interested me. Unless new blood came to town, I'd be single indefinitely, which wasn't so bad. I liked my freedom.

His smile turned condescending. "When are you going to accept the fact that you have needs, Charley? You need a man."

I walked back over to him and leaned onto the bar, showing him a little cleavage just to torture him. "When are you going to admit that you're an asshole?" Any shred of guilt for shooting him down went right out the window.

The look on his face was priceless, and the comment was worth losing a customer over it, if it came to that. Mike was really starting to get on my nerves anyway. But instead of getting offended, he laughed and finished his beer, jiggling his glass for another.

Some guys just never learn.

Beau was standing behind me when I turned around. "You know that's foreplay to that dimwit."

"Just get him another beer."

"Roger that, boss. I got you."

As I was walking away, Patrick squeezed up to the bar

wearing those ridiculous sunglasses again. "Is it too bright in here for you?" I could smell alcohol on his breath. "Where'd you end up tonight?"

"The Rusty Nail." He huffed a laugh. "Waste of a perfectly good Friday night."

"It's a rednecks' bar with karaoke on Friday nights. What did you expect? I'm surprised they let you through the front door wearing that shirt." He didn't give a rat's ass what people thought about his flamboyant wardrobe. It was one of the reasons I loved him so much.

He rolled his eyes. "Girl, you need to learn how to have fun." The word *fun* rolled off his tongue with a drawl.

"So you've told me a hundred times."

"Especially after that fiasco earlier tonight. Speaking of which, we need to reschedule those deliveries."

I lowered my voice. "Can we talk about it later when I have time to think?"

"You're the boss." He leaned in and removed his shades. "Now, let's get out of here."

"I can't just leave, and you know it." Although a night out with my ride or die was tempting.

Our first introduction freshman year of high school had been serendipitous. Patrick was awkward and small for his age back then. Perfect bully bait. Wallace Tillman, a sophomore with a mean streak, thought it would be funny to assault a kid half his size. When I witnessed Wally drag Patrick into an old shed behind the school, I ran over to put an end to whatever was about to happen in there. When I pulled the door open, Patrick's face was pressed into the side of the shed, and Wally was standing behind him with his pants hanging down around his knees. I can't really say what happened next because I don't remember. By the time Patrick got the guts to turn around and look, Wally Tillman was pinned to the wall by a pair of garden shears and a hand spade, with his pants still hugging his knees. The tools had pierced clear through his palms and embedded into the wooden wall of the shed. Neither one of us knew exactly what had happened in there, but Patrick swears it was me who did it.

In any event, Wally wisely kept his mouth shut when we threatened to kill him if he didn't. To this day, Tillman gives us both a wide berth whenever he runs into us on the street. Patrick and I have been thick as thieves ever since. I didn't give a damn if he was a vampire now. I'd walk through fire for that man, and I was pretty sure he'd do the same for me, even though you couldn't tell by the way he talked to me sometimes.

Sighing dramatically, Patrick looked at me with disinterest. "Being responsible is overrated. What the hell good is being the boss if you can't take a night off now and then?" He looked to his left as he was about to leave and stopped. "Maybe I'll have me a drink first."

I followed his eyes and rested my elbows on the bar. "See that empty stool next to that guy you're looking at? It belongs to his girlfriend who's in the ladies' room." Which was where I was about to go to drag Lucy back out here. I had other work to do.

"Then I guess I'm out of here." He leaned over the bar and gave me an air kiss on the cheek. "I'll call you tomorrow." As he was walking away, he turned around. "By the way, have you heard about that girl who went missing?"

"What girl?"

He snapped his fingers a few times trying to recall. "What's her name?"

"You mean the Henderson girl?" a woman sitting at the bar said.

"Yeah, Patrice Henderson." He shot her a look like she should mind her own business.

I muttered to him, "Well, technically you did ask."

Something like that usually spread like wildfire in Crimson, so I was surprised I hadn't heard about it. Willy Henderson was well known around here. He owned a gas station in town. "You said she's missing?"

"It looks that way." Patrick took a seat. "I didn't know her that well, but she was nice."

"Patrick!" I shot him a chastising look. "Don't talk about her in the past tense. She's probably just hooking up with some guy." That was usually what had happened when girls around here disappeared for a day or two. What else were they going to do for fun?

He gave me a flat look. "Patrice Henderson?"

I couldn't argue with him about that. Patrice was several years younger than us and never got into any trouble that I knew of. I remembered her being kind of shy, the one time she came into the Stag with her older brother. But even good girls had to have a little fun now and then.

Beau wandered over to us. "Y'all talking about Patrice Henderson?"

I glanced back and forth between him and Patrick. "How am I the only person in this place who hasn't heard about this until now?" I ran the only bar in town. Gossip central. "What exactly happened?"

Patrick shrugged. "All I know is she's missing."

We both looked at Beau. He always had the skinny on anything interesting happening in town. I was pretty sure he was sleeping with someone with connections.

He lowered his voice. "I heard she drove over to the farmers' market yesterday and hasn't been seen since. They found her car in the parking lot with bags of food in the back seat and everything. Her keys were even in the ignition."

I squinted at him. "Do the police think someone took her?"

"See, here's the strange part. There was no sign of a struggle, and no one saw anything except her leaving the market with her bags. It's like she was abducted by aliens."

Patrick lowered his sunglasses and looked at Beau. "Boy, have you ever been tested?"

Beau's brows knitted together. "For what?"

"I rest my case." He spotted Lucy coming out of the ladies' room and got up. "That girl is my cue to leave."

The two weren't exactly on each other's Christmas list. Lucy didn't have a filter and tended to say stupid things she didn't even realize were offensive. It was just how she was wired. Patrick was halfway to the door before she made it across the room.

"It's about time," I said when she walked around the bar. God only knows what she was doing in there for so long. I glanced at the ladies' room door. "I better not see some guy walking out of there in a second."

She glanced at one of our regulars who was listening to the conversation with a grin on his face. "Are you trying to make me look cheap in front of a customer?"

"Aw, Lucy." I gave her a commiserative smile. "You don't need me to do that."

As she glared at me, I walked around the bar and went to the back room. I had orders to place, and I still needed to figure out when to reschedule the blood deliveries. The thought of people out there hurting because of that nutcase nearly crashing her car through my front window made me both angry and sad. But before I did anything, I needed to sit down for a few seconds to breathe.

As soon as my butt hit the chair, I heard scratching coming from the back door. The cat must have shown up again. I guess I needed to give him a name.

I got up and opened the door, expecting him to brush past me and start demanding food, but there was nothing there. No cat, no possum, no nothing. "Cat!" I called into the alley when I stuck my head out. A sound came from behind the dumpster, startling me. My nerves were getting the better of me with all this talk about missing girls and alien abductions.

Before I could shut the door and double-check the lock, I caught a glimpse of something down the alley. A shadow climbed along the wall and disappeared around the corner—a very tall shadow.

FIVE

I got to the Stag around seven a.m. the next morning, which I had no intention of making a habit of. I'd had another restless night, with a slide show of yesterday's events—including that shadow I'd seen in the alley—running through my mind until the early hours of the morning. But I had a cat now, and he needed to be fed. He'd polished off that can of tuna yesterday evening in about twenty seconds flat and yowled incessantly until I let him back out into the alley. I hadn't seen him since, so I had a feeling he'd be waiting for me with a ravenous appetite. For no particular reason, I decided to call him Bob. He just looked like a Bob.

After closing up last night, I'd stopped by Candy's shop to see if she had anything to heal a feline eye infection and to get rid of fleas, and to see if I could convince her to take Bob off my hands. But she already had a cat, and Odin had earned his name appropriately. Bringing another cat into her house would have incited war. I also considered taking him home with me, but I was worried about leaving a cat alone with a crow. Rex would probably traumatize him.

As I was getting out of my truck, I spotted the lights on in the empty building across the street. It was an old machine shop that had sat vacant for well over a decade. Nobody would lease the place because it would have cost a fortune to convert it into anything except another machine shop, and Crimson already had one too many of those. There was a truck parked on the side street, and I could hear the squeal of power tools inside. Someone was definitely working in the building.

I grabbed a bag of cat food from the bed of the truck and walked to the door, looking up as the light above it went out and then flicked back on a second later. On the drive in, I'd noticed all the lights around the square flickering.

"Please, not today," I muttered, willing the lights to stay on. It would be the first time we'd had a power outage since someone crashed into a transformer last year.

As I was fumbling with my keys, I looked up and nearly jumped out of my skin when I caught Dog's reflection in the glass.

I turned around. "Don't you know better than to sneak up on someone like that? What are you doing here this early anyway?"

He held up a bag of cat food.

I chuckled. "I guess you've got a heart after all."

"Just don't tell anyone. I have a reputation to protect." He glanced across the street at the old building. "Looks like some-one's moving in."

"Yeah, I noticed. Do you know anything about our new neighbor?"

"About as much as you."

If it was a local, half the town would have known about it by now. "Maybe I should go over there with a housewarming gift." I finally managed to get my key in the door to unlock it. "I could put a bow around the cat?"

He reached over me to push it open. "A cat person wouldn't be stupid enough to rent that place."

"Good point."

When I got to the back room, I opened the door to the alley. Bob walked in like he owned the place, looking a hundred percent better than he had when he showed up. After getting a bellyful of food last night, he must have felt content enough to give himself a good bath. Even his bad eye had healed completely.

"How did you pull that off?" I said, bending down to run my hand over his back.

I went into the kitchen and grabbed two bowls, filling one with water and the other with food. Then I took them down the hallway and set them on the floor next to the back door. Bob looked at the dry food and then back up at me. "That's it, buddy. Tuna is for special occasions only, so take it or leave it." I'd splurged on quality food, which was probably why he turned his nose up to it. Animals weren't so different from people when it came to healthy food choices.

After dabbing some of Candy's ointment on his eye, I went back into the bar and looked out the front window. There was a man standing outside the building across the street, and he was staring at me. Dog walked up behind me with two cups of coffee in his hands and let out a humph.

"What?" I said.

He handed me one of the cups while keeping his eyes on the stranger. "I can smell the money on him from here. What's a guy like that doing in Crimson?"

"That's a hell of a nose you've got there." I continued to study my new neighbor, wondering why he was wearing a fancy suit in the middle of all that construction. It had to be dusty in there. "Maybe he's looking for a nice little mountain town to retire to."

"Looks like he's done looking. Must have bought the place."

"Then he's not very smart."

Dog shook his head. "Never trust a man wearing a suit that costs as much as a car."

Dog was the last person I expected to judge a man by his appearance. My mother had told me he'd quickly gained a reputation of being a hothead when he first showed up in Crimson. He took on anyone who looked at him wrong. But that aggression got him to the top of his pack in record time. He'd mellowed over the years, and I trusted him with my life. So did my mother, and I can't say that about many people.

He grunted and took a sip of his coffee. "I was thinking about that accident when I got home last night."

"Oh yeah? Me too." I nodded to my truck. "I need to get that dent fixed." I didn't care how old that truck was. A dent was a dent, and I didn't need any more rust creeping into the paint job.

"It was real interesting how that car stopped on a dime and missed the bar completely. Kinda like it hit an invisible wall."

"That was interesting." I was starting to regret mentioning that light to him because now he was looking at me the same way Candy always did. Like I was some closeted witch waiting to be outed.

He took another sip and looked at me sideways. "How's that adrenaline flowing today?"

I held my hand out and splayed my fingers. "Steady as a rock."

Candy referred to it as me starting to bloom. My mother could put you in your place from a hundred yards away. Summon thunder with a flick of her hand. Some of that magic had to run in the family, and Candy urged me to explore it. But between running the Stag and an illegal venture out of the back room, I only had time to focus on the tangible.

While we were spying on our new neighbor, a patrol car pulled up to the building across the street. Murphy got out and started talking to the man. After a brief conversation, he got back in the car.

I groaned when he pulled up to the bar. "That's all I need."

"At least he can tell us who the new guy is."

It also meant I'd have to spend more painful time with Murphy and get a grilling about what happened Thursday night. "I'm hiding in the back. Let me know when he's gone."

"Come on, Charley. He's not that bad."

I gave him a blank stare. "Yeah, he is." As much as I wanted to duck out, Murphy had seen my truck and was looking at me through the window. He was holding a piece of paper and knocked on the door. The police report, probably.

"It's open," Dog said.

Murphy walked inside and strode up to me. "I figured I'd save you a trip and stick it through the mail slot on the door, but since you're here." He handed me the report. "You're in a little early, aren't you?"

Ignoring his question, I took the paper from his hand and looked across the street again. "I see you were talking to the new tenant leasing the old machine shop. Who is he?" Murphy would probably be tight-lipped about the guy just to get under my skin.

For a change, he was forthcoming. "He's not a tenant. He bought the building."

I guess Dog was right.

"Who is he?" Dog asked.

Murphy hesitated, as if providing such information was breaking privacy laws. Nothing was private in this town. As usual, he was just trying to control the conversation.

"It's public record," I said. "And you didn't have any problem giving me the information about that nutcase who tried to drive her car through my bar last night, so why don't you save me the time of having to look up the property records and just tell me who he is."

After a brief hesitation and a watch-your-mouth glare that didn't faze me one bit, he relented. "The man's name is Atticus Devereaux. He's from New York."

Great. A rich Yankee coming down here to buy up the town. It explained the expensive suit. "What's he doing down here?"

Murphy shrugged. "Says he's opening a restaurant in the building. He also bought the old Simpson house over on Davenport Street."

I stared at him like he had two heads. "A restaurant? In Crimson? What the hell for?"

"Well, I don't know, Charley." His head cocked as he put his hands on his hips. "Want me to go back over there and get his Social Security number for you too?"

I stepped up to him and looked him in the eye with just as much attitude. "Yeah, would you?" The man really got to me, and I hated it when I took the bait.

His face tightened. The same way it used to when my mother would stand up to him. Sometimes I wished he'd lose his temper, but not today. Dog couldn't afford to go to jail, and that's exactly where he'd end up if Murphy was stupid enough to lay a hand on me. Wouldn't be the first time he tried.

After backing down, I grabbed the extra bag of cat food Dog had bought and walked away before the conversation escalated. "Thanks for the accident report."

Bob was pacing back and forth, anxiously waiting for me to let him back out after eating his breakfast. He slipped through the crack in the door before I even got it halfway open.

"Have a good day," I yelled to him. "No need to thank me for the food." I watched him disappear around the corner and found myself questioning if I was being a bad person letting him run loose like that around town. Maybe I should have taken him home even if that meant subjecting him to Rex's antics.

After shutting the door, my phone rang.

"I was just about to call you," I said to Patrick. "Can we reschedule the pickups for this afternoon?"

"We've got a problem, Charley." Patrick could be dramatic at times, but there was an urgency in his voice that said otherwise.

"What is it?" I had a sinking feeling my week was about to get even worse.

"It's Dickie. He's out."

"Out of what?" I knew what he meant, but I needed to hear the actual words come out of his mouth before I started to panic. Dickie was the reason the co-op existed on a sustainable level. He was our most prolific donor, and he'd never pulled a stunt like this before.

"He's sitting right here next to me and says he's through with the co-op. Says he's *seen the light.*"

"Where are you?" I asked.

"My place. You better get here fast. He's eyeing the front door."

I shoved my phone in my pocket and went back into the bar where Dog was enjoying his cup of coffee. "I have to go. I'll see you tonight."

The man knew me too well. "What's wrong?"

"Nothing you need to worry about. I've got a small fire to put out, that's all."

"You want company?"

I shook my head. "Thanks, but I've got this."

When I walked outside, the new guy was still standing in front of the building. If I wasn't in such a hurry to get over to Patrick's place to talk Dickie off the ledge, I would have walked over to say hello. But it would have to wait.

After climbing into my truck, I detoured around the square so I could drive past the future restaurant to get a closer look. I slowed down and did the neighborly thing, waving at him with a smile as I cruised by. He was tall and easy on the eyes. Well-dressed. The kind of man who didn't wander into a town like Crimson very often.

There was a contractor's van parked at the side of the building, and a larger commercial truck was pulling around back, probably to unload supplies for whatever work was being done inside. There was definitely a renovation taking place, and a costly one. May's cafeteria represented fine dining around here, so I'd give him a month before he realized his mistake.

"Good luck to you, Mr. Devereaux," I said to myself as I made a mental note to stop by and properly introduce myself next time I saw him. We were neighbors now, and I wanted to assess the man personally. See if he was just eccentric or only playing with half a deck. That building was a joke, and the old Simpson house was more suited for a wrecking ball than habitation. It was rumored to be haunted by old man Simpson himself.

Along with some money, Patrick inherited a house when his father died several years back, but he ended up selling it and moving down to Little Crimson. It was a nice house in one of Crimson's better areas, but after Patrick was turned, things changed. He started finding messages around his property: roadkill tossed in the bushes, people letting their dogs shit on his lawn. He even got his mailbox mowed down a couple of times. But it was the word BLOODSUCKER painted on his front door that was the last straw. Patrick didn't scare easily, but he didn't want to live around a bunch of hateful assholes either.

I drove ten minutes south and turned onto the main street of Little Crimson. It was just a two-block stretch with a gas station, a few shops, and a tiny grocery store that carried mostly junk food and beer. Other than blood, vampires didn't eat much, although they were perfectly capable of enjoying food. They just didn't need it to survive.

The houses were small. Most of them were in need of maintenance, like a paint job or roof repair. But the properties were tidy if you overlooked the garden gnomes and plastic flamingos. But who was I to say what was tacky and what was art. It didn't really matter. There wasn't much traffic during daylight hours to see it.

I made a right on Patrick's street, noticing how quiet it was. There wasn't a person in sight, and I felt kind of like a trespasser. Like an intruder creeping around in the dark, only the sun was starting to peek through the trees. Most vampires had gone inside for the day, so I guess you could say I was creeping around in the light. Patrick lived in the last house on the street. It was nothing fancy, but it was colorful, painted bright green with a rainbow flag strung over the front door that he dared anyone to touch.

As I rounded a curb and approached the house, something ran out in the road in front of my truck. I slammed on my brakes.

It was Dickie, and he was on fire.

SIX

I swerved and veered off the road, coming to a stop at the edge of Patrick's yard. It was late morning, and the sun was starting to stream through the clouds. I jumped out and ran around to the bed of the truck to grab the wool blanket I kept in the utility chest for emergencies, although I never imagined needing it for this kind of emergency.

Dickie was flailing around in the road directly in the sunlight. I ran and threw the blanket over him, trying to stay out of striking range as he lashed out in a panic.

"Get away from the fool, Charley!" Patrick had taken cover under one of the tall oaks in his front yard. "I can't help you if he attacks!" He was stuck under the tree, shaded from the murderous rays of the sun.

Ignoring his warning, I tried to herd Dickie off the road. His arm came out from under the blanket and punched me in the chest, slamming me back against the truck. When I caught my breath and tried to climb to my feet, he came at me again, losing his footing when I jumped out of the way. He hit the ground and rolled several feet, coming to a stop under the cover of a tree. The flames extinguished, but he was badly burned.

"Dickie?" As I crept toward him, his eyes flew open. There was something wild in them. I was no longer looking at the vampire I knew. His charred lips curled back as a set of fangs descended, and a guttural growl snaked up his throat.

"Run, Charley!"

I tried, but my legs wouldn't move. I was frozen in place. Caught in his hypnotic gaze.

As Dickie lunged, something streaked past me, knocking me off my feet. When I climbed to my feet, all I could see was a spinning ball of fur and flames in the middle of the road.

I focused on the canopy of the giant oak as my adrenaline surged. A loud crack filled my ears, and the limb started to split. Before I could warn Dog, it came crashing down, fracturing as it hit the ground a few feet away.

The wolf skidded back, shaking his head violently. He dug his fangs into the vampire's charred arm and dragged him toward the tree out of the sun's rays. Dickie was unconscious, but he was still alive.

"You followed me?" I said to Dog. Still in wolf form, his hindquarters hit the ground as he started to pant and whine. "Are you okay?"

Patrick gave him a once-over. "He got him a mouthful of vampire blood. He'll be fine when the rush passes."

That was another reason Dickie's blood was so valuable—it was potent.

"Let me see if I can find something to fit his big ass," Patrick said. Dog started to come around, squirming and moaning. Gurgling out words that made no sense. Patrick returned with a pair of pants and tossed them to Dog as he shifted. "They might be a little tight."

Dog managed to pull them on but couldn't zip them up. The bottoms didn't even reach his ankles. "Is this necessary?"

I'd seen Dog naked so many times, I don't know why he bothered. "Suit yourself."

He opted to leave them on and looked down at Dickie. "Let's just get him in the house."

"Damn fool," Patrick said. "We should leave him out here and let the sun finish him off."

I looked up at the rays starting to break through the tree. "It'll finish you both off if we don't get inside."

He bent down to grab Dickie's ankles. "Get his shoulders," he said to Dog. "Charley can slip that blanket under him after we lift him up. We'll lose less skin that way."

I shuddered.

After getting the vampire positioned on top of the blanket, we took him into the house and laid him on the couch.

Dog threw me a glance. "You weren't kidding when you said you had a fire to put out."

"I guess not. What the hell happened this morning, Patrick?"

"I don't know what got into that vampire. One minute we were having coffee, and next thing I know he was running out the front door."

"Back up. You said he told you he wanted out of the co-op?" Something was off. I was missing a piece somewhere. "Did he seem suicidal?"

Dog nodded to the vampire on the couch. "Dickie's always been a little off. Ain't nothing right about him."

Patrick scratched his head, like he was trying to put the pieces together himself. "He came over before the crack of dawn and said he was leaving the co-op. Said he'd had a vision."

Did I hear him right? "A vision? Dickie?"

"He said God spoke to him and told him he was an abomination. Said it was time to pay the piper, whatever the hell that means. That's when I called you." He let out a short laugh. "I went to use the little boys' room. When I came back out, the front door was wide open and he was smoking like a marshmallow in the street."

"Isn't that something?" I said to Dog. "Good thing you decided to follow me. Just don't do it again."

"Are you kidding me? I could smell you when you walked out of the Stag."

"Okay, that's a little creepy."

"You smelled like fear, Charley." He shrugged. "So I followed you. Sue me."

Dickie began to stir on the couch.

"What do we do with him?" I asked. There were no vampire urgent care facilities.

Patrick let out a groan. "I guess he can stay on my couch for a few days while he recovers. After that, I don't know. And there's no way of knowing what's going on in that messed-up head of his, so he might try to do it again."

I got an image of Janice Wilson passed out in her car while her face burned to a crisp. "You think he'll be scarred like that for life?"

"No way to tell. But knowing Dickie's blood, he'll be right as rain."

In the meantime, we needed to find another donor. Hell, we needed to find ten more donors. Even if Dickie did make a full recovery, there was no guarantee he'd come to his senses and continue with the co-op. "We need a lot more donors."

Patrick nodded in agreement. "Yeah, you're right. We're going to need more supply whether Dickie comes around or not. I'll put the word out."

I'd been avoiding the inevitable. With growth came two things: spreading myself even thinner than I already was and more risk of ending up in jail. The co-op had stayed under the radar so far, but that seemed to be changing. And the Crimson PD was always a threat, especially with Tom Murphy sniffing around lately.

"Let's reschedule the pickups for tomorrow night," I said to

Patrick. "Eight o'clock. Make some calls to let everyone know." I motioned to Dog. "Come on, I'll give you a ride back to the Stag."

We climbed into my truck and started back toward town, but Dog was unusually quiet. "What's on your mind?"

Glancing out the window, he let out a steady groan. "The pack has been restless lately."

"So, what else is new?" The pack was always restless.

"It's different this time. The moon is too full too soon. The energy is out of balance."

I laughed quietly. "Maybe that's what made Dickie go kamikaze this morning."

He turned to look at me. "This is serious, Charley."

"I know, but if I don't joke about it, I'll end up crying. Would you rather see that?"

Another soft groan escaped his mouth.

We pulled up to the Stag and got out. On my way to the door, Dog started walking in the other direction. "Where are you going?"

"To check out the neighbor."

I glanced at the building across the street. "Looks like they quit for the day." The contractor's van was gone, and the front door was shut. It was Saturday after all.

He kept walking. "Good. It'll make it easier."

"Make what easier?" For some stupid reason, I followed him.

I gave him a wary look when we walked around the building. "What are we doing, Dog?"

"Relax. We're just looking around."

I walked over to one of the rear windows to look inside. The glass was filthy, obstructing the view.

Dog waved me over to the back door, which was ajar. I guess the man didn't feel the need to lock his doors in a small town like Crimson. He didn't even bother to shut it, which was a little too convenient.

"We can't just walk in there," I said.

"Why not?"

"It's called breaking and entering."

He pushed the door all the way open. "No one broke anything. Looks like an invitation to me."

Something told me I was going to regret this, but my curiosity got the best of me. I followed him inside. The place had been gutted, and a full-scale renovation was obviously underway. Devereaux was sinking a lot of cash into a business venture that was destined to fail.

"They got a lot done in one morning, unless they worked through the night. Remind me to write down that contractor's number next time I see the truck parked outside." Good contractors are worth their weight in gold.

Dog looked over his shoulder at me. "Why? Planning to expand the Stag?"

"You never know." I nodded to some red marks on the wall above the front door. "What do you think those are?"

With his considerable height, Dog was able to reach up and run his hand over one of the symbols. He held his fingers to his nose and sniffed. "It's not blood, if that's what you were thinking."

"I wasn't, but thanks for the clarification."

He studied the symbols again. "Looks like some kind of chalking."

"Chalking? What's that?"

"You know. Chalking the door. If Mr. Devereaux is a Christian man, it might be some kind of blessing for the place."

I looked around and spotted a door on the other side of the room. "I wonder what that leads to." I went over and opened it, getting an overwhelming whiff of mildew. The air beyond it felt damp, and the steps descended into darkness. "Must be the basement."

Dog looked over my shoulder. "Probably. Just don't ask me to go down there to find out."

I shut the door. "Let's just assume it is." I wasn't going down there either.

After nosing around the rest of the building, I started to get nervous. "Have you seen enough? We need to get out of here before we get caught." I was not a lucky person. Never had been. With my track record, Devereaux would walk in on us, and I doubted he'd be sympathetic about our curiosity. What a way to introduce yourself to your new neighbor.

"Yeah, let's get out of here."

The moment we walked out the back door, a crow swooped down in front of us. I stumbled back against the wall and clutched my pounding chest. "I am too old to be doing this."

"Old? Do you need me to carry you across the street?"

"Would you?"

He snickered. "I've got almost ten years on you. I don't want to hear another word about being old." He headed around the building. "Come on. Let's get out of here before Murphy decides to cruise by."

When we got back to the Stag, Bob was lounging on top of the bar with one of his orange paws curled up to his mouth. He was washing it contentedly. "Did you let him in?"

Dog shrugged on his way to the kitchen. "He must have slipped in when one of us was on our way out."

I glanced at the cat while I poured myself a glass of water from the sink behind the bar. My mouth had gone extremely dry after the misdemeanor we'd just committed. As I was raising the glass to my lips, I looked out the window. Atticus Devereaux was standing outside his building looking across the street at the bar. "Dog!"

Hearing the urgency in my voice, he rushed out of the kitchen. "What's wrong?"

I turned to look at him. "I think we just got lucky, and I'm never lucky. Guess who's back?"

He walked over to the window and gave me a puzzled look. "Who?"

When I looked across the street again, Devereaux was gone.

SEVEN

Saturday nights were our busiest night of the week, and tonight was no exception.

"What are you drinking?" I asked my customer sitting at the bar.

Then I waited for it.

"You, if I'm lucky." He gave me that stupid grin that always followed one of his bad pickup lines. "What time do you get off?"

I smiled, avoiding eye contact. "Come on, Danny. You've got a bar full of women just waiting for a guy like you to hit on them, and you're wasting your time on the least likely one to take you up on your offer." He was a decent guy but not my type, not by a long shot. He kept trying, though.

As he blathered away with his next proposition, Beau waved me over to the other end of the bar. He was talking to one of our regulars.

"Did you hear about the break-in?" Beau said when I walked up to them.

"No. Who got broken into?"

Break-ins were rare in Crimson. That accident yesterday was probably the most action Crimson PD had seen all year. And it certainly wasn't the guy who'd tried to rip off the co-op the other night, because he was eating dirt somewhere out in the woods.

"The feedstore over on Adler Street," Keith Barnes said.

"Pete's place?" I let out a light chuckle. "What did they take? A few bales of hay?" I shouldn't have made light of it. A break-in was a break-in.

He took a sip of his beer and leaned closer. "Nothing. They just trashed the place. They'll be cleaning up fifty-pound bags of hog feed for a week." He shifted his eyes around the room as his voice lowered. "Pete said a couple of vampires came into the store yesterday evening just before closing. He said he'd never seen them before, and all they did was stroll up and down the aisles making his customers nervous."

I suddenly got serious. "How did he know they were vampires?"

"Because one of them walked up to Pete and lowered his shades. His eyes looked like firepits. That's how Pete described them. Then he flashed a set of fangs and asked Pete if he had any live chicks for sale. So yeah, probably a vampire."

The customer sitting next to Keith muttered something about bloodsuckers.

"What's that?" I asked him.

He took a sip of his beer and snickered under his breath. "I said, them *bloodsuckers* are getting out of hand around here. They need to stay right where they belong down there in Little Crimson. Bunch of freaks."

Before I could remind him that half the bar was filled with *freaks*, he got up and finished his beer before walking out the front door.

"Is it just my imagination," I said as we watched the jerk

disappear down the sidewalk, "or have people around here gotten more hateful lately?"

Keith pulled his eyes away from the window. "No, you're right. We're reaching our asshole quota in town."

Getting back to the discussion, Beau cocked his head. "What would a vampire want with a bunch of chickens?"

"I don't know," I said, "but I doubt it would have ended well for those poor birds. I hope he didn't sell them any."

Keith shook his head. "Pete went in the back to pretend to check his stock, but when he came back out to tell them he didn't have any left, they were gone." He took another swallow of his beer and nodded once firmly. "I think it was them who came back and tore the place up."

"Why would they bother if they weren't going to take anything?" I said. "It was probably kids."

Beau snorted. "Probably them degenerates on the football team."

"You ought to know." If I recalled, he used to be one of those degenerates. "Whatever happened to smoking weed and drinking beer in the woods?"

Keith let out a sigh. "I guess it could be worse. They could be getting high on that vampire blood."

I glanced at Beau. "Yeah, wouldn't that be tragic. I hear that stuff isn't addictive, though. Like meth or opioids."

"Says who?" He scoffed. "I say drugs are drugs."

"Then you've never met someone addicted to opioids."

His brows arched. "Have you?"

It was time to change the subject before I started sounding like an expert. I pointed to the other end of the bar. "Speaking of drugs, someone down there needs a drink."

"Hey," Keith said as I started to walk away. "Have you met the guy who bought the old machine shop across the street?"

I glanced out the window and saw the place lit up again. "Not yet. Have you?"

"No, but Becky said he came into the hardware store this afternoon and introduced himself to everyone in the place. Said he's opening a restaurant."

"So I hear." I recalled the fancy suit he was wearing. "He doesn't look like the burger and fries type, so maybe he's planning to open a steak house." Or God forbid a sushi bar. That would sink like a stone in Crimson. Around here, the only thing people did with raw fish was use it as bait.

"Nope," Keith said. "Something called 'French fusion cuisine.'"

Beau got a sour look on his face. "What the hell is French fusion?"

"Hell if I know," I said. "But *French* sounds expensive. Hope he has a backup plan when it fails." The last thing a small town like Crimson needed was a pricy restaurant. Even the mom-and-pop eateries around here had a hard time staying afloat.

"It's not like you to talk poorly about someone before you've even met them," Marcy Bedford said to me. She was sitting next to Keith with her big ears perked.

"Don't you know it's rude to listen to someone else's conversation?" I said back to her, even though she was right. I shouldn't have been talking about the man without meeting him first, but that was about to change. Through the window, I spotted Devereaux crossing the street and heading straight toward the Stag.

Beau tapped me on the arm. "Look who's about to walk in."

"I noticed."

The front door opened, and Atticus Devereaux came inside. The hum of conversation went silent as every eye in the place turned toward him. He was attractive, I'd give him that. Tall with a lean but muscular build, I'd say he was around forty. His deep brown eyes oozed with confidence, and I couldn't help but stare at him for a moment.

I pulled my gaze away from him and started to wipe down the bar when he looked over at me. From the corner of my eye, I saw him walking toward me, his expensive cologne filling my nose as he neared the bar.

He walked up and extended his hand. "Atticus Devereaux. I believe we're neighbors."

For a second, I found myself at a loss for what to do. Had a brain freeze. I finally snapped out of it and shook his hand. "Charlotte Underwood. I prefer Charley."

A slight smile crossed his face as his eyes lingered on mine. "Charley. How charming."

He was the one doing the charming.

"May I?" he said.

May he what?

Finally getting a clue, I glanced up and down the packed bar. "We're pretty busy on Saturday nights. You might have better luck with a table." One of the guys sitting in front of him got up. He didn't even finish the drink I'd just served him. After throwing a few bills on the bar, he looked at Atticus, smiled, and then headed for the door.

"Or you can take that one before someone beats you to it," I said, taking the money.

Atticus sat down and continued to stare at me with unabashed boldness. His intense eyes ignited an annoying flutter deep inside my stomach. To be honest, it caught me off guard and made me uncomfortable, and I was never uncomfortable in my own bar. He was definitely laying the charm on thick.

Pulling myself together, I got back to tending bar. "What are you drinking?"

"Scotch. Neat."

I reached for a bottle of Dewar's on the lower shelf, but then I came to my senses. "Do you have a preference?"

He glanced at the top shelf. "Glenlivet, please."

That bottle had been collecting dust for some time, and I was starting to regret buying it. If it had been anyone else, I would have mentioned the price before pouring him a glass. Folks around here frowned on surprises when it came time to pay up. But something told me he already knew it was the most expensive bottle in the bar.

I poured him a drink and set it in front of him. "I hear you're from New York."

He gave me a lukewarm smile. "Yes."

So much for conversation.

After a moment of awkward silence, I started to walk away.

"I'd like to invite you to dinner," he said before I could make a clean break. "My restaurant opens on Tuesday." When I stood there gawking at him, he added, "As my guest, of course."

"Tuesday as in this coming Tuesday?" How was that even possible? The place was gutted when Dog and I went in there this afternoon.

"Yes. *This* Tuesday."

I glanced out the window at the lights from inside the building across the street. "Do you mind if I ask how you're planning to get a restaurant up and running in four days?" Even a shitty diner took longer to build out than that. But this was Crimson, and strange things happened around here on a regular basis.

"I pay my contractors handsomely. They're quite motivated. They'll be working night and day, so I hope the noise doesn't bother you."

I could spare an hour, and I was curious to see what he could pull off in that old shop in four days. "Sure. Why not." It would also give me a chance to get to know the man.

"Good." He tossed a hundred-dollar bill on the bar. "I'll see you Tuesday."

I glanced down at it. "You can buy the whole bottle for that." And he hadn't even touched his drink.

Holding my gaze, he finally got up to leave. Turning around, he asked, "What are you, Ms. Underwood?"

"I'm just a bar owner, Mr. Devereaux."

"Oh, you're much more than that. Perhaps you just don't know it yet. I'm looking forward to getting to know you."

Butterflies started flapping around in my stomach, and I began to regret agreeing to dinner. Atticus was a handsome man, but I didn't have time for a distraction. My hands were full at the moment.

After he left, Lucy walked up behind me and eyed his untouched glass. "If no one's going to drink that fancy scotch, I will."

"Like hell." I grabbed the glass and put the hundred in the register before she tried to help herself to that too. Then I headed for the kitchen, downing the scotch on my way.

Our sous-chef, aka dishwasher, nearly slammed into me with a bin full of dirty glasses when I walked through the swinging door. Walter "Mutt" Kramer was a big guy. Six foot four and a good two hundred and fifty pounds on a slim day. But he didn't have a mean bone in his body. Having no family, Dog and his wolves had all but adopted him as an honorary member of the pack. He called himself Mutt because he'd been orphaned at a young age and had no idea what his heritage was. He just assumed he had a little bit of everything in him.

"Sorry, Charley." He nearly bumped into a shelf when he backed up. The tall one where we stored all the new glassware I'd recently purchased.

"Don't apologize," I said. "I wasn't watching where I was going."

He set the box on a rolling cart and let out a nervous laugh, stuffing his fidgeting hands in the pockets of his apron. "It was my fault, Charley." A goofy grin appeared on his face every time I walked into the room.

"Do yourself a favor, Mutt. Take a win when someone

hands it to you." Before he could start praising me for how right I was, I set the empty glass into the bin he was carrying and continued into the kitchen.

Dog stopped chopping the head of lettuce on the cutting board and nodded through the order window. "Was that him?"

"Yep. That was Atticus Devereaux himself."

"What's he like?"

I shrugged. "He seems... nice. A little formal for my taste, but he is from New York." I couldn't shake the smell of his cologne. Most of the men around here either smelled like sweat and beer or Old Spice. "He stopped in to introduce himself and to invite me to dinner at his restaurant."

Dog slammed the knife into the head of lettuce again. "Oh yeah? Did you take him up on it?"

Why did I say yes? Now I had to dig out something to wear to a French restaurant—a *French* restaurant. "Yes, but I'm already starting to regret it." I glanced at him sideways when a grin slid up his face. "What are you smiling about?"

"Nothing." He set the knife down and wiped his hands with a towel. "It's just nice to see you going on a date."

"Date? Who said anything about a date? The man's old enough to be my... older brother. I'm just getting to know our new neighbor. And the competition," I added. "Well, maybe not exactly competition."

"Does he know that?"

"He will on Tuesday night. It's his grand opening."

Dog cocked his head. "Tuesday of what week?"

It would have been laughable if this wasn't true. "This coming week. That's what he said."

He chuckled, sweeping the chopped lettuce into a container. "I hope you like eating with construction dust settling on your plate."

"Hopefully Devereaux will come to his senses and cancel."

I needed to find Bob and fill his food bowl before going back out to see if Beau and Lucy needed help at the bar. Since I also needed to catch up on some admin tasks in the back, I was hoping for once that the place didn't get any busier.

Mutt must have been standing behind me, because when I turned around, he backed up and stumbled into that shelf he'd had a near miss with earlier. He hit it so hard it shook, sending the heavy boxes of glassware sliding forward.

"Charley!" Dog yelled.

I looked up as it tipped. Mutt had stepped away from it, and the boxes were sliding off the shelves toward me. I startled and lost my balance, throwing my hands up instinctively as I hit the floor and shut my eyes.

Instead of the boxes crashing down on top of me, the room went quiet. Hear-a-pin-drop quiet. Even the noise from the bar faded. When I opened my eyes, the boxes were hovering in the air above me, and the shelf was suspended at an angle.

I glanced around the kitchen, spotting Mutt plastered against the wall. He seemed frozen, with his eyes wide open and his mouth gaping. Before I could comprehend what was happening, Dog grabbed me and pulled me out of the way just before the shelf and boxes came crashing down on the spot where I'd fallen.

Dog let go of me and stared at the mess in disbelief. Then he slowly turned to look at me. "How's that adrenaline flowing tonight?"

"Uh... worse than usual?"

A bunch of customers were gawking at us through the order window, and Beau came running into the kitchen with Lucy on his heels. "What the hell, Charley? It sounded like a bomb went off in here!"

Lucy stepped around him and gazed at the colossal mess on the floor. Then she looked at me and grinned. "Awesome."

* * *

By the time I pulled up to the house, I was bone tired. The past few days had been exhausting, and all I wanted to do was climb in bed and sleep uninterrupted for a solid eight hours. Like that was going to happen. My adrenaline was still rushing. But instead of being wired with energy, I felt drained. My mother used to get like that. She'd go for days like the Energizer Bunny and then crash hard, like I was doing right now.

I turned off the ignition and sat in my truck for a moment to stare at the moon. It wasn't even full yet, and I was already swimming in chaos. And that look Dog gave me tonight. My spells, as I quaintly referred to them, were coming on more frequently, and they were getting stronger.

Dog had noticed them for weeks. Like Candy, he was quick to point out that I was more like my mother than I wanted to admit. But she always told me I was straight as an arrow. Straight meaning one hundred percent human. The events of the past few days had me wondering.

I shook it off and got out of the truck, looking up at the tree overhead. "Rex!"

Most nights he preferred to stay out, being a wild bird and all, but I took him inside when he let me. Nights were prime hunting time, and crow brains are an owl delicacy.

Something moved on the side of the house as I walked toward it, a shadow slipping around back and out of the moonlight. My adrenaline started surfing through my veins again. "Who's there?"

I almost went back to my truck to grab the rifle I kept behind the seat but figured it was probably just an animal lurking around the house. One of the many deer that wandered onto the property. The gun had belonged to my mother. I never got rid of it after she died. I'd never had to use it either, but she made sure I knew how.

Not wanting to find out what it was, I hurried up the steps to the porch and fumbled with my keys. I nearly dropped them twice but finally managed to unlock the door. As I was pushing it open, someone grabbed my shoulder.

I turned around and body-slammed whoever was behind me, sending them tumbling down the steps.

"Patrick!" I ran down to help him up.

He threw his hands up to stave me off. "*Don't* touch me, psycho."

"What the hell is wrong with you?" I glared down at him. "You know better than to sneak up on me like that. What if I'd had a knife in my hand?" Thank God I didn't go back for the rifle, although I probably would have shot my foot off with it.

He flashed his fangs with a wince as he climbed to his feet and felt the back of his head. "Didn't you see my car?" He nodded toward the garage.

All I could see was my truck. "Is it invisible?"

"It's parked on the side. I didn't want to take your space."

"Well, that makes a hell of a lot of sense." Sometimes I wondered about him.

After following me inside, he plunked himself down on the couch and swung his feet up on the coffee table. "I need a drink."

"You want a beer? I think I have one in the back of the fridge."

"I'd rather have a mojito."

I sat down next to him. "I've got some mint out in the garden and a couple of limes, but unless you brought the rum, you're out of luck. What are you doing here this late anyway?"

"I wanted to see if you found out anything more about what happened to the Henderson girl."

"Patrice?"

"Is there another Henderson girl?" He sank deeper into the couch cushions and sighed. "Why am I always the last person to hear juicy gossip in this town? I should be on speed dial for news like this."

Patrick was never the last to know.

"What do you mean? You're the one who told me she was missing."

He gave me a surprised look. "Then I guess I'm not the last to know this time. Welcome to the club, baby."

My patience was wearing thin. "Did they find her or not?"

"Oh, they found her all right. Buck naked in the woods with her hands nailed to a tree. Someone crucified that poor girl."

I flinched at the image that popped into my head. "Is she dead?"

"Not yet, but that girl's in bad shape." He leaned forward and lowered his voice. "What kind of crazy motherfucker does that? I'll tell you—a vampire, and not the good kind."

"A vampire? Why would you think that?"

"Because she had bite marks on her neck when they found her."

This was bad news, and not just for Patrice Henderson. It was fuel for the fire building between the humans and vampires in town. Tension that had been getting worse for the past few years. "Tell me they have a suspect."

"I was hoping you could tell me. Things are heating up in Little Crimson, and it ain't looking good for public relations around here."

"Did something else happen?"

He snickered. "Half the vampires in Little Crimson have been finding bags of flaming dog shit on their porches for the past few days. It's just the beginning."

"That sounds like kids to me."

Patrick pinned me with his stare. "Have you seen kids these days? They're just as mean as their parents. Who do you think taught them how to be assholes?" He reached into his pocket and pulled out a piece of paper. "I found this in my mailbox." He handed it to me. "Everyone in the neighborhood got one."

The note said: THE ONLY GOOD VAMPIRE IS A DEAD VAMPIRE.

"Well," I said, handing it back to him. "At least they know how to spell."

He stuffed it back inside his pocket with a chuckle. "Gird your loins, girl. It's about to get ugly around here."

I thought he was right. Patrice Henderson's attack was about to push people over the edge. Incite a civil war that had been just waiting to erupt.

"We can talk about it more tomorrow," I said. "Right now, I need to get some sleep." Sleep deprivation was catching up to me, and now this would have me tossing and turning all night. "You can crash here if you want."

He glanced down at the couch. "On this? No thanks."

"How about the spare bedroom?"

"I think I'll just take my ass home." He planted a kiss on my cheek and got up to leave. "You need to get you a big dog, living all the way out here in the boonies."

"It's ten minutes from town, Patrick."

When I walked him outside, Rex came flying down from the tree and landed on my shoulder. "Well, look at that. My feathered pit bull just arrived."

"Or Sunday dinner."

"Caw! Caw!"

"I think you insulted him."

He chuckled on his way down the steps. "Wouldn't be the first time."

"Do me a favor," I said. "Next time you show up before I get home, use the spare key under the planter instead of creeping around the back of the house. I almost grabbed the rifle from the truck when I saw you."

He threw me a strange look over his shoulder. "I wasn't creeping around anywhere. I was getting some shut-eye in my car. Your headlights and that loud-ass engine woke me up."

I glanced around the darkness, suddenly feeling a chill in the warm summer air. Maybe it was time to get that dog. A very large one.

EIGHT

When I drove into town the next evening, I passed two squad cars in the square. I pulled into my parking spot in front of the Stag and watched them circle around and speed past me, stopping in front of Candy's shop two blocks down. The last thing I needed was to have the cops nosing around when people would be lining up in the alley to pick up their vampire blood from the co-op.

I got out of my truck and watched them walk into Hecate's Cauldron. It was seven p.m., and Candy's shop had already closed. Patrick was supposed to be here in half an hour so we could open the co-op at eight. It gave me enough time to walk down there to see what was up.

When I stuck my head inside, Candy was leaning against the glass display case having a conversation with Officer Carter while Murphy snooped around her shop.

Murphy walked over to the pole in the corner and looked it up and down. "Getting any use out of this thing?"

She raised her chin and gave him a smile. "Why? You interested in a private session, officer?"

With the smirk disappearing from his face, he strolled over to the door leading to the back room. It was locked when he tried the knob. "What's in here?"

"None of your business," I said, walking inside. I was no lawyer, but I'd watched enough TV to know you needed a warrant to search an establishment. A formality Crimson PD rarely bothered with, but it was worth a shot.

Murphy's jaw tensed. "This is police business, Charley. You need to step back outside."

Candy pushed away from the display case and walked around to the other side. She flattened her hands on top of the counter and leaned over it. "This is my shop. Charley doesn't have to go anywhere. Unless I'm under arrest." She straightened back up and held her wrists out. "Would you like to handcuff me, Officer Carter?"

Carter cleared his throat and took an involuntary step back. "Stop that, Candy. No one's under arrest."

"Yet," Murphy commented. "Now, open this door so we can have a look around back there."

She laughed softly and reached under the counter for a cigarette, clenching it between her teeth as she spoke around it. "Show me a warrant."

So much for quitting.

Murphy stomped up to her and stuck his finger dangerously close to her face. "I just might. I've had about enough of you, woman."

"Careful, officer." She looked at his finger, and it started to shake. So much so that he lowered it and clenched his hand a few times to steady it.

He was lucky she didn't set it on fire.

"We found a girl half-dead in the woods last night," Murphy continued. "A witness spotted her walking in here Thursday morning. That makes you one of the last people to see her before she disappeared." He looked back at the locked door.

"You wouldn't know anything about vampire blood going around or sex parties, would you?"

She threw me a glance and got that salacious smile on her face again. "Sex parties? How eighties. Could you be more specific?"

I couldn't help but snicker, but Murphy didn't find it amusing. "You think this is funny?" He glanced back and forth between us with a classic cop look. "Patrice Henderson is lying in a hospital bed unconscious with her throat ripped up and holes in the palms of her hands. The girl was crucified."

He probably should have shut his mouth before revealing information that wasn't officially public yet, although obviously word had spread like wildfire. God forbid the perpetrator was one of us. I knew one thing with absolute certainty—Candy had nothing to do with it. What she did in that back room was between two consenting adults, and as far as I knew, nobody ever got hurt.

Losing patience, Candy tossed the unlit cigarette on the counter. "I don't harm people. I give them what they need." She walked over to the front door and leaned against the frame. "If you're through with your interrogation, either arrest me for something or get out of my shop."

Murphy tapped his partner on the arm. "Let's go."

On their way out, Carter stopped and looked Candy in the eye. "Don't even think about leaving town."

"And miss our session next week? I wouldn't dream of it, officer."

Carter started to flush, but Murphy just shook his head and walked toward his car.

After they left, I gave Candy an incredulous look. "Rick Carter?"

She waved me off. "Not with a ten-foot pole. It shut him up, though."

"Why would they question you about what happened to Patrice Henderson?"

"Why do you think? Any crime in this town that involves sex leads them straight to my door. Stupid fools!" She made a sweeping motion down her torso. "There isn't a human in this town who gets to put his hands on this."

I was starting to wonder exactly what she did during her private sessions.

Her eyes snapped to mine. "Like I said, I give them what they need."

Stay out of my head.

Her hands landed on her hips. "Then stop wondering about my business."

Fair enough.

"I still don't get it. Why would they think it was a sex crime? They found Patrice nailed to a tree with her throat gnawed on."

Candy took a deep breath and let it rush back out while she straightened the top of the display case. "Because it was. At least it probably started that way. I'm going to tell you something because I love you and I promised your mama I'd look after you. But I better never hear you utter these words to anyone. Understand? You're a beautiful young woman, so you need to be careful out there at night."

Did I even want to hear this?

"The police were right about Patrice Henderson coming by Thursday morning. She's been having thoughts. Cravings. Her only options were to talk to me or the pastor over at the church." She stopped messing with the top of the case and looked at me. "Which would you choose?"

No contest. The local pastor was awful. He would have paraded Patrice through town naked while everyone shamed her for having ungodly thoughts.

"The poor girl was terrified about the things running

through her head. Said she'd been having them for months, and she was afraid she might do something reckless."

I let out a short laugh. "You mean she wanted to have her way with some random guy?"

"Well, it's funny unless you've been raised to believe you're going to hell for just thinking about it."

My grin vanished. "You're right. I shouldn't joke about it. But she did make the same assumption about you as those cops."

Candy shook her head. "She thought I could give her something to make the thoughts go away. A spell or an elixir." She grumbled something under her breath and got back to straightening up. "And I could have, but it's best not to mess with hormones. Especially *young* hormones. Had I known she was going to act out her fantasy, I would have done something about it."

"Fantasy? What are you talking about?"

She hesitated, a row of creases filling her forehead as her brow tightened. "She mentioned something about a dating app, only it's for humans looking to hook up with vampires."

There were apps for everything else, so why not? "It's not your fault, Candy. Anyone with a phone or a computer can use a dating app."

She dropped the dust rag in her hand. "Patrice had already done that by the time she came to see me. There was a group of vampires looking for a girl. One girl for all of them. She asked me to give her something to fight her cravings so she wouldn't keep that date, but all I did was tell her to go home and turn off her phone. And she said she would," she quickly added with that guilt-ridden look creeping back into her eyes. "I might as well have thrown that little girl to the wolves myself."

"Stop it, Candy. Patrice Henderson is a grown woman. Sheltered and naive, yes, but grown and capable of making adult decisions. Why didn't you tell Murphy and Carter any of this?"

"Because we have a bigger problem on our hands. If the humans in town find out about this, it'll be open season on vampires. We need to find those bastards and put an end to this before Patrice Henderson wakes up and talks to the press."

It was too late for that. "Half the town already knows."

She looked horrified. "How?"

"The cops around here have loose lips. Patrick told me she had bite marks all over her neck, so it's obvious it was a vampire. The entire town will know within the next few days."

"Those idiots!" She looked like steam was about to come out of her ears. "I've got a good mind to gather the Squad and put together a stitching spell. We'll see how much those cops talk with their mouths sewn shut."

The mention of the Squad sent a shiver down my spine. "Please don't. You know what always happens when those four come to town."

They were witches straight out of "Hansel and Gretel," and they scared the hell out of me when I was a kid. Whenever they came over to the house to do a working with my mother, I'd slip out the back door and disappear until they left. I couldn't take the energy in the house. It was like an electrical storm would roll in the moment they arrived.

The women lived together in an old house at the edge of the woods in an area where four towns, including Crimson, intersected. Technically, they were citizens of all four, so the Quad Squad was probably a more appropriate name for them. Every time they set foot in town, we'd all pay for it with inconvenience. The sky would turn dark gray. The electricity would go wonky. Last time they made an appearance, vultures showed up and roosted on top of buildings for weeks. It was just better for everyone if they stayed in their neck of the woods.

Candy let out a frustrated sigh. "I doubt they'd show up for less than an emergency anyway."

I looked at the time. "I need to get going. Patrick is meeting me at the Stag in a few minutes."

"Charley," Candy said as I was heading for the door. "I meant it when I said I'd look out for you. Whoever did this is evil and won't stop at one victim. Promise me you'll be careful."

"Don't worry. I have no intention of signing up for any dating apps." A big dog wasn't going to stop a bunch of horny vampires if they came to my house.

As I pulled the door open and walked out, I saw a man coming out of the café across the street. "Who's that?" I said to Candy when she walked up behind me. He was tall, with jet-black hair and a face that would make any woman with a pulse look twice. And he sure didn't dress like the men around here. He was covered in black clothing from head to toe. The only thing that broke up all the darkness was his fair skin.

Candy stepped outside and squinted at him, a smile rising on her face. "I don't know, but I think you should go find out."

"Really? You want me to walk up to a complete stranger and start a conversation?"

"Well, why not?"

"Because I'm not that desperate."

She just stared at me with a flat expression.

I looked back at him and caught his eye. Even from a distance I could see the intensity in them. He held my gaze for a moment, stirring up sensations I hadn't felt in a while. Maybe Candy was right.

She gave me a gentle shove onto the sidewalk. "Go introduce yourself."

"Take it easy," I said over my shoulder. When I looked back at the café, he was gone. "So much for that."

Candy shook her head at me and walked back inside. "Text me when you get back to the Stag."

I started up the street, keeping an eye out for the man while I walked back to the bar. Patrick pulled up as I got there. After making sure Beau didn't need me at the bar, we went to the back room to set up.

"How's Dickie doing?" I was praying he'd bounced back and was eager to resume his blood donations. Wishful thinking.

Patrick hesitated and scratched the back of his neck. "Yeah... we need to talk about that."

"Just spit it out."

"He isn't coming around. I tried to talk him off the ledge this morning, but he says he's done."

Fantastic.

Dickie was a beast. A blood gold mine. He donated as much as all our other donors combined. By my estimate, we only had enough blood in Patrick's freezer to last another week at best, and that was without supplying any new members, and more were being referred to the co-op daily. We wouldn't be able to keep up with the demand.

"Kenny is supposed to come by tomorrow to fill out the paperwork," I said. "We can try to fast-track his screening, unless you have other interested donors."

Patrick groaned. "I already thought about that. I swung by Kenny's house after I left you last night, but he's suddenly refusing to get tested. How much you want to bet he's carrying hepatitis or something worse? I got another lead," he quickly added, "but it's a little iffy."

"Iffy meaning what?"

There was that hesitation again. "I got a call from a vampire. Said he got my number from someone in town. He's looking to make some cash."

None of what he was saying sat well with me. "And?"

He quickly validated my uneasy feeling. "He's down in Reaperstown."

"Reaperstown?" I stared at him for a moment. "You're serious?"

Reaperstown used to *be* an actual town, but these days it

was just a stretch of derelict buildings ten miles south of Crimson. The town dissolved over a decade ago, so you couldn't even find it on a map if you wanted to. Now it was known for nothing but trouble. There were some genuinely bad vamps down there. The kind who wouldn't think twice about staking a young woman to a tree and having their way with her, and I wasn't interested in ending up like Patrice Henderson.

"I'm not sure we're on the same page here, Patrick."

"It's a temporary solution. Just until we can find more permanent donors. But you have to understand something, Charley. Vampires and the law don't mix around here. They're scared. It's gonna take some time to gain their trust."

There were days when I wanted to shut the whole operation down, but people were depending on us. Right now we just needed enough supply to hold us over until we could hatch a miracle and convince Dickie to come back or find more locals.

"Has this vampire even been tested?" I had a hard time believing any vampire from Reaperstown was clean.

"He says he has. We'll take a sample and have Doc run it. If he tests clean, we have a donor. And he says he has friends who might be interested."

I was getting a headache just thinking about working with vampires down there. Everything seemed to be spiraling out of control. "Fine, but we're going down there with the pack. Tell your vampire that's the deal." Now all I had to do was convince Dog to go with us. Vampires and wolves generally didn't mix well until they got to know each other, so it was going to get interesting.

I heard a soft knock at the back door. When I opened it, Bob slipped past my legs and ran to his food bowl, which was empty. A customer was standing at the bottom of the steps, looking pale and weak. "You're early, Mary. We haven't even set up yet, but come on in."

She climbed the steps with difficulty and walked inside.

After giving me a strained smile, she braced her shaking hand against the wall and looked around the room. "Would you mind if I sat down?"

"Of course." I pulled up a chair for her.

Mary had been a regular for the past six months. Breast cancer had taken a toll on her, but for a while there she seemed to be responding well to the blood. But vampire blood wasn't a cure for her advanced disease. It just made the pain tolerable.

"I'm sorry to be so early, but I wanted to get a jump on the line." She forced another smile.

I held my hand out to Patrick. "Give me a vial."

"Can you let me set up first?"

"No. And would you mind feeding my cat?" I nodded to the bag on the floor next to his bowl.

Seeing the look on my face, he didn't argue. He opened the briefcase and quickly handed me a vial and then filled Bob's bowl. Patrick was a keeper.

Mary eagerly took it from me and placed it to her lips, careful not to guzzle the whole thing, even though she looked like she wanted to. Within seconds of coating her tongue with a few drops, the color in her face came back and her hands stopped shaking. I never got tired of seeing pain go away. It was like a black cloud lifting from someone's face. Opioids did that too, but with ugly consequences. Despite what some people thought, vampire blood left no trail of destruction. It didn't destroy lives.

Another knock came at the door. When I looked out, there were more people lined up in the alley. After quickly hustling them all inside, we got busy handing out the vials of blood.

"Have you met Mr. Devereaux?" Debra Owens asked.

"He came into the bar last night." I left it at that.

But Hank, a recovering addict who used vampire blood like methadone, wouldn't let it lie. "He stopped by the barbershop yesterday afternoon to introduce himself. He seems all right. He invited everyone in the shop to his grand opening." He scratched his head. "How the hell is he going to have that old building whipped into shape to pass inspection by next week?"

I hadn't even thought about the inspection. Maybe his opening wasn't going to happen after all. Not without a permit. "That's a good question, Hank. I've been wondering that myself."

He kept the questions coming. "Did you hear about Willy Henderson's girl?"

Word traveled fast, and right now I needed to slow it down. "Yeah, that was a real shame. Let's hope they find whoever did it to her."

"It was one of those bloodsuckers, that's who it was." Hank glanced at Patrick. "No offense."

Patrick kept his cool better than I would have. After handing Debra her order, he checked the list and pulled two vials from the briefcase. "Here you go, Hank." As Hank went to grab them, Patrick held them out of reach. "You might want to remember who this came from. Without us *bloodsuckers*, you'd be curled up on your floor with a needle sticking out of your arm."

Hank lost his grin. "Sorry, Patrick. It wasn't right for me to say that."

"No, it wasn't," I said. "Words are powerful. If you want to keep getting a safe supply of blood that doesn't cost you a mortgage payment every week, I'd suggest you keep comments like that to yourself."

We quickly finished handing out the product and sent our last customer on his way. Bob slipped out the door as I was getting ready to shut it. "Where do you go when you leave here?" I said as he trotted down the alley with his tail straight up in the air. I was starting to think I was feeding someone else's cat.

I checked the time. It was nine o'clock and I needed to get

up front. "What are you doing tomorrow night?" I asked Patrick.

He closed his briefcase and stood up. "Going down to Reaperstown with you."

"Good. Set up a meeting. And find out what you can about this vampire before we get down there. I'll call you in the morning." Then I went into the kitchen to convince Dog that he and his pack needed to join us.

NINE

Dog wasn't happy when I told him we were heading to Reaperstown tomorrow night, but he reluctantly agreed to go with us. It wasn't his own safety that had him worried. He and the pack would enjoy a little exercise if that vampire misbehaved, but he was concerned about mine.

The order-up bell rang. I pinched a french fry from the plate on the window ledge before setting it down in front of Patrick. "Did you go to church today?"

"Sure did." He shot me a grin. "The church of sin."

I tossed a fry at him. "You're horrible, you know that?"

"Every chance I get."

I glanced out the front window at the workers going in and out of the building across the street—at ten p.m. on a Sunday. "Devereaux's got them working night and day over there."

"Yeah, and he's probably paying them a boatload of money to get that dump whipped into a restaurant by... when did you say that place is opening?"

"Tuesday."

He chuckled. "I'll believe it when I see it. Unless that man's got him a pack of elves working over there."

"Maybe he does. This is Crimson."

Business was slow, so I decided to take a break. "Can you and Lucy look after the bar by yourselves for a few minutes?" I asked Beau.

He looked at all the empty stools and shrugged. "I think we can handle it."

I stepped around the bar and headed for the front door. Patrick grabbed a handful of fries and followed me. "Could you let me finish my dinner first?"

"Did I ask you to come?"

He stuffed them in his mouth and mumbled around his food, "Girl, you're a pain in the ass sometimes."

"I know." I kept moving before I changed my mind about walking into that building uninvited. When we crossed the street, I looked at the sign next to the front door that said MORCEAU. "What kind of name is that?" It was definitely French.

"An overpriced one. You better make sure your date is paying for dinner Tuesday night."

"It's not a date."

"Does he know that?"

I gave him an annoyed glance over my shoulder. "You're starting to sound like Dog."

"Better Dog than that himbo you got working your bar back there."

The glass door was covered up, and so was the front window that hadn't been there yesterday. I tried the handle, but the door was locked, so we decided to go around back and see if any of the rear windows would give us a glimpse inside. As we were walking away, it opened. Atticus Devereaux stepped out.

"Well, hey there." Patrick sauntered up to him and extended his hand. "You must be the new guy. I'm Patrick Aldean. Resident expert on Crimson, if you need a tour guide."

They shook hands, and a funny little sound slipped from

Patrick's mouth. For a second, I wondered if he planned to let go of the man.

Atticus pulled his hand away and shifted his eyes to mine. "Would you like to come inside?"

I shrugged. "Sure." After sidestepping Patrick, who was still gazing at Atticus, I walked inside and suppressed a gasp. What a difference twenty-four hours had made. In fact, it was unbelievable. I was starting to think that Crimson had been calling Atticus Devereaux's name. He fit right in here.

"Would you like me to show you around?" Devereaux asked.

I turned and nearly collided with the man who was standing inches away from me. "I don't think so." I backed up to put some distance between us, but his eyes locked on mine. I'd noticed how tall he was before, but now that there wasn't a bar between us, he seemed to tower over me.

There wasn't a single worker in the place, not even an elf.

"Where's Patrick?" I didn't see him in the room, so I went back outside. He was standing in the same spot with his eyes fixed forward and his hand extended.

Atticus walked around me and took Patrick's hand, gripping it tightly as he gazed into his eyes. "It's a pleasure to meet you, Patrick."

Snapping out of whatever stupor had come over him, Patrick looked down at his hand. "It's... nice to meet you too."

Atticus walked back inside and beckoned for us to follow him, and for reasons I couldn't begin to understand, we did. Suddenly the place was filled with workers. There was a guy plastering a wall on my left and another polishing the marble floor.

Marble.

"How did you do this?" I asked him, wondering if I was losing my mind.

His lips rose slowly into a smile. "Magic."

I guess we could add magician to the list of residents in Crimson.

Patrick's brows arched. "Seriously, dude, how'd you pull it off?"

"As I said, my contractors are quite motivated."

A man came through one of the doorways wearing a white jacket. "Would you like to sample the venison, Mr. Devereaux?"

Atticus smiled at me. "Shall we?"

It seemed a little late to be testing recipes, but it was also late to be plastering walls.

We followed him into a spectacular kitchen, which was another impossible feat. The chef lifted a cloche from a platter and revealed two medallions of rare meat that didn't look like any venison I'd ever eaten. And I'd eaten a lot of it, living up in these mountains. All the same, my mouth watered at the sight of it.

Atticus picked up a fork and handed it to me. "I hope you don't mind sharing from the same platter."

Patrick grabbed one for himself. "I'm willing to share my fork with you if I get to eat that."

The chef carefully cut the medallions into bite-size pieces. "The meat is infused with smoked blueberries and topped with a butterbur tapenade."

It would probably crush him if we didn't like it, but when I sampled a piece of the venison, I had to fight the urge to spit it back out. It tasted bitter. Like unsweetened chocolate. I had to force myself to swallow it.

Atticus watched me closely. "Do you like it?"

Patrick spared me from having to lie. "That's some good cooking right there. I think I'll have me another piece." He helped himself to a second bite and then a third. When he saw the look on my face, he spared me from having to take a second courtesy bite. "Since no one else is eating it, I'll have that last piece."

Atticus waved the chef away. "Not a fan of venison?"

"It's a little gamey for me. I'm more of a burger kind of girl." I loved venison, but I preferred it cooked the simple way.

"Then the chef will have a challenge for dinner Tuesday night. I'm sure he can win you over."

Patrick was practically smacking his lips when I glanced at him. If I didn't get him out of here, he'd probably ask to sample some desserts.

"I left my bartender alone over there, so I better get back," I said to Atticus. "Thanks for the samples."

As we were leaving, he followed us to the door. "Eight o'clock on Tuesday?"

"Better make it seven. I'll need to get back to the Stag before it gets too busy." It also gave me an excuse to end the meal early.

Patrick weaved his arm around mine as we crossed the street. "You okay?"

"I'm fine. I just don't have time to be dining out. And I'm not looking forward to having to eat that crap."

He looked at me sideways. "Girl, were we eating the same food? That was some of the tastiest meat I've ever put in my mouth." A grin spread across his face.

"You're disgusting, Patrick."

"And I'm enjoying every minute of it, which is what you should be doing. You're too young to be all jaded and zipped up so tight. As a matter of fact, I'm on my way over to have me some fun right now." A wicked grin spread across his face. "I'm heading to a party, and I hear there's gonna be some choice goodie bags at the door."

"What kind of goodies?"

"Oh, I don't know. A little of this. A little of that. Maybe a little DT."

I stopped in the middle of the street to look at him. "Patrick? Don't tell me you're doing drugs."

Just the mention of dragon's tears made me nervous. No one really knew much about it other than it was formulated by a mage and got its name because it turned people into beasts, especially in the bedroom, which was why it was becoming so popular. It was stronger than a little blue pill.

He put on a pout. "Now you're mad at me."

"I'm not mad, I'm worried."

"Don't be. I won't touch the stuff." He gave me a three-finger salute. "Scout's honor."

"Then get out of here. But you better call me when you get home."

He climbed into his car and blew me a kiss.

After watching him pull away, I turned around and got an eyeful of what was happening inside the bar. "Those idiots!"

I ran inside, pushing past the people who'd shown up to watch Richie and Wes Wyatt put on a show. They were stomping up and down the top of the bar like a couple of drunk frat boys. Richie had the Glenlivet in his hand while his brother sucked on a bottle of cheap tequila.

"Do you have any idea how much that bottle costs?" I yelled to Richie.

He brought it to his mouth. "This? Shit tastes like turpentine." It went sailing across the room and shattered against the wall.

"Well, it's an expensive bottle of turpentine, and you just bought it." I glanced around the room wondering where the hell my bartender and cook were at. "Get off my bar!"

Wes walked up to the edge and looked down at me. "Where's my sister?"

I glanced around the room but didn't see her. "Probably taking one of her marathon breaks." She'd be lucky to have a job at the end of the night. The Wyatt family was nothing but a liability, and Lucy being on my payroll was an invitation for trouble. I knew it was just a matter of time before those redneck brothers of hers went off the rails and did something astronomically stupid, like this. "You're drunk. Get down before I call the police."

"The police?" He growled, taking another sip of tequila. "Eat this, bitch!" His foot kicked out, the steel tip of his boot barely grazing my cheek as I ducked and twisted.

I looked down at my hands as they started to shake. Then my eyes settled on the row of liquor bottles behind him. A moment later, one of them flew from the shelf and smashed into the back of Wes Wyatt's head, sending him stumbling forward and crashing to the floor. I glanced at my hands again in disbelief as the shaking subsided to vibrations. Then I kicked him in the side and stepped back. "Eat that, asshole!"

A huge wolf suddenly came out of nowhere and jumped on top of the bar between Richie and Wes. A second later, Richie jumped off and shifted, followed by his brother to make it an even fight—two scrawny drunk wolves against a much bigger and sober one.

Half the bar cleared out when Beau came running from the kitchen with a meat cleaver in his hand. He whistled to get everyone's attention as he slammed the blade into the top of the bar, struggling to pull it back out when the wolves turned to look at him.

"Take it easy, cowboy," I said when he finally freed the cleaver and started swinging.

Dog took advantage of the distraction and attacked from above. He was on top of one of them a moment later, pinning him to the floor by his throat. The other wolf leaped toward Beau but stopped in midair when the cleaver left Beau's hand and landed dead center in the thick fur of his chest. The wolf let out a sharp yip and fell to the floor, panting rapidly as he lay on his side with blood flowing from the wound.

Just as everything was settling down, a war cry filled the room. Mutt came flying from the hallway with a broom gripped tightly in his hand. He came to an abrupt stop, looking like he wasn't sure what to do next.

"It's okay," I said. "It's over."

Mutt nodded several times, his eyes wide as he caught his breath. "Yeah?"

"Yeah." I went over and pried the broom stick out of his hand, which wasn't easy. "I appreciate the backup, though."

"Sure, sure. Anytime."

When I turned around, Beau was standing near the wolf he'd just nailed, and he looked kind of pale.

Dog released Wes and trotted over to me.

Wes shifted instantly and stared down at Richie. "You killed him." He shot Beau a lethal look. "You killed my brother!"

"I-I didn't mean to kill him," he stammered, staring at Richie Wyatt's naked body as he shifted back into human form.

Beau's eyes flew wide. "It was self-defense." He glanced around the room at all the witnesses. "Y'all saw it. Richie Wyatt tried to kill me!"

The bathroom door swung open, and Lucy stepped out. "What the hell is going on out here?" She looked at her brother lying motionless on the floor and then at Wes. After taking it all in, she grabbed Wes's clothes off the floor and threw them at him. "You damn idiot. You probably just got me fired."

To say the least.

She shoved him so hard he fell back against the bar and stared at her in disbelief. Like I said, she probably knew how to beat the crap out of someone by the age of three.

"Damn it, Lucy! Beau killed Richie!"

"He ain't dead." She walked over to him and kicked him in the side. "Get up!"

To my surprise, Richie started to stir. A minute later, he

climbed to his feet, looking sober. With all the eyes in the room staring at his privates, he turned around to face everyone and started to gyrate his hips. "Get a good look, ladies. It's not like most of you haven't seen it already."

"Don't look at me," I said.

Dog took off toward the kitchen while Richie gathered his clothes. After pulling his pants on, he glared at Beau and ran his hand over the wound on his chest that had almost healed. "You better watch your back, boy. We know where you live."

"And I know where you live," Dog said, emerging from the hallway fully dressed. "It's over. Got it?"

Lucy gave her brothers a warning look. "They've got it, and they're leaving."

On their way out, I gave them a warning of my own. "You're banned for life. And you owe me for that bottle of scotch, Richie." I was fully aware that I'd never see a dime for it. At least it was half-empty before he shattered it against the wall.

After they left, my few remaining customers migrated back to their stools. Beau got back to work serving drinks and cleaning up the footprints on top of the bar while Mutt mopped the floor. In ten minutes it would be business as usual. Never underestimate the draw of a cold beer.

Lucy put on her tough face as she approached me, but I could see fear in her eyes. There weren't a lot of people in town who would hire a Wyatt. For obvious reasons. "Am I fired? It's not my fault my brothers are assholes."

And your mother and father, I wanted to say. The whole clan was trouble, but at least Lucy was half-civilized. She managed to yank my chain on a daily basis, but she was a good bartender, and it didn't feel right to fire her over her brothers' bad behavior. Besides, I needed her here tomorrow night so Dog and I could go down to Reaperstown to talk to that vampire.

I decided to milk it a little bit longer to keep her in line for a while. "As long as you show up on time for your shifts, you still have a job."

A brief smile appeared on her face, but it quickly vanished. "I appreciate that, Charley."

"Go home, Lucy. Tell your brothers they almost got you fired." As she was leaving, I added, "But if they ever show up here again, I can't guarantee anything."

* * *

I spent the next couple of hours catching up on the paperwork that kept eluding me. Either I got it done tonight or I had to come in early the next day. But we were taking a trip to Reaperstown, and I'd be useless at focusing on anything else tomorrow afternoon.

After checking the alley for Bob and not finding him out there, I went back up front to the bar. Beau was pouring a couple of shots, but he kept missing the glasses. "I think your aim is off. Are you okay?"

"Why wouldn't I be?"

"You almost got your ass handed to you by a wolf tonight. No one's going to fault you for feeling a little shaky."

His brow twisted. "I ain't shaky." Then he leaned closer. "Besides, I've got Louie under my seat out in the car."

"If you're not careful, you'll shoot yourself with that thing."

He laughed. "I know how to use a gun, Charley."

So did I, but it still made me nervous every time I handled that rifle in my truck.

I sat down and yawned a couple of times, fighting to keep my eyes open.

Beau nudged me. "Why don't you get out of here before you fall asleep on the bar."

Normally I would have scoffed at the suggestion and found

something to keep me busy, but I was dead tired, and the place was nearly empty. "You sure?"

"Yeah. It's Sunday night. We're closing in half an hour anyway."

I dragged myself back up. "I need to check on Bob one more time to see if he's shown up yet. I don't trust the Wyatts not to eat him if they decide to retaliate, so he's staying inside tonight."

When I went to the back room and opened the door, Bob walked inside and made a beeline for his bowl. As I was closing it, I heard something in the alley. I stepped outside, careful not to stray too far from the door. "Is someone out here?" The rustling sounds continued. "I better not have another cat to feed," I muttered as I got braver and took a few steps in the direction it was coming from.

There was a small trash bag wedged between the dumpster and the wall. Someone had missed the opening and just left it there. I pulled it out and walked around to throw it through the door on the other side. What I saw hunched down on the ground nearly knocked the breath out of me.

"Patrick?"

TEN

"How is he?" Dog asked when he walked inside my spare bedroom with Beau behind him.

I looked at my best friend sprawled out on the bed in a deep sleep. "I don't know. I can't get him to wake up. He's been like this since I got up this morning."

Dog pulled up a chair next to me when I sat on the edge of the bed. "Tell me exactly what happened last night."

"I already told you everything. I found him out back hunched up next to the dumpster. Then I pulled my truck around, got him in, and brought him here."

Dog took one of my hands in his. "It's me, Charley. You need to tell me everything, and right now, you're not."

I glanced between him and Beau. "You're both going to think Patrick's lost his mind, but he hasn't."

Beau let out an exasperated sigh. "Look, Charley. We can't help him unless we know what we're dealing with."

"I already told you two or three times. I went to check on Bob, and I heard strange noises in the alley. When I walked over to the dumpster, I found him..."

Dog gripped my hand tighter. "I've heard and seen it all, so just say it."

I let go of his hand and took a deep breath before spitting it out. "He was down on his haunches eating a chicken carcass."

"Well," Beau said, nodding his head, "maybe he was hungry."

And maybe Patrick was right about Beau needing to be tested.

"It was raw."

Beau snorted a laugh. "Now, that is crazy."

Dog glared at him. "Nice."

"You want me to lie?"

Suddenly feeling queasy, I got up and ran for the bathroom, hugging the toilet as I felt the urge to hurl again.

Beau stuck his head through the door with a concerned look. "You okay, Charley?"

I gave him a thumbs-up. "I'm puking my guts out, but I'm doing great." Another retch came, but there was nothing left in my stomach.

He squinted at me. "You ain't pregnant, are you?"

I lifted my face from the bowl. "Jesus, Beau. I throw up, and the first thing you think to ask is if I'm pregnant?"

Shifting his feet nervously, he shoved his hands in his pockets and shrugged. "Well, I don't know."

"Are you speaking from personal experience?" Looks like someone needed to keep their pecker in their pants. I heaved a few more times before climbing to my feet and going back into the bedroom. "To answer your question, I'm definitely not pregnant." My love life was nonexistent.

I'd been nauseous since seeing Patrick with that raw chicken in his mouth the night before, but I was pretty sure that wasn't the reason for my sudden love affair with the toilet. I was starting to think that venison was bad. Not a good start for a new restaurant in town. It could also explain Patrick's mental state. But I was more concerned about that "goodie bag" he'd probably gotten at that party. For the moment, I decided to keep that to myself and focus the attention on a more sympathetic explanation for his sudden display of insanity.

"I think we might have gotten food poisoning last night. Devereaux served us a sample of the new menu, and it didn't taste right. I only had one bite, but Patrick had several."

"Then we should get him to a hospital," Beau said.

"He's a vampire, Beau. There's nothing they can do for him."

He started to pace. "Well, we can't just do nothing. How are you going to explain to Tom Murphy how your best friend died in your house? He'll have a field day with you, and then he'll come after me and Dog as accessories."

I shot him a horrified look. "Who said anyone's dying? Candy is on her way over. She'll know what to do." If anyone could help Patrick, it was her.

The five minutes that passed before I heard her walk through the front door felt like hours. Strutting into the bedroom wearing paisley pants and a crisp white blouse with wide lapels, she looked like she'd stepped out of a seventies time warp. There wasn't a hint of urgency in her eyes.

"Candy," Dog acknowledged.

She walked up to him and put her hand on his shoulder, resting her hip against his arm. "Aren't you a sight for sore eyes. How've you been, sugar?"

"Can't complain."

"If you two are done flirting with each other," I said, "can we get down to business?"

She gave me a chastising look. "You call this flirting? Honey, you'll know it when I'm flirting."

Dog chuckled and nodded to Patrick. "Better get to it before she accuses us of having an affair."

Candy winked at him and set her purse on the nightstand. Then she bent down close to Patrick's face. "Wake up, sleepy head."

"I already tried that," I said. "I can't get him to open his eyes."

"Don't you worry. Candy knows how to wake a man up." She reached into her purse and pulled out a small vial no bigger than a perfume sample and twisted the top off. After placing it under Patrick's nose and getting no response, she straightened up and narrowed her eyes. "Now, that's a first."

I glanced at the vial. "Smelling salts?"

"Something like that." She studied him, eventually pulling up a chair next to the bed. "I think this is going to require a more drastic diagnostic test."

I didn't like the look on her face. "What kind of test?"

She finally pulled her eyes away from Patrick to look at me. "You said you found him eating a dead chicken last night?"

"Well... it was more like a leftover carcass from the dumpster. It didn't have a head or feathers or anything."

"It was *raw*, right?" She patted me on the thigh. "It's the same thing, honey, but whatever makes you feel better."

Every time I got an image of what I saw last night, I got nauseous all over again. "Maybe it's just that venison I was telling you about."

She held her hand out. "I need a hair tie?"

"Uh..." I glanced around the room and spotted one on the dresser.

After I handed it to Candy, she pulled her long red hair back and secured it into a bun. Then she reached into her purse again. "And I was stupid enough to wear my favorite white blouse today." She pulled something out of her bag that looked like a syringe. "Y'all might want to back up."

"What is that?" I said.

"The diagnostic test I mentioned."

Instead of taking her advice, I stepped closer and watched her prep the syringe by flicking her finger against the tube of black liquid, coaxing an air bubble to the surface. Then she pressed the plunger gently until a drop of the liquid came from the tip of the needle. It looked like black ink.

My brow tightened. "I don't think this is a good idea."

She set the syringe down and pulled a pack of cigarettes from her purse, placing one between her teeth.

"Candy Palmer, don't you dare light that cigarette in my house. You said you quit."

"Well, obviously it didn't work." She grabbed the syringe and spit the cigarette out of her mouth, quickly jabbing the needle into Patrick's arm. Then she steadily started to plunge the contents into his vein. "Go grab a couple of towels."

"For what?"

She glanced at me like I was stupid. "For the splatter."

"Splatter?" Beau looked horrified. "What the hell are you doing to him!"

The dark liquid raced up his vein toward his shoulder as she slowly injected it.

Dog nodded his head knowingly. "A demon reckoning."

Patrick didn't even stir as every visible vein in his body started to turn black, making him look like one of those diagrams detailing the veins and arteries of the human anatomy. When the liquid reached his face, his lips parted. He inhaled sharply as it snaked toward his eyes.

Candy straightened up and took a step back. "Here we go."

Patrick's entire body started to tremble as his closed eyelids began to bulge.

"What's happening to him?" I wanted to shake her when she didn't answer me.

She nodded to Patrick instead. "See for yourself."

"Holy mother of God!" Beau's back hit the wall with a thud

when Patrick sat straight up and opened his eyes. Blood spurted from his sockets.

Candy looked down at her blouse and let out a sigh. "What a mess. It confirms it, though."

"For the love of God, Candy, confirms what?" I said.

"Honey, your friend is possessed."

Dog gave me a sympathetic smile. "She's right, Charley. You might want to back up."

"That won't be necessary." Candy leaned over the bed and came face-to-face with Patrick. His eyes tracked hers, but other than that, he didn't move a millimeter. "He's in there all right, but he's trapped. He isn't going anywhere with that blood in his veins. Now we just have to figure out who his daddy is."

"His daddy? Can we back up a little bit?" I looked him in the eye, but it wasn't Patrick I was seeing. "What was that stuff you injected into him? And how do you know he's possessed?" I actually caught myself hoping it was true. Either he was possessed—which I assumed was curable—or my best friend was going mad and had a hankering for raw meat.

"Zombie blood," Dog said. "Isn't that right, Candy?"

Zombie blood?

She put the cap back on the needle and stuffed it into her purse. "It's the easiest way to tell, and it has the added benefit of incapacitating the patient. It's either that or a cell, and the one in my back room is in use."

Beau cocked his head. "Oh yeah? What kind of cell?"

"Focus, please." I wasn't done with my questions by a long shot. "Now what do we do?"

"Like I said," Candy continued. "We need to find out who or what did this to him. Find his daddy."

"Or mommy," Dog said. "There are just as many female demons as male."

Candy smiled. "I stand corrected."

We were talking about demons now?

I let out a nervous laugh. "Of course. Why didn't I think of that?"

Candy pulled a pair of handcuffs from her purse. How she fit all that stuff in that little bag of hers was a mystery. "You can start by telling us your exact steps leading up to finding him behind that dumpster. Somewhere along the way, something got to him."

"He went to a party last night. Maybe it was someone he met there." I left out the part about the dragon's tears because drugs didn't equal demonic possession. But then I remembered seeing that shadow in the alley the other night and then again on the side of my house when Patrick was waiting for me Saturday. It gave me a serious case of the creeps. "I think someone is stalking me."

Dog narrowed his eyes. "You didn't mention that before."

"I didn't think I had to. I thought I was being paranoid, but now I'm not so sure. I saw a shadow in the alley behind the bar Friday night when I went out to call the cat. The next night I saw something on the side of my house when Patrick came to see me. I thought it was him, but it wasn't."

"That's it," Beau said. "You're not leaving the Stag after closing without an escort to your truck."

"And I'll be following you home," Dog added. "Better yet, I'll have the pack take turns keeping an eye on the house until we figure out what's going on."

I wasn't thrilled about having my house surveilled by a pack of wolves, but I knew they'd be out there watching whether I agreed to it or not. "I appreciate that, but don't go overboard with the surveillance. It might be nothing."

Candy motioned to Patrick who was still staring at us with that strange look in his eyes. "That over there isn't *nothing*. In the meantime, I've got a little insurance to keep him in line."

She held up the handcuffs. "I'm assuming he'll be a guest here until this is over."

A strange little laugh came from Patrick's mouth, making me second-guess if my house was the best place to quarantine him, or whatever we were doing. I loved Patrick, but I still had to sleep in the other room. "If he is possessed, do you think those are going to stop him from escaping?"

"Oh, he's possessed all right," Candy said. "That zombie blood would have killed him if he wasn't."

A shiver ran down my spine. "What? You risked his life?" My anger was starting to build.

She stepped up to me and took my chin in her hand, raising my eyes up to hers. "Now, you listen to me. I knew damn well what I was doing." She pulled out another syringe. "I also brought something to flush that zombie blood right out of him if I was wrong, which I wasn't."

I considered asking what was in the second syringe, but I wasn't sure I wanted to know.

"And don't you worry." She dangled the handcuffs in front of me. "These are special. I infused them myself with a little mojo."

"Why is he so calm?" The look in Patrick's eyes said he wanted to harm me, but he just sat on the bed with an eerie gaze.

"Well, technically he is dead until I reverse that black death running through his veins, so he doesn't have the strength to do much moving around." She grabbed his forearm and flapped his limp wrist. His eyes slowly shifted to hers without moving his head. "See? You'll be safe as a baby in your mother's loving arms."

"What do we do now?" Beau said before the mood got any heavier in the room.

Candy slapped one of the cuffs on Patrick's wrist and secured the other one to the metal bed frame. "We find whoever did this to him. Then we'll kill the bastard." She headed for the door. "I need to open the shop in less than an hour, so I'll leave you to babysit your boy here. I'll call you later."

I was glad she was leaving because there was other business we needed to discuss, and neither she nor Beau was going to like it. But someone had to take Patrick's place tonight. I wasn't walking into that meeting alone, and that vampire would peg Dog as a wolf the second he got a whiff of him. I just hoped we didn't scare him off. But as far as I knew, he and Patrick had never met face-to-face, and I was counting on getting neck-deep into the negotiations before the vampire realized he wasn't dealing directly with my partner. We had nothing to lose by trying.

"What do you know about Reaperstown?" I asked Beau as soon as Candy walked out the door.

"I know enough to stay the hell away from that place. Nothing but bad news comes out of Reaperstown. Especially that club down there. The Beast. You want to die with a smile on your face, that's the place to do it."

Dog gave me a look. "You're not seriously considering what I think you are?"

"As a heart attack. Do you have a better idea?"

Beau glanced back and forth at us. "What are you two talking about?"

No sense beating around the bush, so I got right to it. "We lost Dickie, and he was our biggest donor. Patrick has a lead on a vampire in Reaperstown who's interested in joining the co-op."

His eyes widened. "Are you out of your minds?" Then he started talking out of the corner of his mouth like the room was bugged. "God only knows what kind of diseases those vampires down there are carrying."

"It's not like we plan to sign him up without testing him first. Besides, we're desperate. There aren't a lot of candidates in town, and the alternative is to shut down for a while. You know people around here can't put their suffering on hold while we figure it out."

He finally settled down. "What does this have to do with me?"

I locked eyes with Dog for a second before breaking the news to Beau. "Because you're going down there with me tonight. You're my new Patrick."

ELEVEN

The woods were so quiet I could practically hear the squirrels snoring in their nests. "Where are they?" I asked Dog. It was getting late, and we had a meeting with a vampire in Reaperstown. As much as we were desperate for product, I had no intention of going down there without backup. Backup that was nowhere in sight at the moment.

Beau let out a nervous laugh. "We're all going to get killed."

"Keep your pants on, boy." Dog scanned the woods at the edge of the clearing and brought his eyes back around to mine. "They're here."

I glanced at the tree line and spotted glowing eyes from one end to the other. Wolves started to emerge from the forest, and a moment later we were surrounded. One of them shifted and walked up to us. It was Dog's second-in-command, Loki.

Beau got an eyeful of the naked shifter and looked everywhere but at Loki. I, on the other hand, was used to seeing buck-naked wolves standing in front of me.

Dog glared at him and growled, "You're late."

Loki lowered his head and averted his eyes. "We had a little trouble on the way over."

Dog ran the pack like a drill sergeant. There wasn't a lot that could constitute trouble for wolves their size, so I didn't think he was interested in hearing excuses. He heard Loki out, though. "What kind of trouble?"

Loki kept his eyes lowered. "We got ambushed."

"By?"

He gritted his teeth. "Crows."

Another wolf shifted and stepped forward before Dog could lay into Loki. It was Lux, one of the females of the pack. This time Beau's eyes wouldn't look at anything *but* the wolf.

A grin slid up the side of her face. "Whatcha lookin' at?"

Beau cleared his throat and brought his eyes up to hers and managed to keep them there. "Nothing."

After letting him squirm for a moment, she looked back at Dog. "Something wasn't right about those crows. There had to be fifty or sixty of them. I've never seen anything like it."

Dog approached the tall redhead with an amused look in his eyes, but it was laced with aggression. "You're telling me the pack was intimidated by a bunch of birds?"

I looked up at the sky. "Crows don't fly at night." They didn't see well in the dark and usually settled in to roost before sunset. Before raptors came out to hunt. "Something must have flushed them out."

"Like I said, they weren't acting right. One of them nearly took out Max's eye." She looked over her shoulder at the gray wolf behind her with bloodstains on the fur of his face. "If I didn't know better, I'd swear the damn things were rabid."

"Birds don't get rabies," Beau blurted out.

She looked back at him, her nostrils flaring as she took in his scent.

He stepped back. "What? Want me to drop my pants so you can sniff my ass too?"

"Careful, sweetheart. I bite."

Dog stepped between them. "That's enough," he said to

Lux. "Go." After she and Loki shifted and ran back toward the woods, he turned back to me. "You need to get going. See you down there."

Thanks to the pack taking their time, we were running late. We were meeting this vampire at an old warehouse at ten p.m., and if we were lucky, he'd still be there when we finally showed up.

After watching the pack disappear into the woods, Beau and I climbed into the truck and drove south of town, my foot heavy on the pedal to make up for time.

Beau bounced his leg nervously. "What do you know about this vampire?"

"Not much. Patrick said his name is Ian Masterson."

"Masterson?" Beau dropped his face in his hands and let out a steady groan. "Christ, Charley! That vampire is seriously bad news."

"You know him?"

"Hell no, but I've heard of him. He's part of some vampire *organization*," he said with air quotes. "They rule the roost down there."

I almost slammed on the brakes. "You mean a gang?" Great. We were on our way to meet a thug with fangs.

"It's too late to freak out about it now."

"Oh, I haven't even begun to freak out yet." I turned my head to look at him. "Tell me you're joking."

"Eyes on the road." He nodded to an oncoming vehicle we were veering toward.

I pulled the steering wheel to the right as the approaching driver lay on the horn.

"Damn it, Charley. You'll get us killed before we even get there."

As much as I wanted to, I wasn't turning around now. We needed that blood. And the pack was meeting us down there just in case, and this was definitely a just-in-case scenario.

"Give me the directions," I said.

He pulled up the text message I'd forwarded to him. "Take the next exit and turn right. It's a few miles down from there."

The stretch of road we turned on didn't have any street-lights. It was so dark outside from the thick cloud cover that I could barely see ten feet in front of me. "Is it just my imagination, or is it unusually dark tonight?"

"It's dark all right. That's Reaperstown for you."

We came to a stop sign at the edge of what looked like a blink-and-you-miss-it town. There were a few shops lining the street that all appeared to be permanently closed. "Yep. This is it." I'd only driven through the place once, and it was years ago with my mother. Back then Reaperstown was still alive. Barely, but alive. Now the only business that appeared to be up and running was a club on the corner of the two blocks that made up the entire town. There was no sign on the place, but the lights were on inside and I could hear music coming from it as we approached.

"Is that the bar you mentioned?" I asked.

Beau slid down in his seat. "Yep. That's it. The Beast."

A guy who looked half-dead stepped outside and lit a cigarette as we cruised by. He took a drag and smiled at us, revealing a set of fangs. Through my side mirror, I watched him pull out his phone. "I think this Ian guy is about to find out we're here."

Beau looked out the back window at the vampire. "I don't like this one bit."

"I'm right there with you, buddy." What the hell had we gotten ourselves into? As we drove through another stop sign, exiting the town, I considered our options. There was no sign of the pack, but I didn't expect there to be. They were out there, though. Dog wouldn't let me down.

"We can always hang a U-turn and make a run for it," Beau said, still eyeing the vampire through the rear window.

I hit the brakes. "No, I don't think we can." Standing in the road in the beam of the headlights were several vampires. There were more approaching the truck from the rear, so kicking it into reverse would only complicate things.

Beau let out a heavy sigh. "I guess we found the place."

I put the truck in park and rolled down my window when one of them walked up. "Are you Ian?"

Without answering, he motioned to a run-down building on the side of the road. "Park over there." It was an old garage or auto repair shop. Some of the vampires followed him over to it, but the rest remained standing in the road. Probably to make sure we didn't try to make a run for it.

After parking the truck in front of the building, we got out and went up to the guy who appeared to be in charge. "Where's Masterson?" I said.

"You're late. Ian doesn't like to be kept waiting."

"And I don't like being lied to." I figured boldness would command more respect than acting like a petrified rabbit. Having the pack around here somewhere as backup fueled my bravado. "Take me to him, or we're leaving."

Beau slid his eyes to me and whispered, "Tone it down, Charley."

The vampire was clearly amused. "Well, all right then. Follow me."

We went inside the building. The clouds had mercifully started to part, allowing the moonlight to stream through the dirty windows and partially illuminate the dark room. I didn't see any sign of this Ian guy, but there was enough crunchy debris on the floor to announce us. I also didn't want to press my luck by continuously asking where he was, so I kept my mouth shut and waited patiently. It didn't take long to hear steady footsteps coming from somewhere in the large space.

The vampires all stepped back. The one who'd led us into

the building grabbed my arm roughly to pull me with him when I didn't fall in line.

Beau boldly grabbed his wrist. "Take your hand off of her."

The others moved so fast we didn't see them coming. They slammed Beau against the wall, and the vampire let go of my arm and grabbed me around the waist, grazing his fangs against my neck. "Give me a reason, sweetheart."

"Marcus, show the lady some manners." The deep voice came from across the room, and I was released instantly.

He stepped out of the shadows and into the moonlight, a long leather jacket hugging his tall, lean physique. His shirt was undone down to the middle of his chest, revealing a gold pendant. A symbol or a sigil. After assessing the situation, he cocked his head and looked at Beau, finally settling his dark eyes on mine.

"I guess you're Ian," I said when he wouldn't stop staring at me.

"Shut up!" Marcus barked at me.

Without taking his eyes off mine, Ian held his hand up to silence the vampire. "And you must be Charley. Is that a nick-name, or were your parents rebellious?"

"Both." I held his gaze until it was almost painful to continue. Vampires could outstare anyone or anything, and it usually ended badly for the one being gazed upon.

He looked back at Beau. "And who is this?"

"My partner," I said before Beau could answer.

His slight smile vanished as he gave Beau another look. "I was told you worked with a vampire. *That* is no vampire."

"Patrick had a family emergency, so Beau is stepping in for him temporarily. You can trust him."

In the blink of an eye, he was towering over me. "I don't trust anyone." After staring at me for a moment, he asked, "Do you know who I am?"

"Not really." I kept my eyes glued to his, refusing to cower under his intense gaze. "But I'm assuming we're not here to discuss a partnership or to collect a sample of your blood, so why don't you cut to the chase and tell us why we *are* here."

He started to walk away, snapping his fingers once as he leisurely strolled toward the center of the room. In a streak of movement, one of the vampires disappeared into the other room and returned with a chair. He moved so fast my eyes couldn't track him.

I glanced at Beau, but he was still being held against the wall by a bunch of vampires who had no intention of letting him contribute to the conversation, which was probably a good thing.

Ian sat in the chair and finally got down to business. "I run things in this town. I guess you could call me the mayor of Reaperstown."

"No offense, but this dust bowl isn't much of a town anymore, so I wouldn't be bragging about that." As soon as I said it, I regretted it. My mouth had a mind of its own sometimes.

A grin spread across his face. "I like you, Charley. You're not afraid to die."

Actually, I was, but I decided to use his assumption to my advantage. "It wouldn't be the first time I almost met my maker."

His grin widened. "Interesting choice of words."

He continued to stare at me silently, studying me like he was trying to figure me out. I, on the other hand, was calculating how long it would take to reach the door if it came down to fight or flight, but I was pretty sure the vampires would win that race.

"We have a problem," he finally said.

I couldn't have agreed more. "Mind telling me what that is?"

"I understand you have a thriving business operating out of that bar of yours. A business that's cutting into mine."

So that's what this was about. He had his own vampire

blood operation. Ian Masterson was just another thug profiting off of people's pain and misery. "You're a dealer." It wasn't a question.

He was in my face before I could blink, but I held my ground, even though my legs were shaking.

"Is that what you think I am?" His face was so close to mine, I could feel his breath on my skin. "Some lowlife who stands on a corner peddling vials of blood? You insult me, Charley." He stepped back and ran his hand through his jet-black hair and then went back to his chair. "I'm a businessman. I think we might be able to work together after all."

I could feel a shakedown coming. "We're not in it for the money. We run a blood co-op. People around here are simple folks, but they have big-city problems. Illness and addiction. All we're doing is providing the community with some relief they can afford." I doubted I could say the same thing about him.

There wasn't a drop of sympathy in his cold eyes. "Vampire blood isn't free, so someone is making a profit."

I shrugged. "Our donors get paid for their blood, and we take a small cut to cover expenses." As I said the words, it did kind of sound like a profitable side hustle. "But let me make something clear. We sell it at a fraction of the street price so our members can still eat, and we don't sell to kids. Or for recreational use."

After hearing me out, he cocked his head. "You're a regular Florence Nightingale, aren't you?" But that was the end of his reasonable demeanor. He stood up and walked back over to me, any trace of amicability gone from his face. "I'll be taking a twenty-five percent cut of every vial you sell."

"Twenty-five percent? We'll have to jack the price up to a level our customers can't afford."

"That's not my problem."

I shook my head. "No deal."

"Charley," Beau warned between clenched teeth.

"I'm no hustler." I took a bold step toward him. "I'll shut it all down before I take food from my neighbors' mouths."

He pinned me to the wall by my throat. "No, you won't. You came here for a partnership, and now you have it."

"I came here for a donor," I manage to get out as his hand tightened around my neck.

The windows suddenly shattered. Glass flew in every direction as wolves flooded into the building.

Ian released me. I was so relieved to have his hand off my throat, I nearly sank to the floor. But then I saw his fangs descend.

I reached inside my boot and pulled out a knife. Something else my mother had taught me was to never walk into a dangerous situation unprepared, and a vampire meetup in Reaperstown certainly qualified as dangerous.

Ian gave it a curious look as I waved it in front of me. "Are you planning to cut me with that?"

"Come any closer and you'll find out." I lashed out when he tested me, slicing through the sleeve of his leather jacket.

He looked down at his arm, and his curiosity turned to anger. "You'll pay for that."

When he came at me again, I held the knife at arm's length, pointing the tip at his face. A blue light illuminated from my hand, traveling over my skin and into the steel blade as my body started to vibrate. The light shot from the tip and hit him square in the forehead, knocking him backward a good six feet.

"Charley!" Beau yelled from across the room.

I looked up as a vampire was coming toward me. Instinctively, I gripped the knife tighter and pointed it straight up as he came down on top of me, impaling him on the blade. He rolled off me when we hit the ground, and I sliced it across his throat with enough force to sever it halfway. Dog came out of nowhere and finished him off, while I stared at my hand in disbelief.

Climbing to my feet, I spotted Ian on the other side of the

room. As our eyes met, he nodded to the vampires holding Beau against the wall. They shoved him to the floor at Ian's feet and backed away.

Ian pressed the sole of his boot against Beau's neck, pinning him to the concrete floor. He scanned the room and brought his eyes back around to mine. "Call off your wolves, or your friend here will find himself with a broken neck." He pressed harder, eliciting a moan from Beau.

"We didn't come here for a fight," I said. "You threw the first punches." I gave Dog a pleading look.

He shifted and took a step toward Ian. "Let him up."

Ian pressed down harder. "Why would I do that?"

My adrenaline started to race again when Beau's face turned purple. When he let out a strangled cry, I panicked. "*Let him go!*" It felt like a hurricane coming out of my mouth.

Ian's cocky grin suddenly vanished as he lifted off the ground, hovered for a second, and then slammed into the back wall.

Dog looked at me sideways. "Jesus, Charley."

"It wasn't me."

"Oh, I think it was."

Rubbing his jaw where his face had kissed the wall, Ian steadied himself and fixed his eyes at me, a wicked chuckle coming from his mouth. "You want to play?"

"Get over by the wall," Dog said. "And stay there."

Not wanting to meet Ian's wrath, I backed up toward the windows. They were too high up to reach, so I pressed myself to the wall to stay out of the line of fire.

Dog shifted and stalked toward Ian while the pack kept the rest of the vampires at bay.

Beau coughed a few times and wiped some spit from his mouth. After catching his breath and climbing to his feet, he shot the vampires a hateful look and flipped them the bird. "Who's in charge now?"

That boy had a death wish.

As Dog approached him, Ian looked at the others and gave a silent command. Marcus flew into the air, clearing the line of wolves. The rest followed, and it was a free-for-all.

Staying clear of the brawl, I backed into the corner near the dilapidated garage door. It looked like it was a strong wind away from crumbling.

Dog lunged, digging his teeth into Ian's shoulder, tearing at it violently. Ian reciprocated and latched onto Dog's flank. The two rolled halfway across the room, coming to a stop when Ian jumped like a cat, grabbing a hold of a rafter in the ceiling with one hand while pulling a dagger from his jacket with the other.

"Dog!" Again, my back hit the wall, and suddenly I was staring up at the night sky. I'd broken through a rotted door.

I ran toward the truck and jumped in, cranking the engine. Then I backed up and floored it, crashing through the dilapidated garage door as Ian dropped from the rafter on top of Dog and wrapped his arm around the wolf's neck.

Dog tried to break free, but Ian was already slicing the blade across the thick fur covering his throat. He tossed the knife and dug his fangs in next.

I hit the brakes and grabbed the rifle from behind the seat as I got out, taking aim at the first vampire I saw.

Ian.

The vampire stood up and wiped blood from his mouth with the back of his sleeve. Dog had shifted and lay motionless at his feet with his neck ripped open. The vampire let out a mocking laugh. "You think you can kill me with that?"

"There's one surefire way to kill a vampire," I said. "I reckon this rifle could take your head clean off if I get enough rounds in you before you make it across the room." I shrugged. "Even if I don't, it'll slow you down long enough for one of those wolves behind you to finish the job."

From the corner of my eye, I spotted Beau hiding behind a

table that had been flipped on its side. Loki was pacing back and forth in front of it, keeping the vampires at bay.

Ian moved toward me, but Dog started to come to and managed to sweep the vampire's legs out from under him before collapsing again. Ian hit the floor hard, and Lux pounced.

"Get Dog in the truck!" I yelled to Beau.

Beau ran over to help Dog up, struggling with his weight.

The old building rumbled, and I heard a cracking sound come from the ceiling. When one of the rafters came crashing down, I slung the gun over my shoulder and helped Beau get Dog in the bed of the truck.

"You're driving," I said, climbing into the passenger seat.

Beau threw the truck into drive. "What about the pack?"

"They'll be fine." I prayed I was right, but there was nothing we could do.

After speeding out of there, I looked at Dog sprawled out in the bed through the back window, silently calling in every favor the universe owed me. He'd be all right, I told myself. He had to be.

TWELVE

By the time we got back to my place, Dog was already sitting up in the back of the truck. We got him inside and laid him on the couch.

I covered him with a blanket. "It amazes me how resilient you are."

He threw it off and tried to sit up. "I don't need this."

"I'd prefer not to stare at your naked body," I said, pulling it back over him.

"Why? What's wrong with it?"

"Nothing." That was the problem. It was hard not to stare, and I didn't need any weirdness at work. Not that I hadn't seen his impressive physique many times. When your friends are shifters, it comes with the territory. "I'll go get some towels and bandages so we can take care of those wounds."

He waved me off. "Don't bother. They're almost gone."

Wolves healed fast. So did vampires. Ian was probably fit as a fiddle by now and planning his revenge.

The blood caked to Dog's skin wasn't going to vanish without some soap and water, though. I was about to get something to clean him up with when I heard Beau call my name.

Dog motioned to the hallway. "He went to check on Patrick."

When I walked into the spare bedroom, I gasped. Patrick's skin was as white as bleached flour, and his eyes were milky. He looked dead, and he was hovering a few feet above the mattress. The only thing keeping him anchored was the handcuff attached to the bed frame.

Beau scratched his head. "This is messed up."

I couldn't argue with that. As much as I loved Patrick, right now he was giving me the creeps. "Just promise me you won't breathe a word of this to anyone."

Patrick had enough trouble with bigots around here. The last thing he needed was for the zealots in town to hear that the gayest man in Crimson was also possessed by a demon. They'd probably raise a stake and start gathering firewood.

"They wouldn't believe me if I did. But don't worry. My lips are sealed."

When we went back into the living room, Dog was looking out the window. "The pack is here."

"That was a real shit show back there," Lux said, brushing past me when I opened the front door. She stopped halfway into the living room and turned to look at me. "Where are my manners? Mind if we come inside?"

"Be my guest."

"Where are the others?" Dog asked.

Loki followed her inside. "We didn't think Charley would appreciate a dozen wolves in her house."

I didn't have a problem with the pack. In fact, I was grateful to them. But as I said to Beau, I didn't want to broadcast the news of my houseguest in the back room.

"I appreciate the help tonight," I said to them. "We wouldn't be standing here right now if you guys hadn't shown up when you did."

Dog looked out the window again. "That vampire doesn't

want you dead. The pack, on the other hand, he would have enjoyed killing. He needs you alive and well."

"If he thinks he's getting twenty-five percent of our business, he's dreaming." Just the thought of it infuriated me. "Who does that vampire think he is?"

Dog laughed. "When you drove through the garage door and pulled that rifle on him." He shook his head. "I about pissed my pants."

"You weren't wearing any. If anyone was pissing their pants, it was me." With all the stupid things I'd done in my twenty-eight years, sometimes I wondered how I was still alive.

Lux gave me a lopsided grin. "That was ballsy. You're just a chip off the old block, aren't you?"

"You think my mother would have done something that stupid?"

"Stupid?" Dog's face twisted up. "That took guts. It's probably the only reason I'm breathing right now."

Lux gave him an affectionate punch in the arm. "It'll take more than a vampire to kill an old dog like you."

"Who are you calling old?"

"Speaking of vampires." It was time to get back to the problem at hand. "Ian will come for me. Something tells me he's not the forgiving type, and you can bet he didn't appreciate a woman showing him up tonight. He's probably already planning his revenge for what happened back there."

Dog grunted and nodded. "A young woman at that. You humiliated him in front of his bloodsuckers, so he'll be a problem."

"Problem?" Beau snorted. "He'll be a goddamn nightmare."

Dog glanced at the couch. "Maybe I should bunk down here for a few days."

"I appreciate that, Dog, but no one's bunking down anywhere. He needs an invitation to enter my house, and I'm not planning to give him one."

I moved the conversation forward, knowing I'd have wolves camped out somewhere on my property tonight whether I liked it or not. "We've got another problem to deal with. Someone's been running their mouth. First Kenny walks into the Stag and tries to sell me blood, and now Ian Masterson knows about it? Not to mention that fool who tried to hold us up the other night." Keeping a vampire blood co-op secret when a good portion of the town used it as their pharmacy was never going to be easy, but we screened our members thoroughly and took referrals only. No one in their right mind would risk losing their supply by exposing it. "It's only a matter of time before Carter and Murphy show up with a dollar-store warrant."

"And find what?" Beau said.

"You're missing my point."

"Then I think it's time we have a talk with Kenny."

Dog glanced at Lux and Loki. "Actually, I think it's time the *pack* had a talk with Kenny. We'll get it out of him."

"We can talk about it tomorrow." I pulled some debris from my hair and looked down at my dirty shirt. "I needed a hot shower to wash that vampire off me."

As everyone was getting ready to leave, Lux suddenly stopped in her tracks. Her nose lifted into the air. She sniffed, and a low growl came from her mouth.

Beau leaned into Dog. "Is she okay?"

Dog watched her for a second and suddenly seemed to recognize the look in her eyes. "It's not what you're thinking, Lux."

She dropped down on all fours and ran toward the hallway before Dog could stop her, taking out a small table against the wall in the process. Dog shifted next and went after her.

"Stay!" I said to Loki when he looked like he was about to join in. Then I ran to the guest bedroom, praying Lux didn't have Patrick in her jaws when I got there.

I came through the door and collided with Dog's backside.

It was like hitting a brick wall. I stepped around him and saw Lux next to the bed. She'd shed the wolf and was kneeling in front of Patrick, but it wasn't Patrick's voice coming from his mouth. It was the voice of a woman.

"Lena, please don't hurt me," he said in a soft voice. "I miss you so much."

Lux had tears running down her face. I stepped toward her, but Dog grabbed me. I glanced down at his fingers digging into my arm, and he softened his grip.

"Who's Lena?" I asked.

Without taking his eyes off Patrick, Dog swallowed hard. "It's Lux's birth name. The voice sounds just like her mother's, but she's been dead for years. She was a member of the pack."

"What?" I looked back at the man on the bed, but it wasn't my best friend anymore. If there was a shred of a doubt in me that he was possessed, it was gone now.

"I need to get Lux out of this room," he said. "Then you need to lock this door and stay out." The look in his eyes was as serious as I'd ever seen. "No food. No water. That thing sitting on the bed isn't human, so he'll survive without it."

When I didn't respond, he shook me gently. "Charley!"

"Charley!" Patrick mocked in a voice that sounded just like Dog's.

I snapped out of it and looked at Patrick's grinning face before answering Dog. "You're right. I've got it."

"Good. No one goes in or out until we find out who did this so we can fix him, or..."

"Or what?"

He didn't answer, but I knew what he meant. We either pulled the demon out of Patrick, or we'd be burying him. "Wait. There's no way to lock the door from the outside."

"You got a padlock?"

"No."

A grumble came from his mouth. "I'll be right back."

I followed him down the hallway and onto the front porch. He crossed the yard and went into the garage, coming back out a few minutes later with a board and some tools in his hands. Then he went back inside and started nailing the board to the bedroom door, securing it to the outside frame.

After he was done, I looked at his handiwork. "You think that's going to stop him if he escapes those handcuffs?"

"Probably not, but it'll slow him down and give us a heads-up."

"You mean me."

He took a deep breath and gave me a commiserative smile. "I mean we. Looks like we're going to be roomies for a while."

* * *

I stumbled over a wolf when I walked out of my bedroom the next morning. It was dark in the hallway, and Loki had taken his task a little too seriously. He was sleeping pressed up against my door.

He shifted back to his human form when my foot caught him in the side. "Easy, woman. Watch where you're walking."

"Sorry. I didn't anticipate a wolf sleeping in the hallway."

I went into the kitchen and started some coffee. Then I checked the fridge to see what I could scrounge up for breakfast. Wolves were ravenous creatures, and it was the least I could do to repay them for babysitting me all night. I would have been comfortable with Dog staying over, but *he* was more comfortable with all three of them camping out in my living room. And the hallway apparently.

Lux jumped up on all fours, pointing her tail in the air as she dropped into a downward dog position to stretch her legs. After shifting, she grabbed her clothes and got dressed, which was what I was hoping Loki would do, but he just stood there naked examining the bowl of overripe bananas on my counter. Wolves are also natural exhibitionists.

"Uh..." I looked away from him. "Mind putting your clothes on?"

He glanced down at his naked body and grinned at me. "Sorry about that."

While Loki grabbed his clothes, I went into the living room to find Dog. He wasn't on the couch, but the bedding had been used. "Where's Dog?"

Lux walked over to the window and looked out. "He's sleeping on the porch, and he's got a bird on top of him."

I opened the front door, startling Dog when I stepped outside. Rex cawed and flew onto the railing when the wolf jumped up and let out a growl. "It's just me." Wisely, I took a step back until he calmed down.

Loki came out and looked at the crow. "I guess he made a friend."

"That's Rex. He thinks he lives here."

He flew from the railing and nearly grazed us with his wings as he sailed through the front door.

Lux chuckled. "Looks like he does."

"Did you sleep out here all night?" I asked Dog.

After shifting, he scanned the property. "I got restless inside the house. Besides, I'm used to it. Any problems with Patrick?"

My bedroom was right next to his. I barely slept and even stuck my ear to the wall a few times during the night. "Not a peep. It was a little too quiet in there." The wheels in my head started turning. "You don't think—"

Dog brushed past me and went down the hallway. Lux and I followed him. "Stand back." With both hands, he yanked at the board. Dog was stronger than the average human, but he wasn't stronger than his own handiwork. I went and got the hammer from the kitchen counter so he could use it to wedge the board off.

A minute later, it was on the floor with a chunk of the frame, and the door was swinging open. I breathed a sigh of relief to see Patrick sitting on the edge of the bed, his demonic eyes fixed on mine.

"At least he's still in here," Dog said.

I glance at the damaged doorframe. "Damn it, Patrick. You could have at least made some noise."

Loki sneered. "The bastard did that on purpose."

"Patrick isn't big on behaving even when he isn't possessed." I walked toward the kitchen while Dog did his best to resecure the door. "Anyone hungry?"

Lux rested her elbows on the breakfast bar. "What do you have?"

"Eggs. Bacon." I poured us both a cup of coffee. When I walked over to the stove to start cooking, a box of cereal came down on my head.

Lux glanced up at Rex. "I think your crow has a bone to pick with you."

Dog came into the kitchen. "The door should hold until I can get back here this afternoon with a proper lock."

"At least that vampire didn't show up last night," Loki said, walking up behind him.

I reached up to let Rex climb on my arm. There was something attached to his leg. "I'm not so sure about that." I pulled the string to release a tiny piece of paper tied around it and unfolded the note. "He was here all right."

Dog took it from me and read it. "Looks like the extortion rate just went up." He laid it on the counter for everyone to see. The message said THIRTY-FIVE PERCENT.

THIRTEEN

Halfway across the street, I stopped to get a good look at the place. It was unrecognizable. The dirty white exterior was now covered with chocolate-brown vertical siding, and ornate architectural molding ran along the edges of the building, hiding the fact that it used to be a run-down machine shop. The large picture window in the front was strung with sparkling lights that gave it a charming feel. There wasn't a building in Crimson that looked remotely like it, so it stuck out like a sore thumb when you entered the square. Atticus Devereaux really was a magician.

Atticus was expecting me for dinner, but he would have to settle for a raincheck. I was in crisis mode, so sitting down for a fancy dinner wasn't on my list of priorities. I didn't have the time nor the stomach for it. Glancing down at my outfit, I felt underdressed to even walk in there, but I couldn't find a phone number or anything else about the place online, so here I was.

I went inside Morceau and immediately caught a whiff of something. It wasn't food. I'd say it was incense or some kind of spice. As I glanced around for a greeter, a man wearing a suit walked up to me and smiled. "This way, please," he said before turning toward the dimly lit room.

I hadn't even given him my name.

"Oh, I'm just here to..." I tried to tell him I was here to cancel, but he kept walking.

I followed him to the other end of the room, glancing at all the diners. There were more people than I expected. People who I knew for a fact couldn't afford to eat in a place like this. Marcy Bedford for one. The woman still had an unpaid tab at the Stag, and I intended to collect from her next time she came in. But I had a feeling I wasn't the only one getting a free meal on opening night.

The locals seemed to be enjoying the place, and there were a lot of them. Jim Hardy, Crimson's chief of police, was sitting with his wife, Florence, stroking her hand while he gazed at her. Usually Hardy barely acknowledged he was married, so it must have been the wine.

As I followed the man, my boots clicked against the white floor. It was shiny, with small black diamonds spaced every twenty inches or so. The furniture was understated, but the light fixtures shouted extravagance. Dainty pendants hung above every table, and there was a single crystal dangling from each. In the center of the room was a beautiful chandelier that sparkled brilliantly. I had to resist the urge to reach up and run my fingers over the crystals like a wind chime as I walked under it.

"Charlotte." Atticus Devereaux stood up from a table next to the window. "I was afraid you might not come."

"It's Charley, and unfortunately I can't stay."

He frowned. "Is something wrong?"

"No, nothing's wrong." If he only knew. "I just have some fires to put out, so I have to get back to the Stag." He stared at me for a moment with an unreadable expression, and I had to fight the urge to sit down at the table.

"What a shame." He smiled pleasantly. "At least stay for a glass of wine."

He reached for my hand, and a warm sensation traveled up my arm. I had the strangest feeling that the walls were closing in around me, and suddenly I was gripping the back of the chair to steady myself.

"Charlotte? Are you all right?"

Atticus was coaxing me into a chair when the feeling passed. "I probably just need to eat something." Having lost my appetite that morning after finding that note, I hadn't eaten all day. But I could have kicked myself after saying it to him.

He motioned to a waiter. Before I knew it, I had a plate of food in front of me and a glass of wine. Another magic trick.

"I hope you like duck," he said, taking a seat across from me. "I took the liberty of planning the meal in advance."

I didn't have the heart to tell him I wasn't a fan of duck and that I was leaving after a few bites. I could at least be polite to the man for five minutes. So I took a bite and forced it down with a hefty sip of wine and started in with small talk. "How do you like Crimson so far?"

He relaxed into his chair and settled his warm brown eyes on mine. "I find the people welcoming and the mountain air refreshing."

The duck was growing on me, so I took another bite. "It must be pretty boring compared to New York." The center of town consisted of a four-block stretch of about thirty businesses, a third of which were either shuttered permanently or were only open a few days a week outside of tourist season. It took a certain type of person to thrive in Crimson.

"I've spent a lot of time in small towns." He took a sip of wine and set the glass on the table. "I feel right at home in Crimson. People here are different. You're different, Charley."

We gazed at each other for a moment before my eyes wandered to the window. I found myself staring at the strings of sparkling lights hanging around the square, swaying back and forth as if a storm were coming. For a moment I forgot where I was.

I snapped out of it when I heard the sound of glass breaking. I looked in the direction of the noise and saw Florence Hardy leaning over the table. She was staring at the chief, with her breasts hanging halfway out of her low-cut dress and her tongue tracing the edge of her lips. A glass had fallen from their table and shattered.

"Someone had too much to drink tonight," Atticus said. There was a slight annoyance in his eyes, but it quickly disappeared when they got up to leave.

I looked at the time. Somehow an hour had passed since I left the bar. I got up from the table. "I need to get back. Thank you for dinner."

Glancing at my barely touched meal, he brought his eyes up to mine. "A raincheck?"

Took the words right out of my mouth. "We'll see." He seemed nice enough, and he certainly was handsome. But something was off between us. Maybe it was the age difference.

He got up to walk me out. "Good night, Atticus," I said when we reached the door.

He surprised me with a kiss on the cheek and whispered, "What are you?"

It was the second time he'd asked me that, but I really didn't have an answer for him. I was still discovering that for myself. But he'd obviously picked up on something, which made me wonder what *he* was. He sure knew how to lay on the charm, though.

Without a reply, I smiled awkwardly and started across the street, feeling him watching me until I reached the bar. I was practically vibrating with adrenaline.

After walking inside, I went straight to the kitchen to talk to Dog about the sleeping arrangement for the night. The pack couldn't sleep at my place indefinitely, but for the next few nights I had roommates.

Mutt was standing in the middle of the kitchen with a spatula in his hand when I walked in. He kept looking back and forth between the griddle and the fryer like he wasn't sure which one to deal with first. There was a bun on the floor near his feet.

"Are you okay?" I asked.

"I'm sorry, Charley. I can't keep it all straight."

Seeing the panic in his eyes, I took the spatula out of his hand and flipped a burger on the griddle. "Why don't you get another bun while I take care of this."

His eyes wandered to the deep fryer. "What about the fries?"

"How 'bout I take care of those too?"

He nodded and went to get a fresh bun. He came back with it a moment later and neatly placed a garnish of lettuce and pickles next to it on a plate.

Mutt had concentration issues. As a homeless teenager, he'd never gotten any kind of support or treatment for his severe anxiety, and it didn't take much to set it off. He couldn't handle the slightest bit of pressure, and trying to tend to the grill and the deep fryer at the same time was a recipe for disaster. To this day, he refused to take medication for it.

"Where's Dog?" He knew better than to leave Mutt alone in the kitchen during the busiest time of the night.

He zipped up tight and got a deer-in-headlights look.

"He's not in trouble, Mutt. Just tell me where he is."

"He went to the back room to get something, but he's been gone for a while."

A *while* for Mutt could be anywhere from five minutes to five hours depending on the level of crisis he was experiencing.

I took him out front and sat him down at one of the tables. "Don't go back in that kitchen until I return."

The back room was empty when I walked inside, but the door leading to the alley was ajar. I stuck my head out when I heard noises coming from out there. Someone was standing in the alley by the dumpster.

"Is that you, Dog?"

He walked toward the door. "Stay inside."

"Why? What is it?" I glanced back at the dumpster, remembering the last time I went out there and found Patrick dining on a chicken carcass.

His brows hiked. "Trust me."

Like I wasn't going to look now. I walked down the steps toward the dumpster with Dog right behind me.

He groaned softly as I pulled out my phone to turn on the flashlight.

When I rounded the side of the dumpster, I got an eyeful. "Chief Hardy?" He didn't even flinch. He kept thrusting into his wife against the wall.

Florence Hardy looked over her husband's shoulder at me with a grin on her face, but it was like she was looking straight through me. Her eyes were solid black.

I turned around and stared at Dog for a second.

"I warned you," he said, going back inside. "I need to check on Mutt."

"Yeah, you do that. He just had a mini meltdown in the kitchen." I glanced around the dumpster again, just to make sure I wasn't seeing things. They were still going at it, but who was I to tell the chief of police what he could or couldn't do in the alley?

As I was heading back toward the door, Beau came outside. "Charley? What are you doing out here?"

I motioned to the dumpster. "See for yourself."

He got curious and went over to take a look. "Holy hell!"

"Holy hell is right." I glanced up at the moon over the building. It was almost full. "Figures."

Beau shook his head. "There ain't nothing normal about this alley lately. It's giving me the creeps. Let's get out of here."

"Did you need something?" I asked him on the way back in.

"Oh, yeah. Candy's looking for you."

When we went back up front, she was behind the bar mixing drinks. "What are you doing?" I asked.

"Just helping out, honey." She'd served her share of drinks in the clubs down in Atlanta for decades, so she could teach us all something about bartending. After sliding the glass in front of a patron, she held out her hand. "That'll be six bucks."

"Put it on my tab," he said, winking at her.

She leaned closer to him. "This ain't no open bar, so pay up." Her eyes narrowed as she put a hand on her hip. "Unless you want to be scratching your balls for a week."

He reached into his pocket and tossed a five and a one on the bar, grumbling as he took his drink and went over to a table.

"Remind me to never stiff you," I said.

She grabbed a towel to wipe up the mess he'd left when he spilled some of his drink. "Bill Meadows is nothing but a freeloader."

Lucy walked down the bar to where we were standing, raising her voice. "He's a lousy tipper too."

"Hey, Candy!" Bill stood up and unbuttoned his pants and pulled his zipper down, coming just short of exposing himself. "Ride any poles lately?" He rocked his hips back and forth, laughing as he impressed himself with his dumb wit.

I don't know what had gotten into him lately, but I'd had enough. I started to walk around the bar to show him the door, but Candy clenched my arm in a death grip to stop me. She shot him a toothy grin, and a mirage-like haze drifted across the room in his direction. She'd just made good on her threat, and that idiot would be rubbing himself raw before the end of the night. I'd let him know the next time he came in here that he could take himself right back out.

Bill lost the attitude when the blue haze snaked around his chest and continued down his torso, sending him scurrying toward the men's room.

Dog came out of the kitchen with his trusty meat cleaver and blocked Bill's path. "I think you need to apologize."

With sweat dripping down the side of his face, Bill grabbed his package and focused on the cleaver. "What are you going to do with that thing?"

"This? I was just cutting some potatoes in the kitchen, so don't worry about the knife." His eyes flashed amber as the wolf peeked through. "Now, that's something you do need to worry about."

"I'm sorry!" Bill blurted out.

"Not me, asshole." Dog motioned to Candy. "Her."

His eyes snapped to Candy. "I'm sorry! Please make it stop!"

She leaned her elbows on the bar. "Let me weigh my options here, Bill—you, or every woman who's ever come into contact with you?" She glanced up at the ceiling for a moment to ponder. After straightening back up, she looked him dead in the eye. "I stand with the women of the world. Get him out of here, Dog."

"And stay out," I said.

Dog grabbed Bill by the back of his shirt and dragged him to the door. He shoved him out with a warning look and pointed the cleaver at him. "Don't forget to give us a five-star rating on Yelp."

Half the place gave Dog a round of applause, while the other half kept their heads low, especially Bill's buddies sitting at the bar.

Beau came down the bar with a mischievous grin. "Did you tell Candy about the chief?"

Candy got a sly look in her eyes. "The chief? What about him?"

He leaned in. "He and the missus were out in the alley a few minutes ago wearing out the wall."

"Wearing out—?" A grin slid up Candy's face. "Oh!"

I wanted to make light of it, but something besides the obvious was bothering me about what I'd just seen out there. "The chief and his wife were at Morceau when I was over there earlier tonight, and they were all over each other."

"Jim Hardy?" Candy scoffed. "The man treats his wife like she's his maid."

"I know. They were drinking in the restaurant, but wine doesn't make you go at it like rabbits in public." But dragon's tears might.

Beau chimed in. "No kidding. If they weren't drunk, they were high as hell on something."

"Which is what I'm afraid of," I said. "Patrick told me something the other night. A few hours before I found him back in the alley. He was on his way to a party." I looked at Beau. "What do you know about a drug called dragon's tears?"

He straightened up and got all fidgety. "What makes you think I know about that stuff?"

Candy and I both nailed him with a look. "I didn't ask if you take it. I just want to know if it's going around town."

He thought about it for a minute and came clean. "Look. I don't mess with DT. It'll make you do things."

"You mean like have sex in an alley with an audience?"

He cocked his head. "Yeah."

Candy was giving me the eye. "Get back to Patrick."

"He said there were going to be 'goodie bags' at this party, and guess what was rumored to be in them?"

Beau's brows pulled together. "Why didn't I hear about this party?"

"Seriously?" I wondered about him sometimes. "You just said you didn't mess with DT? And be glad you don't. That's where Patrick was right before he started dumpster diving. And you never answered my question. Is it going around town or not, because what we just witnessed in that alley sure looked like it is?"

"Not that I know of. You want to get your hands on something like that, you need to go down to the Beast."

I nodded. "Reaperstown. And guess who runs things down there?"

"Ian Masterson?" He didn't seem convinced. "I thought he was selling vampire blood?"

"Who's to say he doesn't have multiple revenue streams?"

"Speaking of Reaperstown," Candy said. "Dog called me and told me what happened last night."

I glanced at him through the order window. "Did he?"

"That man loves you almost as much as I do, so don't get all ruffled about it. You need to stay with me for a while."

Shaking my head, I reached under the bar for an apron. "I'm not moving out of my house. Besides, someone's got to take care of Patrick until we can figure out how to fix him."

"Take care of him?" She let out a short laugh. "In his state? It's not like he needs to be fed and watered."

I was aware of that but, possessed or not, he was still my best friend. "So Dog told you about our trip to Reaperstown?"

"He sure did. You're not a stupid woman, Charley, so you need to stop doing stupid things."

I wouldn't call it stupid. We were just desperate. And how was I supposed to know that vampire would end up being the self-proclaimed mayor of Reaperstown?

"If those vampires come looking for me at my house, Patrick will be a sitting duck. I'm not leaving him alone."

"Fine. You can both move in with me for a while. Then you can tell me all about your dinner with Mr. Devereaux."

She was in for a letdown about the dinner that barely happened.

"Get your things," she said. "We're going to your house."

FOURTEEN

The house was dark inside when we pulled up, but I knew for a fact that I'd turned the living room lights on when I left for the Stag. I couldn't see the lights in the spare bedroom either.

Candy looked up at the tree towering over the truck. "What in the world? You might want to move your truck out of the line of fire."

It was filled with small black forms. Crows. They roosted in large numbers, but I'd never seen an army of them in my tree before.

Rex swooped down and landed on my shoulder when I got out of the truck, cawing loudly in my ear. "What is it?" I checked his leg to make sure he wasn't being used as a messenger pigeon again. It was note free.

"I see that bird hasn't gotten tired of you yet." Candy made a clucking sound, and Rex flew off my shoulder and landed on hers. "I like you too, little man, but this blouse was expensive. Go on now. Shoo."

He flew back into the tree, and the entire flock animated and started to make noise.

"Keep it down," I said. "I've got neighbors."

As we walked toward the house, Candy looked back at them. "Does that happen often?"

"You mean dozens of crows taking over my tree? No. This is the first time Rex has brought friends home."

Candy stopped and narrowed her eyes. "I don't sense any trouble, but maybe we should take it slow going inside." She stepped in front of me. "I'll go first. Stay behind me just in case I need to throw down."

"Throw down what?"

She put her hand on her hip and turned around with her brows cocked. "You better not be making fun of me."

"I wouldn't dream of it." I hurried up the steps to get in front of her. "But this is my house, Candy. Those vampires are looking for me, so I'll take the brunt of it if they're waiting inside." Before she could make it up to the porch to argue about it, I unlocked the door and pushed it open.

When I hesitated, she walked up next to me and peered inside. "It's awfully quiet in there."

I stepped through the door and tried the light switch on the wall, but nothing happened. "The lights are dead."

"Well, that's a bad omen." She pushed past me and tried the switch herself. "Maybe the bulb just burned out."

"Both of them? I doubt it."

A sound came from the direction of the bedrooms. I got up the nerve to walk down the hallway, but Candy grabbed my wrist. "Wait. Where's that gun your mama always kept in the house?"

"In the truck behind the seat. It's not going to do us much good against a horde of vampires, though." Even if it did slow them down, we didn't have a pack of wolves ready to pounce this time.

Dog had come back to the house that afternoon to put up stronger boards and a proper padlock on the spare bedroom door, but as we approached it, I used the flashlight on my phone and saw the lock lying on the floor with the boards ripped off. The door was ajar.

Candy took the lead and held her arm out to stop me. "Stay back, Charley."

"Like hell," I said, pushing her arm away.

We compromised and went in together. The bed frame was broken, and Patrick was standing next to the window with the handcuff dangling at his side. His eyes were fixed on the moon.

"Patrick?" I took a step toward him but stopped when I heard his voice.

"Get out." It was barely a whisper. "It's too dangerous here."

"If you wanted to hurt me, you would have done it by now."

He slowly turned. A hiss came from his mouth as he looked at me. "They're coming."

Candy grabbed my arm. "We don't have much time, Charley. We have to get out of here soon."

It was killing me to leave Patrick behind, but she was right.

I went into my bedroom to grab a duffel bag. After stuffing a few things inside, I went back into the living room where Candy was waiting. She had a strange look on her face. "What's wrong?" She nodded to the other side of the room. When I turned around to look, my breath hitched.

Ian Masterson stepped out from the dark corner. Through the wall, several others emerged. They materialized right through it and stood next to him. Six vampires were standing in my living room.

A smile spread across his face. "Where are your wolves now, Charley?"

"How did you get in here?"

He cocked his head. "Your demon friend invited us in."

Patrick?

"Get. Out! All of you!" I commanded in the firmest voice I could muster.

The wall sucked them back out the same way they entered. A few seconds later, Ian was calling my name from the front yard.

I opened the door and stepped onto the porch, staying near the threshold in case he tried something. "You're not welcome in my house. Stay out."

As he took a step closer, his dark eyes bored into mine. "You know that only works for your house." His grin widened. "I guess I'll have to pay you a visit at your place of business. What is it called?" He cocked his head and snapped his fingers. "The White Nag?"

Candy stepped outside next to me. "Didn't your mama teach you any manners?"

His eyes darted to hers. "Saucy, aren't you?"

"You think this is saucy?" She laughed under her breath. "You must have led a sheltered life before you got your fangs."

His grin faded. "Perhaps we'll continue this discussion some other time. Then you can judge for yourself how sheltered I am." Then his eyes turned back to mine. "Now, how about that invitation? Or shall I pay you a visit at your bar tomorrow night?"

Having been raised around civilized vampires who'd never tried to attack me before, I wasn't an expert on deterring one. I'd never had the need before. "I already told you, our members can't afford your extortion."

He raised his finger to shush me when I opened my mouth to continue. "I don't do business from front lawns. Why don't you invite me in so we can have a proper conversation." When I hesitated, he inhaled sharply. "Very well. The bar it is. Perhaps I'll snack on a few of your regulars if I get hungry."

Talk about playing dirty. I could handle him threatening me, but my customers were off-limits.

Candy stared back at him with a calculating gaze. "Why don't you let the vampire in so we can sort this all out."

I glanced at her sideways, not wanting to take my eyes off the bloodsuckers who looked like they were waiting for the opportunity to pounce. All but Ian who was playing it cool and cocky. "Are you out of your mind?" I whispered.

She reached for the sapphire amulet around her neck and narrowed her eyes at the vampire. "Honey, I'm as sane as ever, but we both know this isn't going to end well if we don't hear the vampire out."

Trusting she knew what she was doing, I stepped aside from the front door. "You can come in, but the others have to stay right where they are."

They protested, but Ian threw his hand up to silence them. Then he turned his eyes back to mine. "You'll have to be a little more explicit than that, since you've already kicked me out."

"Oh, for the love of—" I threw him an intolerant glare. "Mr. Masterson, won't you please enter my house."

"Well, if you insist." He took a step forward. Within a second, he was standing in my living room.

I slammed the door shut after Candy and I went back inside. "What do you want?"

"You know what I want."

"The co-op will be out of business in a day when we tell our members the price has gone up twenty-five percent."

"*Thirty*-five percent," he corrected.

"No way."

He took a step closer. "I don't care how you do it. Pass the cost on to your suppliers if you have to."

I laughed. "We're not drug dealers."

"Really? Could have fooled me."

I wanted to smack the smug look off his face, but he'd probably kill me for it. "We provide a community service for the sick in this town. The reason they come to us in the first place is because they can't afford the drugs their doctors prescribe.

Don't you have any compassion?" I glanced down at his chest. "There has to be a heart in there somewhere."

"There isn't." His smirk vanished. "I'm a businessman, and you're eating into my profits. No one sells product around here without paying me my proper cut."

I wanted to ask about the dragon's tears, but I'd ruffled enough feathers for one encounter.

"If I let you slide, I'd look weak." He came closer and cocked his head. "You wouldn't want me to look weak to my colleagues, would you?"

"You think extorting a local blood co-op is going to fix that problem for you?"

He got an amused look on his face. "You have quite a mouth on you."

"So I've been told."

"But you see, that's exactly what would happen. I'd waste a lot of time reining in rogues, and then I'd have to make an example of you." He was in my face before I could take another breath, twirling a strand of my hair between his fingers. "I'd hate to have to destroy a face like yours."

"Ten percent," I said, taking a step back. It was my cut, to cover the expenses of running the co-op, but I'd find a way to manage without it. "That's the best I can do."

His sunny demeanor quickly vanished as his fangs descended. When I opened my mouth to try to diffuse the situation, he slammed me against the wall and brought his face within inches of mine. "Are you trying to bargain with me?"

"Bastard!" Candy clutched her pendant and brought it to her lips, kissing it before running her tongue down the length of the large sapphire nestled in silver. "Here's a bargain for you. Let her go, and I might consider not knocking those fangs right out of your mouth."

A sneer spread across Ian's face. He released me and turned around to face her. "You really do want to die, don't you? And here I thought you were smarter than that. Being a wise, older dame and all."

He was going to regret that comment.

She smiled at him. "I was teaching boys how to be men while you were still entertaining yourself under the covers with dirty magazines." Her smile went flat when his eyes darkened and turned nearly black. "Hold your horses, cowboy. No need to get all hot under the collar over a few words."

He flew across the room at her. She backed up and hit the wall, throwing her hand up with splayed fingers. With her other one gripping the sapphire, a string of strange words came from her mouth, followed by a beam of blue light shooting from the palm of her hand. It struck the vampire between the eyes and absorbed into his body, radiating down his torso toward his legs. In a flash, he lit up like a flare and flew backward, hitting the wall next to the living room window before sliding down to the floor.

The vampires outside pressed against the glass, but without an invitation, they stopped short of breaking it. All they could do was watch their leader get his ass kicked by a *wise, older dame*.

Ian climbed back to his feet, shooting the vampires a look that had them backing away from the window. Then he straightened his jacket and rolled his shoulders. "Now, *that* was exciting." He pushed his hair out of his face and grinned. "But enough foreplay." Crooking his finger at Candy, he stalked toward her. "Bring it."

Candy reached for her pendant again and raised her hand, but this time the beam of light sailed past Ian's head as he ducked out of the line of fire. "Catch me off guard once," he said, grinning wider, "but never twice."

The beams of light kept coming, but Ian dodged Candy's magic like a skilled sensei. He reached her and yanked the amulet from her neck, staring at her pale skin inches away from his fangs. "Now, about that conversation we never finished earlier."

"Get out!" I yelled, expecting him to be sucked back through the wall, but this time nothing happened.

"Too late for that, sweetheart. You gave me an explicit invitation." As his mouth widened for the strike, I looked around the room for a weapon. The handle of my old baseball bat was sticking out from under the sofa. Right where I kept it as a burglar deterrent.

I grabbed it, but as I raised it into the air and charged at Ian, a two-by-four came down on his head. He looked stunned as he stumbled sideways and crashed into the wall.

"Come on!" I said to Candy as Patrick raised the board again. She grabbed the necklace from the floor and followed me toward the back bedroom. "Head for the woods," I said, opening the window. "I'll be right behind you."

"Your mother would kill me if you died before I did, so you're going first."

She could be stubborn as a mule sometimes. "I'm faster than you, so just go!" I helped her climb out, praying those vampires hadn't surrounded the house. But we were dead if we stayed inside, so we had nothing to lose. She hit the ground less than gracefully and started to run, looking back to make sure I was right behind her.

I jumped through the window when I heard footsteps coming down the hallway. After hitting the ground, I glanced from left to right. There wasn't a vampire in sight, but I only made it about ten feet when I saw something jump Candy up ahead of me. One of them had tackled her and was trying to pin her to the ground. She wrestled with him, trying to free her hand holding the amulet. It slipped from her grip and landed in the grass.

A sound had me looking over my shoulder. Another vampire was running toward me. I dropped and rolled, avoiding a collision when he lunged. As I was about to make a run for it, the light coming from the sky suddenly dimmed, and the yard went eerily dark. It was like a cloud had blocked out the moon as a formation of black figures moved across the sky.

Crows.

They hovered over the house and let out a terrifying symphony of caws. One of them flew down from the center. It was Rex, his white feather standing out against the black sky as he came closer. A trail of crows followed, and one by one they slashed their talons at the vampire next to me. Another group dive-bombed the one attacking Candy.

While the vampire flailed under the onslaught of talons, I ran for the truck and climbed in. After pulling the gun out from behind the seat, I started the engine and drove toward Candy.

I'd almost made it to her when a third vampire jumped on the side of the truck and reached his arm through the window to yank the steering wheel. I hit the brakes and scrambled to the passenger side to jump out. When I landed on the ground, the vampire straddled me.

His fangs clicked into place. "Going somewhere?"

I heard a familiar voice as the moon reappeared in the sky, and everything lit up in a blaze of blue. Then a strange feeling of calm washed over me as his fangs came closer.

The vampire suddenly got smaller. He flew straight up into the sky with the crows circling him. The mass of birds became a solid black dot above me as the moon disappeared again. The vampire screamed as they flew in a formation that tightened around him. Then everything went silent, and suddenly the sky opened back up as the crows reversed direction and the dot exploded. Body parts rained down around me.

I rolled out of the way just before the vampire's head hit the ground next to me and cracked open like a watermelon.

"Gross."

Candy ran toward me. "Honey, are you okay?"

"I was more concerned about you."

Both of the vampires who attacked us were gone. Probably off licking their wounds. There was no sign of Ian or the others either.

Candy looked down at the carnage on the ground and shook her head. "We really should bring in the Squad to assess your abilities before you take the wrong person's head off someday."

"Me? I didn't do that. I just helped get the vampire up there. It was those birds circling overhead." I looked up at the sky. The crows were gone, and the moon was shining bright above us.

She followed my eyes. "Maybe. Maybe not."

We spotted Patrick standing at the open bedroom window and went over to him. "What happened to Ian?" I asked him.

"Go," he said. His eyes were still filled with a dead look.

I shook my head. "Not without you. We can stay at Candy's place until we figure out how to help you."

"You can't." Without another word, he turned and walked away from the window.

Candy took me by the arm. "Come on. They might decide to come back."

I gave her an incredulous look. "We can't just leave him here."

"You saw what he did to that vampire. And he is technically dead until that zombie blood runs its course. I doubt those bastards will bother with him." She looked at the tree where the crows had settled in for the night. "Patrick will be just fine. He's safer out here than in town."

"What if he decides to leave?"

She sighed. "If he wanted to leave, he would have done it by now. Besides, we tried to hold him, and you saw how well that went."

Reluctantly, I followed her back to the truck, feeling sick

about leaving him alone and wondering if my best friend would ever be normal again.

"Candy," I said as we were getting into the truck.

"What is it, honey?"

I couldn't get that voice out of my head. The one I'd heard right before the sky lit up in blue. "You're going to think I'm crazy, but I think my mother was with me tonight."

She smiled at me. "Of course she was. Your mama's always been with you."

FIFTEEN

Keeping my eyes out for trouble as we drove back into town, I glanced at Candy. "I don't understand why I couldn't just kick Ian out of my house when he attacked you."

"Like he said, you gave him an explicit invitation to enter, so I guess you needed to do the same to make him leave."

"So I was supposed to formally ask him to get the hell out? By name?"

"How am I supposed to know? I'm not an expert at banishing vampires." She sighed. "Doesn't matter now. We're still alive."

"I'll make a note of it for next time a vampire wears out his welcome in my house."

I pulled up to Hecate's Cauldron and put the truck in park. "I'll be back in a few minutes. Go inside and lock the door."

"Where do you think you're going?"

"The Stag is still open. I'm going to help close up." It was my bar and my responsibility.

She looked at me like I had a screw loose. "Do I need to remind you of what just happened back at your place? There's a vampire out there just waiting to take a bite out of you."

"Don't worry, I'll have Dog escort me back." I also knew I'd have the pack following me for the foreseeable future whether I was aware of it or not.

"Well, I don't like it. You may have a lot of your mama in you, but until you learn how to use those gifts at will, you're no match for that vampire."

Ian Masterson was planning to walk into the Stag tomorrow night, so we'd end this business one way or the other within the next twenty-four hours. I just had to stay alive until then.

I held out my hand. "You got a spare key?"

She pulled it out of her pocket and handed it to me. "If you're not home in an hour, I'm coming after you."

"You worry too much. I'll be fine. And if that vampire shows up here tonight, don't forget to state his full name when you kick him out." Candy lived above the shop, so the whole building counted as her home.

After waiting for her to walk inside and lock the door, I drove back around the square and parked in front of the bar. It was late, but the place still had a handful of customers inside. There was a light on across the street at Morceau, but I couldn't see anyone through the window.

When I walked inside, Dog was eyeing me through the order window with his phone to his ear. I could tell by the way he was staring at me that he already knew what had happened tonight.

I walked into the kitchen as he was hanging up. "That was Candy, wasn't it?"

"Yes ma'am. Sounds like you had an eventful evening."

"That's one way of putting it. Did she tell you that Ian Masterson is planning to show up here tomorrow night?"

"We didn't get that far, but I figured those vampires would be showing up here sooner than later. The pack will be waiting for them when they do."

"No telling what they would have done to us if it wasn't for Rex and a few hundred of his crow buddies."

"Crows? Candy didn't tell me that part. Just that Masterson showed up and threatened you. She also said you used your powers on him."

I laughed. "*Used* is a generous way of putting it. It was more like I aimed it in the general vicinity and got lucky. It was the crows that did all the heavy lifting." I couldn't get the sight of those birds out of my mind. "The crows went after the vampires. That's the only reason we got rid of them."

"Then I guess Rex is a keeper." He set a plate on the ledge of the window and tapped the bell. "Don't underestimate your skills, Charley. You'll get better at it. I'm sure your mother didn't master hers at birth."

"I don't know about that. I can't remember a time when she wasn't magic personified." Noticing Dog was alone, I glanced around the kitchen. "Where's Mutt?"

"Good question. He went to take his break earlier and never came back. He's not answering his phone either. If he wasn't usually so dependable, I'd tell you to fire him."

Not to mention that reliable dishwashers were hard to come by in this town. The only other candidates around here weren't worth their weight in pennies. I know because I'd gone through a lot of them before finally hiring Mutt.

"You don't think something happened to him?" With Mutt's size, he wasn't an easy target. But a gun in a thug's hands leveled the playing field.

Dog stared at the cutting board and shook his head. "I doubt it. He's probably having another meltdown like earlier."

I felt for the man, but I needed employees who actually showed up for work and finish their shifts. "Call him in the morning and find out if he plans to come back, or if I need to put a sign in the window."

He looked at me funny when I rolled up my sleeves. "What are you doing?"

"What does it look like? I'm washing dishes."

"Get out of here. I've got this."

"You sure?"

He took a look around. "Does it look like I need help?"

The kitchen was orderly and tidy, which begged the question of why Dog needed Mutt anyway. It seemed like Mutt needed the Stag more than the Stag needed Mutt.

As I was walking back into the bar, I heard Lucy scream. It came from the back room. Dog flew through the kitchen door with his favorite meat cleaver in his hand. We both took off down the hallway and found her bent over the desk in the back with Bill Meadows on top of her.

"Get the hell off me!" She was fighting him like a wild cat.

Dog grabbed him and threw him across the room. His pants were undone with his zipper halfway down. He hit the wall so hard the whole room shook.

Lucy grabbed the cleaver out of Dog's hand and steadied herself. "I'll kill him! First I'm gonna cut off his sorry excuse of a pecker!"

Dog stepped in front of her when she started to cross the room, with her hair disheveled and her lipstick smeared across her face. "Settle down. If anyone's doing any killing around here, it'll be me." The cleaver was back in his hand a moment later as he went up to Bill and growled.

"Whoa!" I said, stepping between them. "What the hell is going on here? And what are you doing in my bar?" I said to Bill. "I told you to stay out."

Lucy wiped some of the lipstick off her face. Her eyes were brimming with tears, and I could see she was fighting them. Crying would have only made her angrier. "That asshole jumped me!"

Bill snickered. "You little tease." He flicked his tongue at her.

There were no second chances in my bar when it came to violence. If he hadn't gotten the message loud and clear earlier tonight, or when he got a look up Lucy's skirt the other day, I'd make sure he got it now.

"If you ever set foot in my bar again, I'll have the pack take care of you." I glanced at Dog. "Isn't that right?"

Dog nodded. "Yes ma'am."

"You're banned, Bill. Get out."

"Banned?" He looked like I'd just revoked his driver's license. Then his cocky grin disappeared as his eyes darkened and took on a mean look. "You're choosing a customer over that whore." He motioned to Lucy.

Strike four.

"Throw him out the back door," I said to Dog before heading for the hallway. Lucy gave him a departing glare as she followed me out. Bill Meadows was about to be in a world of hurt when her brothers found out he'd tried to force himself on her. He already had a Lucy strike against him, and I doubted she was in a forgiving mood. Was she ever?

The bar had almost emptied out by the time we got back out there, being a few minutes before closing, and Beau was finger combing his hair in the mirror.

"Got a date?" I asked him.

He looked at me in the reflection. "Nah. I'm just taking care of my investment." His sideways grin flattened when he got a look at Lucy standing next to me. "What happened to you?" Her hair was a mess, and there were traces of lipstick still smeared on her face.

"Bill Meadows happened to me, but my brothers are going to make sure it never happens again."

Beau snorted a laugh. "Bill? What did that idiot do now?"

"He attacked Lucy. And by the way, when I kick someone

out of the bar, I mean it." I couldn't believe they let Bill back in here, especially Dog.

"Sorry. We thought it was just a time-out earlier tonight to let him cool off."

"It's permanent now."

He winked at me. "Gotcha, boss."

"We're closing up," I said to the last couple of stragglers at the bar. I had things to discuss with my staff, like an impending visit from a bunch of vampires with a grudge.

Dog locked the door before coming over to the bar to take a seat. "That was a shit show."

Beau seemed confused. "You said Bill attacked Lucy?"

"Why? Don't you believe me?" She shot him a dirty look.

"Of course I believe you!" He shrugged. "It's just kind of strange."

I squinted at him. "What's strange?"

"Bill doing something like that." He scratched his head. "He seemed fine when he came in here. Said he'd had a few drinks before he got here, but then he started to act kind of antsy as the night went on."

"Antsy how?" I asked.

"You know. His whole demeanor changed. He kept fidgeting, and his eyes kept darting around. Then he got up and went to the bathroom and stayed in there for a while. That's the last I saw of him."

I didn't like the sound of that. "You said he parked himself in the bathroom for a while? Like he was doing something in there he shouldn't have been doing?"

"You think he was doing drugs in there?" Dog said to me.

"I don't know, but it's sounding awfully suspicious. It could also explain his lewd behavior tonight."

Beau's mouth went slack. "You think he was doing dragon's tears in there? That son of a—"

The men's room door opened, and Keith walked out and looked around the empty bar. "Did I miss last call?"

"Yeah," Beau said. "What were you doing in there? Sleeping?"

Keith got a goofy look on his face. "I was sitting on the throne."

I threw my hands up. "I don't need to hear this. Just let yourself out."

As he was heading for the front door, something came to mind. "Hey, Keith. I got a question for you. The other day when those vampires came into the feedstore, did Pete say what they looked like?"

He thought about it for a second. "He said they were wearing leather, and one of them was real tall with dark hair. That's about it."

It could have been Masterson—or a dozen other vampires from Reaperstown. They weren't from around here, that's for sure.

"Wait a minute," Keith said. "He mentioned the tall one was wearing a big gold necklace with some kind of symbol on it."

I glanced at Dog who seemed to be having the same thought. Ian Masterson was making himself known in Crimson, and you'd be hard-pressed to convince me he wasn't the source of the DT going around.

"Thanks, Keith. Be safe getting home."

After he left, Dog got down to business. "Speaking of vampires, we need to discuss the ones who are planning to show up here tomorrow night."

Lucy's eyes shifted to mine. "What is Dog talking about?"

No sense beating around the bush. "I've got a bad bunch of vampires down in Reaperstown coming after me." I gave Beau a commiserative look. "Unfortunately, you too."

Beau started to pace behind the bar. "I told you we were all going to get killed."

Dog groaned and ran his hand over his face. "All right, everyone, settle down. We need to prepare." He walked behind the bar and grabbed a bottle of my favorite tequila and poured me a much-needed drink. After handing it to me, he gave me the floor. "Tell us what happened."

"Masterson was waiting at my house when Candy and I got there to check on Patrick. We barely made it out of there by the skin of our teeth."

"Christ, Charley!" Beau was starting to look a little pale. "This is bad!"

"You think? He threatened to show up here tomorrow night, and I can guarantee you he'll make good on that threat."

Lucy was either stunned or fascinated. It was hard to tell. "He's coming here?"

"Yes, here. And he'll bring reinforcements."

She chuckled. "I guess I'll be taking a vacation day tomorrow."

Beau scoffed at her. "Coward!"

Lucy snickered back. "Maybe he'll bring one of your girlfriends from that vampire club down there, and you can beg her to help you out."

"You've been to the Beast?" I said to Beau.

"No, I ain't been there, but I know someone who has."

I should have known. "You mean you're sleeping with someone who partakes in vampire blood and has been down there." Beau Henry had his pecker in half the women in this town, including some of the upper-crust citizens around here. "You mind if I ask who?"

"Never mind who."

Dog reined in the conversation. "Can we focus on the issue at hand so we can all go home and get some sleep? We're going to need it tomorrow night."

"Maybe he won't show," Beau said. "I mean, with the pack being here and all." He looked at Dog. "They are going to be here, right?"

"What do you think?" Dog replied with a condescending grin.

Beau looked relieved. "Does that mean you have a plan?"

"Well, no," I said. "Not yet anyway."

Dog rubbed the bridge of his nose. "Look, we're all tired. Everyone, go home and get some sleep. We can talk about it tomorrow."

I couldn't have agreed with him more. I was dead tired after going head-to-head with a bunch of vampires back at the house. Now I just needed to go back to Candy's place, climb into bed, and get ready to do it all over again tomorrow night.

SIXTEEN

I was nervous all afternoon while I waited for a bunch of crazed vampires to walk into my bar and start trouble. Although the pack was ready to back me up, it wasn't me I was worried about. The bar opened in an hour, and it would fill up quickly with plenty of potential victims if I didn't submit to Masterson's extortion demands.

The clock was ticking, and plan B was sounding better by the minute. But even if I did decide to go with my backup plan and close the Stag for the night, those vampires would just pivot. They'd walk in here tomorrow night or the next until they got what they wanted. Short of shutting the place down indefinitely, I had no choice but to face Ian Masterson head-on.

"Did you find Mutt?" I glanced at the time. My dishwasher was due an hour ago.

Dog shook his head and continued to wipe down one of the tables. A task Mutt should have been doing. "I still haven't heard from him." Instead of being irritated, he seemed concerned. "I don't like it. Mutt is no prize, but he's dependable."

"Have you called Dougie?" Dougie was Mutt's best friend. If something was up, he'd know about it.

Dog nodded. "He hasn't heard from Mutt either. Like I said, I don't like it. I swung by his place on my way in. His car was there and his door was unlocked, but no Mutt. Something's wrong."

Now I was worried. "Maybe we should call the police."

"I already did. It's been less than twenty-four hours, so Carter told me to give it another day or two." He shook his head in disgust. "The asshole said Mutt was probably off on a bender."

"I thought Mutt was sober?"

"He is. Mutt doesn't have much, but what he does have, he worked damn hard for. Just the thought of drinking again makes his skin crawl."

Dog was right about that. I shouldn't have questioned it. Mutt worked in a bar, for God's sake. I'd never seen him once give that wall of liquor bottles a second glance.

The front door opened, and Tom Murphy walked inside. He came over to the bar and leaned against it. That was all I needed. Murphy showing up for no reason but to aggravate me with his mere presence. "We're not open yet, Tom. What can I do for you?"

"I just wanted to stop by to let you know that Helen Stovall, the woman who tried to drive into your bar, was released from the hospital this morning."

"Oh yeah? Good for her. Is she still loony?"

"She seems sane, but she's sticking to her story."

I got busy taking inventory of the liquor bottles, hoping he'd get the message and leave. "As long as her insurance pays for my truck damage, I don't care if she says Jesus himself told her to drive through my front window."

He lingered. The man made an art form out of getting under my skin. "Is there something else I can help you with?"

Tom turned his attention to Dog. "I hear Mutt has gone missing. Is that right?"

"Yeah." Dog threw him an irritated glance. "No one over at the police department seems to give a shit about it, though."

That shut Murphy up, but it also got his attention back on me.

"I noticed your truck was parked out front all night. Did it die on you?"

I'd left it here last night and walked back to Candy's place with Dog and Beau as escorts. I should have known Murphy would notice it. "I didn't go home last night." *Not that it's any of your business*, I wanted to say, but I wasn't in the mood to argue with him.

He narrowed his eyes, waiting for me to expound on that, but I just stared back at him. "You need to be careful, Charley. We still haven't caught the bastards who attacked Patrice Henderson."

If he found out about me going to Reaperstown, his head would probably explode. "How's Patrice doing?"

"Still critical. We're hoping she regains consciousness soon so she can tell us who did this to her."

All hell would break loose if she came to and pointed a finger at a vampire, but it was pretty obvious. A wolf attack would have been messier. The question was, which vampire? I knew who was at the top of my suspect list.

Dog walked toward the kitchen. "I need to prep for opening."

That was my cue to get rid of Murphy. "If there's nothing else, I need to help Dog in the kitchen. We're shorthanded tonight."

He stared at me for a few seconds like he was trying to read me. Then he showed himself out. "Go home tonight, Charley."

I was about to walk into the kitchen when I heard the front

door open again. "We're not open yet," I yelled to whoever it was.

"It's just me." Candy came in and glanced out the front window at the patrol car pulling away. "What did Murphy want?"

"The usual. To stick his nose into my business."

She set her keychain on the bar. The woman had more keys than a dungeon keeper. "I closed the Cauldron up early. Thought I'd come by to wait it out with you."

"We don't open for another forty-five minutes," I said. "Besides, those vampires won't show up until the sun goes down."

"You sure about that? Some of the vamps around here do just fine at dusk."

I chuckled, but it wasn't funny at all. "You saw them. I don't think they're the dusky type."

She glanced around the bar. "There's got to be something I can help you with. Where's your broom?" As she was looking for it, something caught her eye out the window. "I'll be right back."

When I walked over to look out, she was heading across the street to Morceau. Atticus was standing outside puffing on a cigar. Candy strolled up to him and shook his hand before leaning against the lamppost.

Dog came up behind me. "What's so interesting out there?"

"Candy's having a chat with Devereaux." I wondered what they were talking about, but I had a feeling she was just checking out the new man in town.

They talked for a few minutes before she came back across the street with a sly grin on her face. "Now that I got that over with, where's that broom?"

"Not so fast," I said. "What was that all about?"

She took a seat and pointed over her shoulder. "You mean the little conversation across the street? I was just introducing myself. Normally I would have stopped by to roll out the welcome mat by now, but I wanted to let you have a shot at him first."

"Candy!" I slapped her with a bar rag. "The man's too old for me. He's all yours." Based on what I knew of her tastes, he was too old for her too, but I kept that to myself.

"Mr. Devereaux is quite the charmer." She shook her right hand like it had fallen asleep or something. "But his energy is all over the place. He invited me to dinner this evening, but I took a raincheck on account of the fang fest happening tonight."

She should have taken him up on his offer. If things got ugly, I didn't want her anywhere near the Stag. Ian Masterson had a bone to pick with both of us.

"It's up to you if you don't want a free meal," I said, "but you might be passing up a good opportunity. A man like Devereaux probably has all kinds of secrets and things he needs to work through. Your services might come in handy."

She gave me an indignant look, her thick fake lashes lowering. "Charley Underwood, what are you trying to say?"

"I'm suggesting you go back over there and take him up on his offer. It's perfect. You can have an early dinner and make it back over here before the fun starts." And if she was lucky, those vampires would show up early and we'd settle the matter before she finished dessert. Then we could spend the rest of the evening comparing notes about the man over drinks.

She stood back up. "You're right. But I'm going to insist we sit by the window so I don't miss anything."

I watched her walk back across the street and suddenly thought about Bob. "Has anyone fed the cat?"

Dog nodded to the floor when I walked into the kitchen. Bob was sound asleep under the counter on a folded blanket next to a bowl of food. It was official. Bob belonged to us all.

* * *

It was a slow night, so at least the bar wasn't crowded. If Ian Masterson had picked a Friday night to invade the place, we'd have a bigger problem.

"What are you drinking?" I asked one of my regulars.

"The usual."

Resisting the urge to suggest he might want to call it an early night, I grabbed a bottle of beer and set it in front of him. I wanted to tell everyone that it might be wise to leave, but that would require an explanation, and I wasn't about to announce that our illegal blood co-op was being extorted by a greedy vampire. However, I did consider manufacturing a plumbing crisis by breaking a pipe in the kitchen, but I couldn't afford that either.

The clock on the wall ticked loudly in my ears as I watch the hand move at a snail's pace.

"Quit looking at it," Beau said when I glanced up at it again.

"We have a storm coming. I wish it would just get here and pass quickly." I just wanted this night to end without casualties.

As if I'd willed that storm with my words, the front door opened. It was more like a breeze had blown in. I caught a flash of ruby in the man's eyes as he stepped inside, giving away the fact that he was a vampire, and there was something familiar about him.

Beau slid a beer across the bar to a patron, nearly sending it over the edge as he fixed his eyes on the stranger. "Who's that?"

Lucy appeared next to me. "I don't know, but I plan to find out."

"Take it easy, tiger. He's a vampire." She wasn't a fan of them when it came to romance. Vampires could be rough in the sack, and Lucy liked to be in control.

Her grin grew wider. "I'd let that one bite me."

On an average night, the bar was filled with vampires, but this one was different. There was something about him that was even darker than Ian Masterson, and it wasn't just his black hair and intense eyes. And I wanted to get him out of here before those vampires walked in. For all I knew, he was one of Ian's buddies from Reaperstown.

Dog looked at him through the order window, his eyes flashing amber for a moment before he disappeared from view.

"Looks like we're about to have fireworks before Masterson even shows up," Beau said.

"Yeah, get ready to duck."

The vampire strolled up to the bar and perused the liquor bottles behind me. His ruby eyes had faded to a sky blue. "Do you have any better scotch than what's on that shelf?" His voice was deep.

I suddenly realized where I'd seen him before. He was the guy walking out of the café the other night when I was leaving the Cauldron. It was hard to forget a face like his.

With the Glenlivet gone, I grabbed the only other bottle I could recommend to someone who clearly knew their scotch. "This is the best I have right now."

He studied the label for a moment. "If that's the best you have, I'll take a double."

Happy to accommodate your discerning palate. I kept the comment to myself.

As I was pouring the vampire's drink, Dog came out of the kitchen and walked up to him with his hand extended. "Dog."

I guess he was curious about the new vampire in town too. Either that or suspicious of him. He didn't look like any vampire around here.

The vampire looked at it before bringing his eyes up to Dog's. "That explains the scent."

Most of the customers at the bar got up to leave when Dog growled at the vampire. Several less I had to worry about when the party got started.

"You need to leave too," I said to the last straggler, Mike.

"Why? I haven't finished my beer."

"I've got my reasons." I grabbed his nearly empty bottle and set it in the sink. "Go on. The next one's on the house tomorrow night."

I slid the drink to the vampire, who clearly hadn't gotten the message. "I don't mean to be rude, but it would be wise to finish your scotch and head out too."

"You have an interesting way of greeting new customers," he said, raising the glass to his lips.

"If you came in here to start trouble, you picked a bad night."

He set his drink back down. "Why is it that every time I walk into a bar, it's assumed that I want to start trouble?"

"Then why are you still here?" My gut was telling me he wasn't lingering because of the Stag's irresistible ambience.

"I was thirsty, and this seems to be the only bar in town." After taking another sip of his scotch, he looked sideways at Dog. "Would you mind not hovering over me while I enjoy my drink?"

"And you're rude," I muttered.

"I'm rude?" He let out a quiet chuckle. "I thought this was a vampire-friendly establishment."

"You could at least shake a man's hand when he offers it to you," Dog said, holding his hand out again.

The vampire finally shook Dog's hand. "My apologies. Samuel Cain." His mouth slowly lifted into a grin. "You're a shifter."

"A wolf," Dog replied with a flash of his amber eyes.

"Where are you from?" I asked. I didn't detect a Southern accent.

"Here and there. I don't stay in one place very long."

"Are you planning to stay in Crimson for long?"

He shook his head. "I'll be leaving soon. After I finish some business."

I kept pushing for more information. "Oh yeah? What kind of business is that?"

Before he could answer, I caught a glimpse of someone outside. Ian Masterson was looking back at me through the window.

Beau glanced over my shoulder. "Heads-up."

"I see him." He was alone, so we had that going for us.

Samuel followed my gaze, locking eyes with Masterson.

"You walked into my bar on the wrong night," I said to him. "You might want to try to leave while you can."

He pulled his eyes away from Masterson. "I haven't finished my drink yet."

Ian's thugs showed up a moment later, so no one was going anywhere.

They walked inside and Ian's eyes traveled around the room. They came to rest on Samuel. "Well, well, who do we have here?" His grin was downright wicked. "This is going to be fun.

SEVENTEEN

I walked around the bar and stepped between Ian and Samuel, hoping that a bold move might hold Masterson's attention. "This is between you and me." And the pack if they ever showed up.

He glanced at Beau behind the bar. "Don't forget your stand-in partner over there."

"Like I said, this is between you and me. Leave Beau out of it."

He scanned the room again and brought his eyes back to mine. "Where's your friend? She's part of the deal."

Candy? Like hell.

"What deal?" As far as I was concerned, we hadn't made one yet.

"The one that's going to keep you alive."

Samuel moved me aside and stepped dangerously close to Ian. "No need to be ugly to the lady." Baring their fangs, Ian's vampires were nearly on top of him before he could get any closer. "Easy. You wouldn't want to draw the attention of the local police by making a ruckus, would you?"

Ian scoffed. "Why should I care?"

"Well, you could make a mess of the place and leave a few bodies on your way out, but then you'll draw all that unnecessary attention to Charley's side business in the back room."

How did Samuel know about the co-op?

"You'll toss all that easy profit right out the window when they shut her down." He shot Ian a contemptuous smile. "That is why you're here, isn't it? To extort her?"

And how did he know Ian Masterson was trying to shake me down? Who was this guy?

Samuel went back to the bar and said to Beau, "I think I'll have a bourbon this time."

Ian pulled a knife from his jacket and threw it at Samuel. It sailed past the vampire's head, barely missing his ear as it landed in the wall at the other end of the bar.

Samuel didn't flinch. "Neat, please."

Beau stared at the blade protruding from the wall, eventually snapping out of it to pour the vampire a double.

After taking a sip, Samuel turned around and leaned back against the bar. "Don't mind me," he said to Ian. "I'm just here to watch."

Ian's head cocked as a sound came from the back. A few seconds later, wolves flooded into the room.

Samuel calmly watched it all unfold. "Well, I wasn't expecting that."

The vampires backed up when the pack advanced, and Dog whistled at Ian. "I think your knife is over there." He pointed to the blade stuck in the wall. "But good luck to you."

Ian grinned back at him. "No worries." He opened his jacket and revealed an arsenal of knives strapped inside. "I carry backup."

As the wolves came closer with their teeth bared, Ian lashed out, slicing through Loki's thick fur. The wolf howled, and the rest of the vampires attacked.

Dog dropped down on all fours and lunged at Ian, clamping down on his arm to force the knife from his hand. For a moment, it was nothing but fur and fangs as the wolves and vampires went at it, eventually separating and splitting up on opposite sides of the room.

"I guess this is what you call a stalemate," I said to Ian. "I'm tired and cranky after this shitstorm of the past few days, so let's move this along."

He spit out a mouthful of fur. "You know what I want."

"You're not getting thirty-five percent."

Samuel's brow furrowed. "Thirty-five percent? You greedy bastard."

"I shouldn't give you a dime, but I'll stick to the ten percent I offered you last night if it'll get you off my back. Take it or leave it."

Ian glanced to his right where Lucy was foolishly inching her way toward the front door. Before I could figure out what he was up to, he dashed across the room like a streak of lightning and wrapped his arm around her skinny neck.

Beau grabbed a bottle of liquor from the shelf and broke it against the edge of the bar, sending vodka everywhere. "Come on, vamp!" He beckoned Ian with a flick of his hand.

"You underestimate me, Charley." Ian lowered his fangs closer to Lucy's neck. "I'd suggest you have your friends back off before I rip her throat out." He nodded to Beau. "Then I'll kill your stupid bartender over there."

Beau lowered the bottle. "Stupid?"

I glowered at him. "Shut up, Beau."

Dog shifted and walked over to the bar. "Go ahead," he said. "She's nothing but trouble anyway."

Shooting daggers at Dog with her eyes, Lucy struggled but quickly settled down when she realized it was only pissing the vampire off.

I had no idea what Dog was trying to accomplish with that

statement, but if he was attempting reverse psychology, I hoped he knew what he was doing.

Beau was staring at something when I looked back at him. I followed his gaze and saw the knife sticking out of the wall a couple feet away from Dog. I shifted my eyes to my cook to get his attention. Then I discreetly glanced at the wall. Dog wielded a knife better than anyone I knew, so I was ninety-five percent sure he could land that blade between Ian's eyes without shaving a hair off Lucy's head. It was the other five percent I was worried about.

Dog was so fast I barely saw him make his move. He yanked the knife out of the wall and pulled his arm back, preparing to send the blade sailing across the room. But a second before he released it, the front door opened. Everyone, including Ian, turned.

Candy walked inside and looked around the bar. "Good Lord. What in the world is going on in here?" Her surprised look didn't fool me for a second. It was all an act for Devereaux, who was standing on the threshold of the door and about to get an eyeful.

Atticus walked inside and scanned the bar, his eyes landing on the wolves who were retreating toward the back of the room.

Ian shoved Lucy to the floor. She scurried away, climbing to her feet to run to the other side of the room. "You'll pay for this, fanger!"

"Be quiet," I said. The woman was her own worst enemy.

Atticus brought his eyes around to Ian's. "Is there a problem here?"

As I waited for the next catastrophe to happen, something streaked across the room in a blur. Ian and his bloodsuckers had taken off like dust in the wind through the open door. I'd never seen a vampire move so fast.

Seizing the opportunity, Lucy followed. "Someone else can close up. I'm outta here."

"You might want to wait a few minutes," I said. Those vampires barely had time to make it down the block, although they had blown out of here pretty fast. But it was her funeral.

Atticus turned his attention back to the wolves.

"This can all be explained," I said. People came and went from this town, sometimes never knowing the true nature of those who lived right next door to them, but Atticus was about to get a blunt introduction to the real Crimson.

He smiled faintly. "What's to be explained? Did you think I didn't know what this town was like?"

And you still moved here? I wanted to ask him. Not that there was anything wrong with living in a town where the supernatural met the mundane, but most folks kept right on going when they found out their neighbors were vampires. But I had to remember that he wasn't all that he seemed either.

He took a stroll around the bar, looking at the wolves staring back at him. "Do you think Crimson is the only place where the worlds meet?"

"Are you saying you had vampires as neighbors up in New York?" Not to mention shifters and witches to name a few more.

"Many."

A shiver ran through me. "Are you a—"

"A vampire?" He started to laugh but quickly composed himself. "Now, that would be interesting, wouldn't it? A vampire running a French restaurant in the South?" His smile returned. "I believe vampires prefer Italian."

"Is that right?"

After holding my gaze for a moment, he took a deep breath and turned around. The wolves had all shifted, and they were standing there naked, but it was Samuel who caught his eye. "I don't believe we've met." He held out his hand. "Atticus Devereaux."

The vampire shook it. "Samuel Cain."

Devereaux nodded to Dog. "It's good to see you again. You

should come to the restaurant for dinner. As my guest, of course."

Dog barely cracked a smile. "Thanks for the invitation. I'll check my calendar."

He held Dog's gaze for a moment. "Well, I should get back." On his way to the door, Atticus looked at Candy. "Are you sure I can't see you home? I hear there's a criminal on the loose." He must have been referring to the attack on Patrice Henderson. "And of course those vampires who just left."

Candy leaned against the bar and popped a peanut in her mouth, chewing it shell and all. "Thank you, but I can make it home just fine."

"Very well. Good night."

I locked the door behind him, relieved that it was over.

Dog watched him through the window as he crossed the street. "That was odd."

"No kidding," I said. "Did you see how fast Ian and his vampires disappeared the second Devereaux walked in here?"

Dog nodded, his eyes staring off in thought. "Yeah, that was interesting." He snapped out of it and turned to Candy. "You had dinner with the man tonight. What do you think of him?"

Her mouth turned up slightly. "I think he's something this town has never seen before, but I don't know exactly what that is. All I can say is I'm not a fan of French fusion. Give me a burger and fries any day." She laughed. "You should have seen those little piggies in that restaurant stuffing their faces with all that fancy food Atticus was giving out. It wasn't easy swallowing that god-awful quail with a smile on my face. I did like the wine, though."

I agreed with her about Atticus being different, and I couldn't shake the feeling that he was hiding something.

She walked up to Samuel and smiled. "I'm Candy. Who might you be?" Her breath hitched. "Wait a minute. I've seen you before." She gave me a wink. "You were coming out of the café the other night."

"Samuel. You must be the witch from down the street. Hecate's Cauldron, right?"

Her smile grew wider. "That's right. But I've never seen you come in. I'd remember."

"No, but your reputation precedes you."

She got a playful look in her eyes. "I don't know if that's good or bad."

"Oh, it's very good. Perhaps I can inquire about your services sometime."

Beau leaned into me and whispered, "What the hell kind of services are they talking about?"

"That's a very good question."

When she was done chatting him up, she looked at the knife still gripped in Dog's hand. "I take it the meeting with those vampires didn't go well?"

"Can't say we accomplished anything," I said. "But at least now we know who they *don't* like. They hightailed it out of here the second Devereaux arrived."

She shrugged. "Maybe it was me who scared them off."

"You mean like last night when Ian nearly tore your neck open? I'm sure he was petrified to see you again."

"Honey, I was fighting off vampires before you were even born."

I bet she was. "Yeah, but for very different reasons."

I glanced around at the mess. "Let's just get out of here. We can clean up in the morning."

"I second that," Beau said.

On the way to the door, I had a word with him. "We have one more scheduled delivery Saturday morning. After that, we need to take the co-op underground for a while."

"You read my mind," he said. "At least until we can get rid of Ian Masterson."

"You mean *if* we can get rid of him." I was beginning to wonder if the co-op was nearing its end, and this town would go right back to the old days of battling suffering and addiction. Vampires weren't supplying us for free. And if we gave in and somehow managed to meet Ian's extortion demands, it would only be the beginning.

Being the last one out, I locked the front door and turned around to thank Samuel for helping out tonight. I also had some questions for him, like how he knew about the co-op, but he was gone. "Where's Samuel?"

Candy glanced around. "He was just here."

Beau and Dog shook their heads. The mystery man had vanished.

EIGHTEEN

The afternoon had been quiet. Not a vampire in sight. Although the sun had been blazing all day without a cloud in the sky to beckon the daytimers out of their coffins. Bad joke. Vampires didn't really sleep in coffins. At least not the ones I knew.

"Any word from Mutt?" I said to Dog through the order window.

"Nope," he yelled back. "I put the word out that we're looking for a replacement."

Just the thought of hiring someone new made me cringe. Especially when things were so sketchy around here. Not to mention the delicate task of acquainting them with the blood co-op. If you worked at the Stag, discretion was of the utmost importance. My staff was often the front line to staying one step ahead of the cops, and any new employee had to be okay with that.

It suddenly occurred to me that we hadn't checked everywhere for Mutt. "Maybe we should call around to the hospitals."

"I already did. I also talked to Carter this morning and told him it was time to file that missing person report."

"Did he?"

"Said he would, but I got a bad feeling it's too late."

I couldn't wrap my head around the idea that one of my employees was missing, but I had a business to run. "Do you need help in the kitchen or not, Dog?"

He slammed a knife into the cutting board and groaned. "An extra set of hands would help."

"Then I'll go ahead and put a sign in the window."

I went to get the help wanted sign from the back room. After writing the position on the front with a marker, I went back up front and taped it to the window. If Mutt showed up in a day or two with his tail between his legs, I'd consider giving him his job back, but he had to have a damn good reason for the disappearing act.

Bob hopped up on the bar and made his way down to where I was stocking glasses. Something Mutt should have been doing. "Thanks for the paw prints." I'd just wiped down the surface, and now I had to do it all over again.

"Who are you talking to?" Beau asked when he walked through the front door.

I nodded to Bob. "Who do you think?"

"Cats ain't smart like dogs, Charley. He doesn't know what you're saying."

I chuckled. "Says who?" If you asked me, cats had bigger brains than dogs. They just didn't mindlessly obey everything you said to them, and they had selective hearing.

Right behind him was a woman I'd never seen before. For a second, I thought they were together, but Beau usually didn't bring his hookups to work with him.

"Are you the owner?" she asked when he turned around to tell her we weren't open yet.

"Me?" He laughed. "Nah, I'm just the bartender." A flirty grin edged up his face. "I'm Beau."

I intervened before he asked her for her phone number. "I'm the owner. What can I do for you?" She started to speak but hesitated. "It's okay, we don't bite around here."

She seemed a little shy. "I'm looking for a job."

That was fast. The sign had only been in the window for a few minutes.

I gave her a once-over. She was a pretty thing, with chestnut-brown hair and blue eyes. But based on her fancy manicure, she didn't look like the dishwasher type. "Are you sure you want to wash dishes?"

She seemed confused. "Dishes?" Then she glanced at the window. "Oh, no! I'm looking for a waitressing job. I saw the sign in the window and figured if you're hiring, you might need some waitstaff."

I glanced at the two tables in the room. "This is more of a self-service bar."

"Okay. I just thought I'd ask. Thanks anyway."

"You new in town?" I said when she started to leave.

She stopped but didn't turn around. I noticed her fists clenched at her sides. "Yeah."

"I could use another bartender."

Beau gave me a confused look.

Before he could open his mouth and ask who was getting fired, I clarified the position. "I already have two full-time bartenders, so it would only be part-time."

I'd been spending a lot of time behind the bar lately, but I had other things to deal with right now. Like a rogue vampire out to get me. And the Stag was doing well enough that I could afford the extra help if she didn't mind lending a hand in the kitchen.

"Do you have any experience mixing drinks?" She stood

there looking like a deer caught in headlights, and I was starting to regret mentioning the job. The last thing I needed was a timid mouse serving some of our regulars. The kind who got her feelings hurt over a roaming pair of eyes. Lucy would reduce the girl to tears before she made it through her first shift. "Maybe this isn't the right place for you. May's cafeteria a block over is always looking for help, so you might want to check over there."

She finally came to life. "I have experience. I worked at a club down in Atlanta for three years."

Beau crossed his arms and grinned. "Atlanta, huh? Whatcha doing all the way up here?"

She clammed up again, but a moment later she lit up like a switch had been flipped. "I have friends in Blue Ridge."

Blue Ridge wasn't exactly next door.

"I always wanted to move to the mountains," she continued, "but Blue Ridge is a little small for me. I figured I'd check out Crimson, being a bigger city and all."

Beau and I looked at each other. Blue Ridge was a major tourist town that made Crimson look like a grain of sand. But whatever.

"Why don't you have a seat so we can talk." I beckoned her over to the bar.

Her eyes roamed around the place as she took a seat. "The White Stag is an interesting name."

"It was my mother's place. She left it to me when she died." I don't know why I was telling her my life story. It just spilled out of me.

Her nervous smile flattened. "I'm sorry."

"Don't be. She's been gone for a while now."

Dog looked through the order window at us. "That's my cook, Dog, and I'm Charley." She stared at me blankly. "That would be your cue to tell me your name now."

"Oh! I'm Tucker."

"Tucker...?"

"Conroy. Tucker Conroy."

"Tucker?" Beau gave her a funny look. "What kind of name is Tucker for a girl?" He followed the comment with another flirty smile that reminded me to have a word with him later. If I did decide to hire her, there'd be none of that.

"You said you used to work in Atlanta?" I noticed her foot tapping against the bottom rail of the stool.

She nodded and licked her lips. I was getting nervous just looking at her. She was hiding something for sure.

"Look. Why don't we start over." I went from needing a dishwasher to suddenly feeling the urge to prevent a potential bartender from walking out the door. Funny how that worked. "I'm Charley Underwood and this is Beau Henry. Now it's your turn."

That seemed to calm her down a bit. "Sorry about that. It's been a while since I've been on a job interview." She bit her lower lip. "I don't have a resumé or anything."

"That's okay. The White Stag isn't really a resumé type of place. I'll get you an application to fill out." I got up to get one from the desk in the back room.

She froze for a second and then gave me a nervous smile again. "Okay."

When I came back out, Dog was at the bar. He'd pulled up a stool and was having a chat with her. I handed her the form. "Here you go."

Beau and I followed Dog back into the kitchen to give her some privacy while she filled it out. When I looked through the window, she was hunched over the application but there wasn't a lot of writing going on.

"Since when are we looking for a new bartender?" Beau asked when I turned around.

"Since I've been spending too much time mixing drinks. I can't get any other work done, like run the bar, do my taxes, order inventory. A business doesn't magically run itself. She can also help out in the kitchen until we find a replacement for Mutt." I was hoping Tucker wouldn't mind washing a dish now and then so we didn't have to.

His mouth gaped. "You're firing Mutt?"

I glanced around the kitchen. "Do you see him anywhere? As far as I'm concerned, he quit. The man ghosted us." Dog didn't say a word. He just kept on chopping onions, but I could see the tension written all over his face. "If you've got something to say, Dog, say it."

He dropped the knife and looked at me. "You're giving up on him awfully fast."

"What do you expect me to do? I've got a bar to run."

"I know that." He stared at the wall with his jaw clenched. "It just pisses me off. If Mutt was a lily-white churchgoer, the cops would be out there looking for him by now."

I couldn't argue with him because he was probably right. "Look. If he shows up and has a good reason for disappearing, I'll give him his job back."

Without another word, he got back to chopping.

After giving Tucker sufficient time to complete the application, Beau and I went back out to the bar. "Are you done?" I asked, glancing at the paper. It was barely filled out.

She set the pen down and averted her eyes from me. "I don't know all the information off the top of my head."

The section on former employment had the name of the bar she'd worked at and the dates she'd started and left but no address or phone number. "I'll need the work phone number to check your reference."

"I can get it for you. I just can't remember it."

I looked back at the application. "And you forgot to fill in your home address."

She did that nervous lip biting thing again. "Do you really need all that?"

"The IRS does."

Why was I still talking to this woman? I was just asking for trouble if I hired her. But there was something in her eyes that told me she needed help, and it was just a part-time job. If it didn't work out, I'd let her go. "I'll tell you what. Write your address down and get me that employment information. I can start you on a trial basis tonight if you want. You've got two nights to show me you can handle the bar."

"Perfect! Thank you!" She got up and stuck her hand out. "I really appreciate it."

"You're welcome." I awkwardly shook it.

On her way to the door, she looked back. "What time should I be here?"

"Eight o'clock." That would give her a few hours tonight to prove she could mix a drink and stave off the assholes without pissing anyone off. "And I'll need to make a copy of your driver's license or a state ID," I yelled as she disappeared through the door.

Beau was shaking his head when I turned around. "You are such a sucker."

"Aren't you the hypocrite. I seem to recall a young guy with zero experience asking me for a job a while back."

He gave me a pointed look. "Yeah, but I had references. And you already knew me. She didn't even write her address down before she left."

Damn if he wasn't right. I basically had nothing but a name. "I'll get it from her tonight."

On top of everything else going on, I'd just hired myself a new employee. On a trial basis, but still. I just hoped it went smoothly tonight and Lucy didn't chew her up and spit her back out. Hopefully Beau would take her under his wing without trying to sleep with her. If it worked out and I made it official, I'd introduce her to the blood co-op and tell her about the Reaperstown vampires circling the bar. Then I'd get to see what she was really made of.

NINETEEN

The bar started filling up early. More than usual for a Thursday evening, which may or may not have been a good thing for Tucker's first night. I was hoping to have a talk with Lucy before she started her shift, but she showed up twenty minutes late, which was unusual for her.

Beau gave her a funny look when she walked behind the bar sporting a sour face. "What's your problem?" She ignored him and made her way over to a customer, but he kept pushing her buttons. "You got a bug up your ass or something?"

I shook my head at him. "Not now, Beau. She looks like she's in a mood, and I don't want her scaring Tucker off on her first night."

Tom Murphy pushed the door open and came inside with Rick Carter right behind him. The cops rarely showed up while the bar was open, so something was up.

Murphy came up to me. "Can we have a word?"

"Sure."

"In private."

I handed Beau the glass I was holding and followed them

outside, getting a lump in my throat from the look on Murphy's face. It wasn't as smug as usual.

He let out a long sigh and gave his partner a look before speaking. "We found a body down by the river late this afternoon."

"The river? Did someone drown?"

"The victim didn't drown. We found the body on the bank, near where the homeless have been setting up camp."

There had been a problem for the past couple of years with vagrants sleeping down there. Although the real problem was with the unemployment in the region and the lack of shelters.

"Looked like some kind of animal got to him," he continued.

"Animal?" Carter huffed, turning away to swallow back whatever had suddenly obstructed his throat. "Looked like a goddamn pack of dogs tore him apart."

Murphy shot him a look to shut him up. "Let's just say it wasn't pretty."

I got a sick feeling when he spotted Dog coming toward the front door and groaned.

"Why are you telling me about this?" And then it hit me. "Is it Mutt?"

Dog walked outside a second later. "What's going on?"

Carter stepped in front of him. "This is none of your concern, so why don't you go back inside."

Murphy shook his head. "Let him hear it. We're going to have to question him anyway, so we might as well save some time."

Dog saw my expression, and his face quickly turned to stone. "Is this about Mutt?"

"They found a body," I said. "Down by the river."

He ran his hand over the top of his head as his eyes went blank for a moment. "How'd he die?"

Murphy got that old look I knew too well. "It isn't Mutt."

"Jesus, Murphy!" I wanted to punch him. "You enjoyed that, didn't you?"

"I never said it was him."

"But you let me think it was." I reined in my anger. "Why are you telling us about it then?"

"Because Mutt's a suspect. We have witnesses who say he did it."

Did it? It took me a second to reconcile what he'd said. Were they actually suggesting that my gentle giant of a dishwasher had killed someone? "I don't believe it."

"We've got two witnesses down at the encampment who described a man who fits Mutt's description to a tee. You want to tell me how many men in town look like this." He pulled a paper from his pocket and unfolded it, revealing a drawing of what I assumed was the suspect. "They were interviewed separately. Both of them gave the same description. This is the sketch."

Dog snatched the paper from his hand. "It looks like him, but there's no way he's capable of killing someone unless it was in self-defense."

Murphy took the drawing back and stuffed it in his pocket. "When's the last time you saw Walter Kramer?"

Dog practically growled at him. "I already told you all that when I reported him missing. If you did your job, we wouldn't be having this conversation."

Carter got up in Dog's face. "What are you suggesting?"

"Take it easy," I said. "Like Dog told you when he reported Mutt missing, we haven't seen him since Tuesday night. But there's no way he did this. There's got to be an explanation."

Carter backed off. "There's an explanation, all right. Mutt's a killer."

For once, Murphy was the voice of reason. "Look. We just need to talk to him. If he shows up here, call me." He handed me his card.

Like I needed it. "You'll be the first to know."

As Murphy and Carter got back into their patrol car and pulled away, I spotted Atticus across the street. He was sitting on the bench he'd had installed outside the restaurant, puffing away on a cigar. "That man looks like he doesn't have a care in the world."

"He's rich, Charley. Money may not buy you happiness, but it sure makes life easier."

I let out a humorless laugh. "He probably has a meth lab set up in his basement, and that restaurant is the perfect cover."

Dog grunted. "Nothing surprises me anymore."

We were about to go back inside when I saw Tucker walking toward the bar. "Here comes our new bartender. Do me a favor. Give her a tour of the kitchen while I have a word with Lucy."

He followed my gaze down the sidewalk. "And the fun begins."

"I just hope the girl doesn't spook easily."

"You don't have a car?" I asked Tucker when she reached us. She got to Crimson somehow.

"I did, but I sold it." She took a deep breath and smiled as she exhaled. "A fresh start doesn't come for free. I rented a place a few blocks over on Fourth Street."

It must have been the "studio" above Webers' Thrift Shop. They'd been trying to rent it out for over a year, but they were asking too much for the dump.

"Dog is going to give you a tour before you start at the bar." Now for the ask. "Do you mind splitting your time between the bar and the kitchen until I can hire a dishwasher?" She stared at me for a second like she wasn't sure. "We all pitch in around here when we're shorthanded, but it's up to you."

She finally released her pent-up breath and flashed me a quick smile. "Sure. Whatever you need."

"I appreciate that." With any luck, she wouldn't complain

when I made it a permanent thing. It's not like Dog needed a lot of help back there anyway.

We went inside, and Dog ushered her into the kitchen. Lucy already had her eye on the woman, but I suspected Beau had already broken the news about our new employee.

As I walked around the bar, she made a beeline for me. "What's going on?"

"In general, or do you mean the new bartender?"

"Don't play with me, Charley. Am I getting fired?"

I gave her my full attention. "Why? Have you done something to make me want to fire you?" She backed off, and I could see the worry in her eyes. "No one is getting fired, Lucy. The Stag is doing okay financially, and I need some time to be the boss around here instead of tending bar every night."

Beau walked up behind her. "I tried to tell her, but she wouldn't listen to me. Maybe now she'll stop taking twenty-minute bathroom breaks every half hour."

I swear they were worse than siblings.

He glanced out the window. "What was all that about with Murphy and Carter?"

I considered keeping my mouth shut, but the cops didn't seem too concerned about divulging information about an active investigation, so why should I? The entire town would know about the murder by morning anyway. "They found a body down by the river." I took a deep breath before delivering the rest of the news. "They're trying to pin it on Mutt."

Beau stared at me for a few seconds and huffed. "Mutt? You're joking, right?"

"Would I joke about something like that? Murphy told me they have two witnesses who said he did it, but they haven't found him yet to question him."

He gaped at me. "You mean we've been working with a murderer all this time?"

"Don't be stupid. As far as I'm concerned, he's innocent

until proven guilty. These so-called witnesses are living by the encampment, and you know what goes on down there." The people down by the river were always getting drunk or stoned and starting fires. They were prime candidates for vampire-blood therapy. But I was starting to wonder if I was fooling myself. Something was responsible for all the strange happenings in this town lately, and it wasn't the approaching full moon. Maybe this drug going around was more dangerous than any of us thought. And maybe Mutt had gotten his hands on some.

Beau's eyes suddenly flew wide. "Holy shit!"

I turned around to see what he was gawking at. One of my customers was standing on a table with her tank top pulled down below her breasts, dancing for a group of men circled around her.

"Get off that table, Mary Ellen!" Lucy yelled across the room. She shook her head. "Her tits are hanging out."

When I hurried around the bar to put an end to the show, I bumped into Tucker as she was coming from the kitchen. She froze when she saw the spectacle. "What kind of bar is this?" Her eyes shot to mine and then back to the table where the men were getting rowdier by the second. "I can't do this again." Then she took off toward the front door.

"Tucker!" She wouldn't even look back at me. So much for my new bartender.

Dog came from the kitchen and headed for the ruckus. He grabbed two men at a time by their shirts and wrestled them toward the door. Beau grabbed another.

As they cleaned house, I yanked Mary Ellen off the table and dragged her outside. "What's wrong with you? Have you lost your mind?" Or what drugs had she taken? I was starting to think we had another epidemic on our hands.

She laughed and shimmied her skirt higher. "You used to be fun, Charley Underwood. What happened to you?"

"I grew up, that's what happened. Go home, Mary Ellen.

Sleep it off." If the wrong person had wandered past the window, she could have gotten me shut down.

With a grin on her face, she stuck her fingers in her mouth and placed them between her legs, walking backward into the street as she kept her eyes on mine. Eventually she turned around and strolled over to Morceau and went inside.

"Good," I said to myself. "Let Devereaux deal with her."

Dog was straightening the chairs when I walked back in. "What happened to Tucker?"

"She freaked out and left." What a way to start her first shift. Then I remembered her comment just before she walked out. "She said she couldn't do this again, whatever that meant."

He righted the last overturned chair. "Maybe she worked in a strip club down in Atlanta, and that's what she's trying to get away from by coming up here. Seeing a half-naked woman dancing on top of the table might have spooked her."

It could also explain why she was so sketchy about giving me her former employer's information. I didn't give a damn if she worked at a titty bar down there, as long as she didn't steal from the register and could mix a drink.

"I guess you'll have to wait and see if she comes back in here groveling tomorrow," he said.

I wasn't holding my breath.

Beau was having a conversation with a customer when I walked behind the bar. He straightened back up and came over to me. "Danny said Mary Ellen was at Morceau's earlier tonight. She probably got lit on a bunch of free wine before heading over here."

"Yeah, well, she was wagging her privates at me on her way back over there." I looked out the window at the restaurant, visualizing her using one of those dainty chandeliers to pull herself up on a table while Atticus watched in horror. Good luck to the man.

I got back to work and tried to focus, but it was difficult. My best friend was in trouble, vampires were threatening me, and now Mutt was being accused of murder. The man couldn't even step on a bug in the kitchen. Dog and the pack would be out there looking for him the second we closed up for the night. But if they didn't find him before the cops did, he'd be locked away awaiting a biased trial that he had no chance of winning, especially if these witnesses turned out to be legit. And then there was the possibility that he'd done it. I couldn't even fathom it. All we could do now was wait and see.

The night had been busy, even after kicking out half a dozen customers involved in the Mary Ellen incident earlier. But I couldn't stop looking at the clock on the wall. It was fifteen minutes until closing, but it might as well have been an hour, the way time was dragging by.

All night I'd hoped that Tucker would come back and let me explain that what happened wasn't the norm around here, but she never did. Never called either. And since she never filled out the rest of her application, I couldn't even call her. With any luck, she'd show up tomorrow, but I wasn't counting on it.

"Has anyone seen Bob?" I asked. That cat seemed to come and go as he pleased. How he managed to get inside the bar sometimes was still a mystery.

Beau shrugged. "I haven't seen him."

Lucy ignored me and went about her business of pouring a beer, which was her way of saying she hadn't seen him either.

I checked the kitchen, but he wasn't in there. As much as I didn't like the idea of going anywhere near the alley with a dangerous vampire after me, I went to the back door and cracked it open, expecting him to slip past my legs so I could quickly shut it again. There was no sign of him though.

As I was closing the door, I heard a faint meow. I stuck my head out but didn't see him. "Bob?" The sound came again, so I took a deep breath and stepped outside, reminding myself that if Ian Masterson was out there, a door wasn't going to stop him anyway. I also figured Bob would have hightailed it by now if he was.

The meowing continued. It was coming from the other side of that notorious dumpster. I was seriously thinking of having that thing moved down to the other end of the alley as soon as possible.

After looking up and down the moonlit corridor, I went back inside and grabbed a letter opener from the desk. It was better than nothing. Then I walked back out with it gripped tightly in my hand. "I'm not playing with you, cat. Better get over here or you're staying out tonight."

Another meow came.

I took a few steps and stopped, whirling around when I caught movement from the corner of my eye. It was just the shadow of a car driving past the alley at the other end. Shaking off the creeps, I reached the dumpster and stuck my head around the side with my heart feeling like it was about to beat out of my chest.

"Are you trying to give me a heart attack?" I said to Bob when I saw him hunched next to the wall. I looked closer and realized he had something in his mouth. Something dead. A rat or a mouse. "You're not bringing that thing inside." In a blink, he was gone. He darted down the alley with his catch still in his mouth. "Ungrateful little shit. No more tuna for you."

On my way back to the door, something came out of the darkness and slammed into me. It drove me into the wall, smashing my head against the brick so hard everything went black. When my vision finally cleared, I was staring into a set of bloodshot eyes and a face that seemed both familiar and terrifying at the same time. "Mutt?"

He snapped at me like a dog, his red eyes growing wider. With his teeth bared, he lunged, pinning me to the wall. Suddenly he pulled back, and shock rolled over his face. "Charley?"

I nodded quickly. "It's me, Mutt. It's okay, you can let go of me now."

Just as quickly as recognition had set in, his face contorted. His eyes looked rabid. A moment later, he was on top of me again. A sharp pain radiated through my shoulder, and everything faded away as a surge of adrenaline rushed through my veins.

Mutt flew backward and hit the opposite wall. As my vision started to clear, I saw a tall figure standing next to him. It was Samuel. His eyes sparkled in the darkness as he gripped Mutt by the neck and lifted him into the air with one hand.

I tried to get up when he lowered Mutt's feet back to the ground, but, still lightheaded, I slid down the wall.

With his other hand, Samuel reached for Mutt's head and snapped it to the right, dropping my dishwasher's lifeless body to the ground. Then he walked out of the shadows and came toward me. "So, we meet again."

TWENTY

Samuel bent down and held his hand out to me.

"Stay back, or you'll end up like him!" I nodded to Mutt's body heaped on the ground a few yards away.

He straightened up and cocked his head. "Well, I wouldn't want that." His face caught the moonlight, and his ruby eyes faded to blue.

I climbed to my feet and steadied myself against the wall, looking past him at Mutt's lifeless form. "You just killed my dishwasher."

He opened his mouth to speak, but I wasn't interested in anything he had to say. He was lurking in the alley, and he'd just killed Mutt. For all I knew, he'd been watching me all along. He'd probably gotten a real kick out of walking into my bar last night.

I glanced at the back door. "Don't you say another word. Dog is going to come looking for me any second now, and you don't want to mess with a wolf." I was waiting for that adrenaline rush to kick back in, but suddenly I felt surprisingly steady. There wasn't the slightest vibration in my body.

He narrowed his eyes. "You think I'm here to hurt you?"

"Well, you did just kill one of my employees."

"Yes, but he was trying to kill *you*."

His attention suddenly shifted away from me. Bob was winding his lanky body around the vampire's leg when I looked down.

I stomped my foot at the cat. "Run!" But Bob didn't move. He just looked up at me with his eyes brighter than usual.

Samuel reached down and scooped him off the ground. His orange fur practically glowed as the vampire held him up to the moonlight.

"Let him go!" I demanded. Instead, he tucked Bob under his arm and stroked his head. "That's my cat you're manhandling."

"Your cat?" He set Bob back down. "Sit." The cat obeyed, lowering his rear end. "Has he ever done that for you?"

"Well, no." I'd never seen any cat respond to a command like that before.

He stepped dangerously close. "That's because he's *my* cat." He snapped his fingers without taking his eyes off mine. "Sebastian, up!"

Bob jumped, landing on Samuel's shoulder, meowing as he stretched his neck to rub his face against the vampire's chin. It was hard to dispute the connection between them.

"Well, you haven't taken very good care of him. He was full of fleas and starving when he showed up here."

"Really?" Samuel glanced sideways at the cat perched on his shoulder and chuckled. "I'm afraid you've been had. Sebastian can be very persuasive when he wants something."

"You're not seriously trying to tell me your cat faked an eye infection?"

He shrugged. "He's faked worse."

I glanced at Mutt's lifeless form, bringing the situation back into perspective. "What are you going to do to me?"

He frowned. "Do to you?"

The back door swung open, and Dog stepped out. Bob, or...

Sebastian, jumped back to the ground and skedaddled behind the dumpster. Dog took one look at Mutt's body and the vampire crowding me and dropped down on all fours. A howl filled the night air as the wolf emerged and, within seconds, the pack appeared at both ends of the alley.

Samuel glanced at the blocked exits and groaned. "This is the thanks I get?"

Dog lunged, and the vampire flew into the air. "We can continue this game," he said, looking down from the top of the building, "or we can have a civilized conversation. Your choice."

"Civilized?" I said. "You just attacked me."

He crossed his arms. "Attacked you? I did no such thing." He nodded to Mutt's crumpled body near the dumpster. "I saved you. And I came to fetch my cat."

Dog shifted and gave me a questioning look.

"Mutt did try to kill me," I said to him.

"Now, will you call off your wolves so I can come down from this roof?"

I braced myself against the wall as the alley suddenly started to spin. My shoulder was on fire, and there was blood running down my arm. The pain was coming from where Mutt had bitten me.

Dog caught me as I went down. The last thing I remembered was seeing Samuel descend from the rooftop like a giant bat and Dog's grave eyes staring down at me before it all went black.

* * *

A sound kept assaulting my ears. A constant ticking that pounded in my head. "Will someone stop that noise!" I sat straight up and covered my ears with my palms. Odin was curled up at my feet, and Candy was standing next to the bed.

"It's just the clock on the table, honey." She handed me a

mug with something warm inside. "Drink this. It'll help with the sensitivity."

Without question, I drank half of it in a few gulps. It tasted like lemon Pledge. At least that's what I imagined lemon Pledge tasted like. My mouth puckered as I handed the cup back to her. "What in God's name is that?"

"You don't want to know, but you'll be thanking me in a minute." She got up and walked toward the door. On her way out, she glanced at someone sitting in the corner. "Don't eat her while I'm gone."

I did a double take. It was Samuel. "What's he doing here?"

She turned around and placed her hands on her hips. "Is that any way to talk about your savior? Be nice to the man. He's the only reason you're still breathing." A clucking sound came from her mouth, and Odin jumped off the bed and followed her out the door.

After checking to make sure I had clothes on under the blanket, I swung my legs over the side of the bed, but as soon as I stood up, I got dizzy and started to fall. It took Samuel less than a second to cross the room and catch me before I crashed into the side table.

"You might want to wait a while before trying to stand." He lowered me back down to the bed. "The venom hasn't cleared your system completely yet."

"Venom? What are you talking about?"

"The man who attacked you was possessed. He infected you with venom."

I could barely feel the wound when I reached for my shoulder. "It's just a scratch."

"It is now, but you should have seen it before." A mock shudder rolled over his shoulders. "I gave you just a tad of my blood to keep you from dying. As much as I hate to part with it," he added.

I shot him an incredulous look. "You did what?" Just

because I ran a vampire blood co-op, didn't mean I wanted to drink it myself. "You should have asked me first."

"You were unconscious at the time, but no need to thank me for saving your life."

So that's why my senses were heightened. Now that the throbbing in my head was gone, I understood why people used vampire blood recreationally. I definitely needed to thank Candy for whatever was in that mug.

"Thank you," I said.

"You're welcome." He smiled and stuck his hand out. "Truce?"

He was even more beautiful than I remembered. I was surprised at how warm his skin was when I touched his hand. Most vampires were slightly cold. Lukewarm at best.

I let go but held his gaze for a moment. Then I pulled my eyes away and looked awkwardly around the room. "So... what about the cat?"

"Sebastian? What about him?"

"I guess I don't need to feed him anymore."

"You can if you want. He likes you, so I suspect I'll be collecting him from your alleyway again."

The shadows I kept seeing out there must have been him looking for Sebastian.

He suddenly looked at the window. It was just before dawn, which meant I'd been out cold for a while. "I should get going."

"We were just getting to know each other," I said. "I don't know anything about you, other than you're a vampire and you like cats." Which was refreshing. The men around here wouldn't be caught dead admitting they liked cats.

"If I don't leave now, I'll be stuck here until sundown."

I laughed. "There are worse places to be trapped than the Cauldron."

"Yes, this is an interesting place."

It was an interesting place. There were plenty of other

witches in Crimson, but Candy was the only one who hung a shingle out and announced herself.

"Before you go, I need to ask you something. How do you know about the co-op?"

"Last night wasn't the first time I wandered into that alley. I've seen the line outside your back door, so I did some poking around. Your customers really should be a little more tight-lipped with the stranger lining up next to them."

Damn it! No wonder word was getting around. If the co-op survived, I was going to call a member meeting to lay down some stricter rules of discretion.

"Don't be too hard on them," he said, apparently reading my thoughts. "I can be quite persuasive when I want information."

"What about Ian Masterson? How did you know he was trying to extort me?" He showed a slight hesitation, and I felt a story coming on. "I run a bar, so I'm pretty good at detecting bullshit. Don't lie to me, Samuel."

He gazed at me steadily. "I know all about Ian Masterson and his *empire* of blood. You're not the first he's tried to shake down, and you won't be the last."

"But how do you know all this?" I got the impression the other night he was new in town and wasn't staying for long.

There was a tap on the door, and Candy cracked it open. "Dog's here to see you."

He locked eyes with Samuel when he walked into the room. "I appreciate you looking out for Charley, but I'll take it from here."

"I was just on my way out." Samuel looked over his shoulder at me as he was leaving. "I have a feeling Sebastian will be showing up at your back door again, so you haven't seen the last of me."

I detected a slight growl coming from Dog as the vampire left. "What was that all about?" he asked.

"What do you mean? He saved my life. The least I could do was have a conversation with him." Dog was way too protective, but I knew he was just worried about me. We didn't know this vampire from Adam.

He sat on the edge of the bed next to me. "How are you feeling?"

"Like I have a colossal hangover. Nothing that a good breakfast won't fix."

"Good." He went quiet for a moment, and I knew he was still in shock over seeing Mutt dead in the alley. They'd known each other for a while, and he cared about Mutt more than he let on. "We'll take care of the body. Bury him out in the boneyard."

The boneyard was where wolf shifters were laid to rest after they died. The ground was sacred. Hidden somewhere in the mountains. Even I didn't know where it was. "You sure about that?"

His chest rose as he took a deep breath. "As far as I'm concerned, he was a wolf. If any of the pack says otherwise, they'll have to take it up with me." Relaxing his shoulders, he turned away and stared at the wall. "The cops are probably going to use him as a scapegoat for Patrice Henderson's murder, and I know he's not responsible for that one."

"Patrice Henderson? What are you talking about?"

"I heard this morning. She died last night in the hospital. Never woke up from the coma."

It wouldn't have surprised me if Ian Masterson or one of his vampires was connected to the crime, and if people heard Patrice's testimony, we'd be at war. Rumors were already flying, and all they'd have to hear was proof that a vampire had staked an innocent young woman to a tree and viciously attacked her. They'd have their justification for running every vampire out of town. If they didn't kill them first.

"I guess we don't have to worry about her identifying her attacker," I said.

"You're right. They'll try to pin it on Mutt instead, after what happened down at the river."

After what I'd seen in his eyes last night, I couldn't deny that Mutt was capable of committing that murder. But Patrice was attacked even before he went AWOL, and I think Dog or I would have noticed if we had a homicidal maniac working right next to us.

Dog rubbed his eyes. "With no family or money, all the county is going to do is bury him in an indigent plot over at the cemetery with a grave marker no bigger than a dollar bill. Maybe none at all. He'll be known as the infamous Crimson slasher, and people will be pissing on his grave." He shook his head in disgust. "I won't let that happen. He's getting a proper burial where nobody can mess with him, even if I have to dig the hole myself."

"Samuel said Mutt was possessed. Said he poisoned me."

"I know what you're thinking, Charley. It crossed my mind too. Whoever did this to Patrick is also responsible for Mutt." He let out an extended sigh and stood up. "Are you going to be okay if I leave? I need to tend to Mutt."

"I'm fine. Go." I stood up, careful to take it slow so I didn't end up on the floor. Dog would stick to me like glue if he saw that, and he had more important things to do than babysit me. It was bad enough that Candy would probably hover over me for days.

As soon as he left, I looked out the window, hoping to catch a glimpse of Samuel walking down the street. But the sun was already starting to rise, so he was long gone by now.

I was heading for the bedroom door when I heard the sound of glass breaking. Candy's apartment took up the entire second floor, but the noise seemed to be coming from the shop below.

I walked down the hallway and stood at the top of the stairs. "Candy? Is everything okay down there?"

"Everything's fine!" she yelled. "Go back to bed!"

Something else broke.

"Go back to bed, my ass." I went downstairs to the shop. Candy was backed up against the display case with a half-naked man standing a couple feet away from her. His penis was swinging back and forth from the force of his wild gesturing.

"You know Mayor Adams, don't you, Charley?"

"Get the hell away from her!" I didn't care if he was the president.

He glanced at me but didn't seem too concerned about me standing there. Then he grabbed another bottle of God knew what from the counter and threw it against the wall. "This is robbery! I paid you good money to fix it!"

Candy slid out from under him and walked around to the other side of the case. "I warned you, Randy. Three strikes and you're out." She looked at the pile of broken glass on the floor. "You're paying for all those bottles." Then she glanced at the hourglass at the other end of the counter. "And your session's up."

She snapped her fingers once, and Mayor Adams froze for a second before letting out a tiny squeak. He blinked several times and suddenly seemed to realize his pants were pooled around his ankles. Then he gaped at me. "Charley!" He reached down and yanked them up, his face turning beet red as his eyes darted back to Candy. "Are you trying to get me kicked out of office?"

I huffed. "Relax, Randy. What happens at the Cauldron stays at the Cauldron. But I might need a favor from you in the future." The mayor owing me could come in handy.

On his way out, he glared at Candy. "This conversation isn't over."

"Is that right?" She leaned against the case and crossed her arms. "I'll be sure to let your wife know you're requesting my services again."

He shut up and walked out, fighting the pink beads strung across the door like he'd walked into a giant spider web. After climbing into his car, he nearly backed into someone on the street.

"You want to tell me what that was all about?" I said.

She grabbed the broom leaning against the wall. "Just another satisfied customer."

"You mean ex-customer."

She laughed. "He'll be back."

"Why were his pants down around his ankles?"

"He's got a problem with his plumbing. It's going to take more than one session to get it fixed, but he doesn't want to do the work. I'm not a miracle worker."

I was starting to wonder if I was wrong about that side gig of hers. "What are you doing with those men?"

Her expression went from annoyed to amused. "Charley Underwood, are you asking me if I'm a hooker?" Before I could open my mouth to apologize profusely, she put me at ease. "I told you before. I give them exactly what they need— a front-row seat to witness the demons inside their own heads." She pointed to the infamous door at the back of the shop. "If you ever want to see all the fucked-up innards of your mind, all you have to do is take a seat right back in there."

No thanks. I preferred not to meet my demons head-on. And I had enough of everyone else's, being a bartender.

She started sweeping up the glass but stopped and leaned the broom against the counter. "What a mess. I better get a towel to sop up all that flying tonic before the shop lifts off its foundation."

"I'll help you." I reached for one of the towels she'd grabbed from behind the counter.

"No, you won't. You get that stuff on your hands, I'll be scraping you off the ceiling."

Before I could argue about it, the front door opened.

"We're not open yet," Candy said without looking up from the mess on the floor.

It was Loki. I took one look at his face, and my stomach sank. "I think he's here for me. What's wrong?"

"Take a breath, Charley. No one died, but you need to come with me."

TWENTY-ONE

I saw the problem before we even reached the Stag. "Who did this?"

"It's your bar," Loki said. "You'd know better than me who has it out for you."

When we got there, I looked up at the red paint dripping down the sides of the stag head above the door. It was covered, like someone had climbed up there and poured a bucket of the stuff over it. The sidewalk below it was just as bad.

Dog came outside when he saw us standing there.

"Could have been kids," I said to him. "But I doubt it. They would have been more creative." It was a long-standing tradition to vandalize the stag head in a more artistic way. What I was seeing was desecration. The colorful graffiti that had been there for years was completely covered up. "I can fix the head, but I don't know how I'm going to clean this sidewalk."

When I reached for the door to go inside, Dog stepped in front of me. "Wait."

"Why?" When he hesitated, I glanced through the window and saw something that made my heart skip a beat. "Get out of my way, Dog."

He sighed and stepped aside. "We can fix this."

I walked in and slowly panned my eyes around the room, taking in the damage one wall at a time. "Who did this?"

"I don't know. They came in through the back door."

Had we left it open? With all the commotion last night, it wouldn't have surprised me.

He nodded to the wall behind the bar. Half the liquor bottles were smashed, like someone had taken a bat to them. By some miracle, the mirror that ran the length of the wall behind them wasn't even cracked. Probably because they needed a canvas to leave their message on. In bright red letters from the same paint used to vandalize the stag head out front, were the words VAMPIRE LOVERS SUCK!

"You're right," Dog said. "This wasn't kids. Someone targeted you, Charley."

I continued to survey the damage. The back wall that held decades of drawings and the signatures of just about every patron the Stag had ever served was now covered with splashes of paint. The floor was a slippery mess.

Feeling faint, I sat down in a chair next to one of the overturned tables. "Who would do this?"

"I don't know, but I'll have the pack come by to help clean up the place."

Beau walked through the front door and stopped dead in his tracks. His eyes widened as he took in the disaster. "Jesus Christ!"

I let out a disheartened laugh. "Jesus had nothing to do with it." Then I said something stupid that I blamed on shock. "Did you leave the back door open last night?"

Beau looked at me like I'd slapped him. "I didn't leave the damn door open. Lucy was the last one out."

Dog muttered something under his breath and put an end to the finger pointing. "No one left the door open. It was kicked in."

I finally calmed down enough to catch my breath. "I'm sorry, Beau. I shouldn't have said that to you. I'm just having a hard time seeing my whole life trashed." After letting my self-pity run its course, my brain kicked into gear. I needed to call the insurance company and file a claim.

"You can do that later," Dog said. "Let's all just take a minute."

The room fell silent for a moment. "Okay," I said. "I've had my minute. I'm calling the police." Before I could dial the number, a patrol car pulled up out front. Murphy got out and looked up at the stag head, sidestepping the red paint on the sidewalk on his way to the door.

Dog leaned in to Loki. "Go round up the pack so we can get this place cleaned up."

Loki practically growled when he saw Murphy pulling the door open. Crimson PD wasn't exactly on the wolves' valentine list. He disappeared down the hallway toward the back a second later.

Murphy stepped inside and took a good look at the place before heading over to me. "When did this happen?"

"Sometime between midnight and this morning." I pointed to the mirror. "Someone's got a serious bone to pick with vampires." What else was new?

"And the businesses in town that serve them," Dog added.

"Word's getting around about Patrice Henderson dying," Murphy said. "People have already decided that it was a vampire who attacked her, and I tend to agree." He pulled his phone out and took a picture of the message on the mirror.

"So that gives them a right to vandalize vampire-friendly businesses?" I said.

He took a few more pictures. "Not at all, but it's motive for them to do it. Got any idea who might have done this?"

I spotted an unbroken bottle of tequila on the floor and

resisted the urge to have a liquid breakfast. "If I knew that, I'd already be on my way over to collect my pound of flesh."

Murphy gave me a warning look. "You need to let the police handle this."

"Like you did overnight when someone was in here trashing the place? Or when they climbed up on a ladder out front to desecrate the stag head? Jesus, Murphy, don't you cops ever patrol?"

"And you need to get a security system installed," he replied.

"I think you're right. I can't count on the police, can I?"

Dog grabbed me when I took a step toward Murphy. "Come on, Charley. I don't need to be bailing you out."

I settled down, not wanting to give him the satisfaction of threatening me with arrest. Murphy would have loved to cuff me and shove me in the back of his patrol car to ponder my actions.

"Why don't you grab a broom," Dog said to Beau. "I'll get the mop."

That was my cue to get rid of Murphy. "Have you seen enough to file a report? We need to clean this mess up."

He strolled around the room and took a few notes. Then he started in with the questions. "Did anything unusual happen last night? Any disgruntled customers? Fights?"

Yeah, I got attacked by a rabid employee. Then I kicked a bunch of customers out after Mary Ellen did a half-naked table dance in the middle of the bar.

"Nothing out of the ordinary. It was business as usual last night." He did have me wondering, though. Maybe I had pissed one of them off.

He nodded a few times, staring at me like I was hiding something, which I was.

I pulled my eyes away first. "If we're done here, I've got work to do."

"Make sure you document the damage for the insurance company first." On his way out, he stopped and turned back to me. "Have you heard from Mutt?"

"Nope. Not a word."

He noticed Dog shoot me a glance. "You wouldn't be lying to me, would you?"

"Why would I do that?"

His eyes narrowed slightly, but he didn't reply. He just kept a steady gaze on me for a moment. "By the way, has Bill Meadows been in here recently?"

Bill Meadows was in here every chance he got, until he attacked Lucy and got his ass banned. "He was in here a few nights ago, but I haven't seen him since."

"How about Maggie Ferguson?"

Last I heard, Maggie worked at the drugstore down the street. I couldn't recall her ever coming into the Stag. "No. Why?"

"They're both missing. No one's seen either of them for a couple of days."

"You don't think they ran off together, do you?" I doubted it.

"Stranger things have happened."

That threat Ian Masterson made the other night came to mind. The one about dining on a few of my customers if I didn't cooperate. But that wouldn't explain Maggie. "If I see either of them, I'll let them know."

"You do that." He finally walked out the door and took a picture of the vandalized stag head before getting into his patrol car.

Dog stood next to me and watched Murphy drive away. "He didn't believe you. He'll keep snooping around the bar trying to find Mutt."

"Just make sure you bury him good and deep so he never does."

Dog looked over his shoulder at Beau. "Let's go see about securing that back door until we can get it replaced."

After they disappeared down the hallway, I got busy taking pictures of the place before the pack arrived for the cleanup. When I went into the kitchen to check for damage in there, I heard the front door open and the sound of shoes steadily crossing the floor. "We're not open." When the footsteps stopped, I glanced through the order window and saw Atticus Devereaux standing in the middle of the bar.

I walked back out. "Morning, Atticus. Can I help you with something?"

"The stag head out front caught my eye. Did someone vandalize it?"

"What tipped you off? The red color or the paint all over the sidewalk?"

He smiled pleasantly and then looked at the walls. "I see there's been a break-in."

"More like someone who wanted to make my life miserable. They succeeded." I reached down to grab a broken bottle near his feet. "Wouldn't want you to hurt yourself. My insurance rates are about to skyrocket as it is."

He took a stroll around the room, stepping over glass and avoiding pools of booze and paint. "It was quite lively in here last night, wasn't it?"

"You mean Mary Ellen? I saw her walk into the restaurant after I kicked her out of here." If only I could have been a fly on the wall to see what happened over there. "She didn't try to climb on top of one of your tables by any chance, did she?"

Instead of answering me, he continued to circle the room, coming to a stop in front of the mirror. "Is that what you are? A vampire lover?"

He was starting to make me feel anxious. "Is there something I can do for you, Atticus?"

The smile disappeared from his face. "I've offended you."

"No, you haven't. I just need to clean this place up, so I don't have time to chat." As he stepped closer and continued to gaze at me, a strange sensation whirled around in my stomach. The familiar flutter of butterflies.

He looked at the paint splattered on the Stag's famous signature wall. "People can be such animals, don't you think?"

The sensation grew stronger, and the room started to heat up. My eyelids felt like lead weights.

"Dirty, lustful animals," he continued, his voice a purr.

I closed my eyes, feeling the warmth of his breath on my face.

"Charley?" Dog was standing at the entrance of the hallway when they popped back open. His eyes traveled down to my thighs where my hand was wedged between them.

Beau walked up behind him but quickly turned around. "Uh... I'll be in the back room."

"Oh, God!" I pulled my hand away, mortified. For a second, I had to think about what had just happened.

Dog seemed just as uneasy. "Are you okay?"

My eyes darted around the room, but Atticus was gone. Had I imagined it?

I opened my mouth to say something, but Dog threw his hands up. "Nope. It's none of my business." Then he disappeared down the hallway again.

Thankfully, I didn't have time to sink any deeper into my humiliation because the pack arrived.

Lux looked around at the mess. "Who'd you piss off?" She set two gallons of paint down. "Hope you like charcoal gray. The hardware store was out of primer, so it was either that or black. Only things likely to cover that red."

I didn't mind gray. This was a bar after all.

Dog came back out when he heard them, not showing the slightest bit of weirdness when he looked at me. "Let's get this place spick-and-span."

While I got busy sweeping up glass and mopping liquor and paint off the floor, the others tended to the walls. A lump formed in my throat as I watched paint glide over graffiti and signatures, covering up years of the Stag's history. History I'd never get back. But if I had to die trying, someone was going to pay for this.

TWENTY-TWO

After spending the day scrubbing and painting, I decided not to file an insurance claim. Some elbow grease and a few gallons of paint outweighed my rates going up. The back door needed to be replaced, but it was nothing we couldn't fix ourselves, and Dog was already on it.

Candy walked in around five o'clock with a venomous look in her eyes. "When we find out who did this, they'll be pissing sitting down."

"You're assuming they were male," I said.

She took another look around. "Honey, I know testosterone when I smell it."

"Who's watching the Cauldron?"

She waved me off. "I closed up for the rest of the day. Figured I'd see if you needed any more help, but it looks like you did just fine without me."

The back wall looked pristine, though it no longer held decades of memories. The floor was another story. It would take time to refinish it, but at least we were able to clean up some of the paint and dry it enough to walk on it.

I leaned back against the bar and cocked my head, looking at the splotches on the floor. "I kind of like it. With everything looking so sterile now, the floor gives the room some character."

Candy reached for a pen behind the bar and went over to the newly painted wall, touching it to see if it was dry. "It hasn't cured yet, but this'll do." Then she put her John Hancock on it and stepped back to take a look. "There you go. The start of a new era at the White Stag." She glanced at the front door. "You aren't going to leave that head out front painted red, are you?"

That was a good question. "I'll probably paint it white again and let future senior classes vandalize it properly."

"Glad to hear it. It doesn't look right like that. The place isn't called the *Red* Stag."

I pushed away from the bar and stretched my arms. They were sore from all the scrubbing I'd been doing all day. "I'll get to it as soon as I can. I've got more important things to do right now." I also needed to go out to the house. "Do you feel like taking a drive? I need to check on Patrick."

"I was thinking the same thing. We need to see if that zombie blood has run its course."

"And if it has?"

She thought about it for a second. "Then we pray it washed that demon out of him."

"Then let's get going." It was Friday, so it would get busy at the bar early.

We climbed in my truck and drove out of town, with me worrying the whole way about what we'd find when we walked into the house. Patrick had already started to come around when we left him, even fighting off Ian and his vampires. But it wasn't the Patrick I knew that had stared back at me through that window. He was still in there somewhere, though. At least I hoped so.

As we drove past my neighbors' place a few houses down, the Wilsons', I noticed something on their lawn. "What the hell is that?" I slowed down to get a better look at the smoldering object in the middle of their yard. "Is it what I think it is?"

Candy slowly shook her head. "Who would do something like that?"

It was a wooden cross, and it had been set on fire and burned out, leaving a scorched patch in the middle of their perfect manicured lawn.

"Damn Nazis!" Candy pointed to the garage. There was a giant *V* painted on the door with an *X* drawn through it. "It wasn't kids who did that."

Even with all the passive-aggressive hostility in Crimson, I'd never seen anything as outright racist as that.

"What are you doing?" Candy asked when I pulled into their driveway.

"Making sure they're all right." Being vampires, the Wilsons were stuck in their house until dusk. Janice Wilson was testimony to that. "I just want to check on them."

I got out and went up to the front door. I knocked but there was no answer. I didn't hear any footsteps either, so I knocked a little louder. The curtain in the front window fluttered. "Mr. Wilson? Are you all right?"

"Go away!" I heard through the door.

"It's Charley Underwood. Is there anything I can do to help?"

"I think your kind has done enough. Now, get off my property."

I didn't take it personally. They had good reason to be resentful.

As I was leaving, I saw Janice Wilson standing behind the curtain in the dark living room, the scars on her face visible through the sheer fabric.

I hurried back to the truck and pulled out quickly, continuing toward the house.

"Wouldn't answer the door?" Candy said.

"Nope. Someone scared them good, and you can bet it wasn't another vampire."

"You think it was the same person who broke into the Stag?"

I glanced at her sideways. "That's a little far-fetched, don't you think? Why would someone trash my bar and then terrorize a family of vampires on the edge of town?"

Her brows hiked. "You're forgetting about the message they left on your mirror. Someone has it out for bloodsuckers, and anyone who supports them."

"Candy!"

"Sorry, I shouldn't use that word. But that Ian Masterson comes to mind every time I think about a vampire now, and it boils my blood."

We pulled up to the house a few minutes later and got out. The crows were all gone, including Rex, and everything was quiet. As we were walking up the steps to the front porch, I got an eerie feeling. It wasn't like we were being watched. The place just felt empty.

"He's not there," I said, stopping before I even reached the front door. "Patrick is gone."

Candy looked at me funny. "What are you talking about? Let's go inside and see."

She couldn't hide it from me. I could see it in the way she hesitated at the door that she felt it too. But the sooner I walked in that house and verified it, the sooner we could go looking for him.

I opened the front door and stepped inside. "Patrick?" When he didn't answer, we went down the hallway to check the bedroom. It was empty. "I should have come out here yesterday to check on him. This is my fault."

"No, it isn't, so quit beating yourself up. Neither one of us could have stopped him if he decided to leave. Look what he did to that bed frame when we put him in handcuffs."

Deep down I knew she was right, but I couldn't shake the guilt.

"There is another possibility," she said. "And it's a more likely one. Whoever did this to him may have called him."

I was confused. "Like picked up the phone and called him?"

She deadpanned me. "No, Charley, not with a phone. Patrick's a vampire, but he's possessed. Whoever did this to him is his new maker now. If that maker dialed into his mind, not even his mama could have stopped him from following the voice in his head."

* * *

I parked in front of the Stag, the image of Patrick wandering aimlessly around town after some invisible voice stuck in my head.

"Maybe we should drive around and look for him."

Candy got out and released a dramatic sigh. "It's not even dusk yet. If he is out there wandering around, he's toast by now." She headed for the front door. "Come on. I could use a drink."

I noticed a patrol car parked in front of the market on the next block. Someone was waving their arms around, yelling at Carter. "I wonder what's going on over there?"

Candy squinted at them. "That's Marge, and she doesn't look happy."

Resisting the urge to walk down there and stick my nose in someone else's business, I followed Candy inside. "What are you thirsty for?"

"I think I'll have a nice cold beer."

I grabbed a bottle of her favorite and set it down in front of her. I could have used one myself, but we were about to open, and I had a long night ahead of me.

I looked up when Dog came from the hallway with Tucker. "I was just having a talk with the new bartender. She'd like to have a word with you, Charley."

The woman ran out on me on her first night, and he thought she still had a job? Not exactly a solid first impression. "You've got five minutes," I said to her. "Start talking."

She gave me a sheepish grin. "I'm sorry about last night."

"You're sorry? Look, we don't know each other, so first impressions speak volumes. If you walk out on me like that on your first night, how do I know you won't make it a habit? Hell, how can I trust you to even show up?"

She sat down on a stool and let out a steady breath. "I saw that woman dancing on the table and I panicked. That bar I worked in down in Atlanta wasn't exactly on the legal side, if you know what I mean."

"I don't, so maybe you should explain."

She hesitated but finally came clean. "The girls were selling more than just lap dances."

It wouldn't be the first time a stripper bar was selling skin out of the back room. "It still doesn't explain why you ran out of here."

"Because they tried to make me do things!" she blurted out. "I was hired to serve drinks, but then I got cornered in the back room by a customer. When my manager saw it, he told me to shut up and do my job." She practically shrank on the stool and cradled her stomach.

"Did he—"

"No! I managed to get him off me and ran out. I didn't even go back to collect my last paycheck. When I saw that girl on the table last night, I panicked. I thought this was the same kind of place."

"In Crimson?"

Candy, who was pretending not to listen, took a sip of her beer and gave me a judgmental brow cock.

I wanted to laugh. No one had ever accused the White Stag of being a strip joint before. "I can assure you we don't put up with customers like that. You put your hands on an employee in my bar, you're banned for life."

She nodded vigorously. "I know that now. Mrs. Weber over at the thrift shop told me the bar was legit, so I came back to explain and ended up having a conversation with Dog. I'm really sorry for running out on you, Charley. It won't happen again."

"It better not." I felt kind of sorry for her, and I really needed a part-time bartender. "If you still want the job, I'll give you another chance. Friday nights are pretty busy in here, so it'll test your bartending skills thoroughly."

She couldn't contain her grin as she hopped off the stool. "Thank you! You won't regret it."

We were opening shortly, so I told her to get familiar with the bar while I had a word with Dog in the kitchen. When I walked in, he was cleaning the sink. I could tell by the look on his face that the deed had been done. Mutt was dead and buried in the boneyard.

"Are you going to give her another chance?" he asked me without looking up.

"Yeah. But the first time she pulls that stunt again, she's out."

He continued to scrub the spotless sink, and I decided not to ask. I walked past him and patted his shoulder. "I better get back out there before Lucy shows up."

She was coming through the front door as I was walking out of the kitchen. I crooked my finger at her when she zeroed in on Tucker standing behind the bar. "Let's talk."

The second we got to the back room, she started complaining. "I suppose you expect me to train her."

"I expect you to be civil to the woman. And yes, you and Beau need to show her how things are done around here." After working at a busy strip club down in Atlanta, Tucker could probably show Lucy a thing or two. "I need the help, so just act decent and don't run her off."

For a change, Lucy lost the attitude right away. "Got it."

When we walked back out, there were already a few customers sitting at the bar, which wasn't unusual for Fridays. Folks would have started coming in at noon if we were open for lunch, which I'd considered in the past. But that would require serving more than just burgers and fries.

I sat down next to Candy to keep an eye on Tucker for a few minutes. I wanted to see how she handled the bar.

Mike walked in and sat down next to me and asked Beau for a beer. "Boy, Marge down at the market is pissed."

"We saw something happening over there a little while ago," I said. "What's going on?"

"Someone stuck a little present through the mail slot on the front door." He chuckled. "A bag full of chicken guts."

I gave him a funny look. "A bag of chicken guts can fit through a mail slot?"

"It was messy. Let's just say they *squeezed* it through."

Beau set his beer down in front of him. "Probably the same assholes who—"

I shot him a look to shut him up. If I wanted to announce the trashing of my bar, I'd do it myself. No need to worry the patrons. They'd notice the painted back wall soon enough and start asking questions.

"Kids," Beau said, nodding his head. "Yeah, probably kids."

Mike got an iffy look on his face. "I don't think so. They painted a note on the door that said 'Vampire lovers suck.' The market is open late, so a lot of vamps shop there at night. I guess someone doesn't like it."

Candy and I glanced at each other. The vandalism around town was no joke.

"Have you heard about Bill Meadows and Maggie Ferguson?" he said.

I shrugged. "Tom Murphy mentioned they haven't been seen for a few days."

"They ain't the only ones." He leaned closer and lowered his voice. "Frank Webb and his wife." He shook his head and sipped his beer. "People are dropping like flies around here."

"Maybe people are taking vacations." I didn't really believe that, but it was possible. And it wasn't like the Webbs were socialites in town. In fact, I couldn't remember the last time I'd seen either one of them.

He scoffed. "Bill Meadows? He's too cheap to drive two hours east to the beach."

I was about to get up when Murphy came into the bar. "Can I have a word with you, Charley?"

"If you make it fast. I've got work to do."

"In private." He motioned for me to follow him.

"What is it?" I asked when we got to the other side of the room.

When he was satisfied no one was within earshot, he continued. "You need to keep an eye on the bar."

I laughed. "Seriously? It's a little late for that."

"This isn't a joke, Charley. What they did to the place last night might just be the beginning."

My patience was wearing thin. "Get to the point."

"I shouldn't be telling you this, but I'm worried about you. A few more people have gone missing this week, and there's a rumor that folks in town are blaming the vampires. People are whispering about their 'true nature' starting to show." He lowered his voice. "They're saying the vampires are getting thirsty."

"That's the stupidest thing I've ever heard. Vampires built this town as much as anyone. Why would they suddenly decide to destroy it? Jesus, Tom, they're just trying to live their lives in peace like you and me." But then there was Ian Masterson. Not to mention his cronies.

"Keep your voice down." He glanced around the room. "Don't you think I know that? It doesn't change what's happening around here. They're targeting vampire-friendly businesses, and the Stag qualifies."

If he only knew about the co-op. "Then do your job and arrest them."

There was that signature look of his. The one he got when he wanted to throttle me. "We need actual evidence before we go around arresting people." He took a step back. "Look, Charley. You know as well as I do there's been tension for years around these parts between vampires and humans."

"You mean the bigots who think anything non-human should have been run out of Crimson decades ago? That back-woods preacher over at the church has been spreading lies to his congregation for years. They're brainwashed."

"That may be, but it is what it is. The market down the street was hit when Marge closed up for an hour to take her dinner break." He put his hands on his holster and shook his head. "There's some kind of meeting taking place over at the church right now. So far it's peaceful, so there's nothing I can do about it. But I've got a good idea I know what's on the agenda."

"Great. We're all sitting ducks."

"Carter and I are going to take turns patrolling the square at night. To keep a closer eye on things until we can get a handle on who's causing all the trouble. But you need to keep an eye on the bar and your house."

"I'm staying at Candy's for a few days for that very reason." The explanation seemed to satisfy him, so I didn't have to tell him the real reason, which I had no intention of doing.

"Good."

It got quiet between us. "Are we done here?"

"For now. I've got another report of vandalism to check out, so I better get going."

"You might also want to drive over to the Wilsons' place." I couldn't get the sound of Mr. Wilson's voice out of my mind. "They got hit too."

He slowly nodded. "I'll swing by."

I headed back over to the bar as he was leaving. "Hey, Tom," I said before he could walk out the door. "Thanks for the warning."

Candy eyed me as I sat down. "Warning? What was that all about?"

"Frank and Milli Webb are missing. That makes four people this week. Murphy said there's talk in town that vampires are responsible for the disappearances. People are getting stirred up about it. You can bet they'll be getting stirred up about shifters and witches next."

Candy stood up and straightened her blouse. "I better get going."

"I didn't mean to scare you off."

She let out a curt laugh. "Honey, nothing scares this broad. But the sun is starting to go down, and if those bastards decide to hit the Cauldron, they'll have to go through me to do it."

"Wait. I'll ask Dog to walk you home." I was probably being paranoid, but Ian wasn't the forgiving type, and Candy was still at the top of his shit list right alongside me.

"Don't bother. I'm only two blocks down." She was on her way to the door before I could argue with her.

As she reached for the handle, Samuel walked in. His shoulder-length hair caught a breeze coming through the door and whirled around his chiseled face as he brushed past her.

"My, my." She ran her eyes up and down his tall form. "I think you get more handsome every time I run into you."

He smiled, his blue eyes finding me behind the bar before settling back on Candy. "Are you on your way out?"

She threw me a wicked smile over her shoulder. "Sadly, yes." As she walked through the door, her eyes lingered on him a moment longer. "You two have a nice night."

"Well, look who's here," I said, trying to play it cool, but it was difficult when he turned his gaze back on me. It was like I'd swallowed a bunch of bees.

I was in big trouble.

TWENTY-THREE

My adrenaline was racing so fast my hands were trembling. What the hell was wrong with me? I needed to put some distance between me and the vampire gazing back at me.

"You want a drink?" I asked Samuel as I tried not to trip over my own feet while I walked over to the tap to pour another customer a beer. The smile sliding up his face didn't help matters.

"Whiskey. Neat."

Beau had his eye on Samuel when I looked down the bar. "Get him a drink. It's on the house." Then I headed for the kitchen to pull myself together before he smelled my nerves. It was a vampire thing. He probably sensed them the second he walked in. When I glanced back at him, he was watching me walk away.

I entered the kitchen and grabbed an apron from the hook. "You need any help in here?"

Dog glanced through the order window. "You hiding from that vampire?"

"I'm not hiding. I'm avoiding a complication I don't need in my life right now. He makes me uncomfortable."

"At least he makes you feel something," he muttered, hacking a large potato in half.

"What's that supposed to mean?"

The knife went still in his hand, but he didn't look up from the cutting board. "You've got nothing to prove, Charley. Have a little fun, for God's sake. If Delia knew this place would turn you into a nun, she never would have left it to you."

The comment stung. "You want me to hook up with a vampire that just happened to show up in town in the middle of all this mess?" I took off the apron and hung it back on the hook.

"Charley," he called after me as I left the kitchen.

I ignored him because I needed to get out of there before I said something that would sting him back. People in this town had no problem telling me to my face that the bar would fail after my mother died. Said I was too young to run it, and I'd squander it away. It took everything I had to keep the place going for the first year. So, I did have something to prove, even if it cost me. But Dog was right. I hadn't so much as looked at a guy since the day I took over the Stag.

When I went back out front, Samuel was walking out the door. To say I was relieved was an understatement, but I also got a lump in my throat. "So much for that," I muttered.

I startled when something rubbed against my legs. Sebastian was sitting next to my feet, staring up at me. "How did you get in here?" After scooping him off the floor, I carried him to the back room and opened the door to let him into the alley. "Go on, you little con artist. It's been fun, but you've got a home."

I found myself wondering where that was. Where Samuel was staying.

He wouldn't budge. Instead, he padded over to the desk and jumped up, flopping down on top of it to groom himself like he owned the place. I guessed Samuel and I would be seeing each other again when he came to get his cat.

After closing the door, I poured some food into his bowl. "Eat up. I'm sure Daddy will be dropping by again to collect you soon when he realizes you've gone AWOL."

When I went back up front to check on Tucker, I was pleasantly surprised. She was moving quickly up and down the bar, mixing drinks like a pro. Lucy was at the other end trying to keep up. She kept watching her new co-worker from the corner of her eye like the competition was making her nervous. I hadn't seen her work that fast in ages, let alone give a damn about customer service.

Beau was watching too, enjoying every minute of it. He leaned over the bar when I sat down. "Where did Tucker say she worked before?"

"Some strip joint down in Atlanta." I marveled at the woman. Tucker had walked in here with zero confidence and was now killing it, mixing three drinks in the time it took Lucy to mix one. "She definitely knows her way around a bar."

"Yep. Lucy's been trying to keep up with her since she got here. I think she's worried about her job."

I chuckled. "Good. Maybe she'll tone down the attitude."

"She's a Wyatt, Charley. I doubt it."

Jake, one of our regulars, came in and took a seat next to me at the bar. He pushed his hair out of his gaunt face and nodded to Beau. "I'll have a shot of Wild Turkey." He kept glancing around the room, with his foot bouncing against the rail of the stool.

When Beau set his drink down in front of him, his fangs descended. He shot it back and slid the glass back to Beau. "Give me another."

"How've you been, Jake?" I wondered why he seemed so nervous. He was usually pretty laid-back.

He scratched his ear. "Okay, considering." His fangs kept popping in and out, a sure sign that something was bothering him.

"You look a little nervous. Is everything okay?"

Realizing his fangs were showing, he quickly retracted them. "Sorry about that. Things have been sketchy around town lately, so I'm a little on edge." He grabbed his replenished glass when Beau set it down in front of him. "A few more of these should do the trick."

"Oh yeah? What's going on?"

He shot me an are-you-blind look. "Have you seen what's going on around here? Vampires are open season in this town lately." He finished his whiskey and slid the glass back to Beau for a third round. "Another."

"You might want to pace yourself, Jake. You just got here." Vampires could be ugly drunks.

He swiveled around on his stool to face me. "Pace myself? I've got a burned-out car sitting in my lot that I'm gonna have to pay for. Believe me, I'm just getting started."

Jake owned Midnight Auto Repair at the edge of town. While all the other mechanics in Crimson were closing up for the day, his shop was just opening for business. When you were a vampire, you had to get creative with your hours, and a lot of people broke down in the middle of the night.

"I'm sorry to hear that. What happened?"

"What happened? Haven't you been watching the news lately?" He looked at Beau. "How about that drink?"

I nodded to Beau, and he poured Jake a third and final shot. "I stopped watching the news a long time ago, so why don't you just tell me."

"Someone sent a Molotov cocktail over my fence this afternoon when the shop was closed. It torched a customer's car. My insurance rates are about to go through the roof when I submit the claim."

"I'm sorry to hear that." From the corner of my eye, I spotted someone standing outside the bar looking in through the window. It was Mary from the co-op. She started walking toward the door when I turned to look at her, but I shook my head to keep her from coming inside.

"I'll be right back," I said to Beau. "Then you and I need to have a talk in the back."

I walked outside to have what I knew was about to be an uncomfortable conversation. "What are you doing here, Mary?" She never came into the bar, and she knew better than to show up here for co-op business. But I could see it in her eyes. She was desperate.

"I'm really sorry," she said. "I wasn't going to come inside. I just needed to get your attention so I could talk to you." She licked her dry lips before continuing. "I haven't gotten a phone call from Patrick to confirm my order for tomorrow morning, so I got kind of nervous about it."

With all the chaos around here, I hadn't even thought about confirming with the members. Patrick took care of all that.

"I'm sorry, Mary. Patrick's been under the weather for a few days, and I completely forgot he usually calls you a few days before. But we're still on schedule for tomorrow morning."

Her face brightened up for a moment. "Oh, thank you. I was worried there might be a problem, and I'd need to call my doctor to get something for the pain." She opened her mouth to say something else but went quiet.

"If there's nothing else, I'll see you early in the morning."

As I started to go back inside, she stopped me. "Is there any chance I could get it now?"

I could see she was hurting. "I wish I could, but I won't have it until late tonight."

She waved me off, doing a poor job of trying to hide her disappointment. "It's all right. I just thought I'd ask. I'll see you in the morning."

I watched her walk away, feeling sick to my stomach about the news I'd be delivering soon if a miracle didn't happen. The news that the co-op was on shaky ground. But for now, we needed to get through the deliveries in the morning.

When I walked back inside, Beau motioned me over. "Candy just called over here looking for you."

"On the landline?" That was odd.

He nodded to my phone lying on the bar. "I answered it when I saw her name come up."

"Why didn't you come out and get me?"

He threw the bar rag he was holding over his shoulder and shot me an irritated look. "Because she told me not to."

I grabbed my phone and called her back. "Is everything okay?" I asked her when she answered.

"I didn't mean to worry you, honey. It can wait until you get to the Cauldron tonight."

The sound of her voice was off. "Are you sure?"

"It's nothing. Go back to work. I'll see you later."

She didn't fool me for a second. Something was definitely up, and I needed to find out what it was.

I beckoned Beau to follow me. At dawn we'd have a line of people waiting in the alley, and someone needed to pick up the product.

"Is something wrong?" he asked when we got to the back room.

Something was always wrong lately.

I reached into the top drawer of the desk and handed him a key to Patrick's house. "I need a favor."

He eyed me suspiciously. "What kind of favor?"

"I need to go check on Candy, so *you* need to go out to Patrick's house and pick up the blood for the co-op deliveries in the morning. There's a small table inside against the kitchen door where the donors leave it." Patrick had installed a slot in the door so the donors could slip it through.

"Me? Why don't you send Dog?"

"You want to flip burgers for him while he's gone?" Beau

didn't know how to boil water. "I'll have him send the pack out there with you. They're watching the bar anyway."

"Then what do you need me for? Have Loki get it for you."

He was starting to irritate me. "Because Loki isn't my errand boy."

"And I am?"

"Well, technically it is your job, since you're standing in as my business partner in the co-op."

He put his hands on his hips and nodded. "A job I didn't ask for."

"You're right, now get going. Eight o'clock is the cutoff, so it should all be there by the time you get to the house. Patrick's got a setup in his kitchen to fill the vials, so I need you to do that too."

He looked at me like I'd asked him to use his own blood. "You know how long that's going to take me?"

"Jesus, Beau! I need your help right now. I'd do it myself if I didn't need to check on Candy."

"All right, I'll do it."

"I appreciate it. And grab Patrick's briefcase while you're there. It has all the order information inside."

I went to the kitchen to tell Dog that Beau needed an escort. While he made a call to Loki, I slipped out the front door. Half the pack would still be around, and there were a lot of people out and about on Friday night. I doubted Ian would be lurking around the bar until closing anyway, and the Cauldron was two measly blocks away. I'd be back before Dog knew I was gone.

Realizing I hadn't eaten all day, I stopped in Murray's deli a block down. After grabbing a pre-packaged sandwich from the refrigerator, I got in line to check out.

The woman in front of me was jabbering to the cashier. "Them vampires got it coming to them, if you ask me. No matter how civilized they pretend to be, they're all dying to sink their teeth into us."

The cashier didn't say a word. She just glanced at me over the woman's shoulder with a smirk.

"I was over at the hardware store the other night," the woman continued. "One of them was shopping right next to me." She leaned over the counter and lowered her voice. "I was afraid he was going to take a bite out of me right there in the store. Damn vampire lovers over there. I might have to drive out of town to buy a box of nails from now on."

"That'll be ten fifty." The cashier's tone was flat.

The woman paid and grabbed her bag, nearly bumping into me when she turned around. "I'm sorry." When she realized she was apologizing to one of those vampire lovers she was spouting off about, she backed up and lost her manners, muttering under her breath as she stepped around me and left the store.

The cashier rang up my sandwich with a commiserative smile. "Sorry about that."

"You don't have to apologize for that idiot."

She pressed the keys on the register forcefully. "I've got a good mind to put a sign up in my window saying 'Vampires welcome'."

"You'll be greeted by a pile of chicken guts on your floor," I said.

She chuckled. "I heard about what happened over at the market, but she *is* the competition." After composing herself, she gave me a serious look. "I also heard about what happened to your bar. I'm real sorry about that, Charley. Your mama would have been seeing red after what they did to the stag head out front. No pun intended."

"I'm not too happy about it myself, but we'll survive." I grabbed my sandwich and smiled. "It gives the seniors at the high school something fresh to vandalize."

When I walked outside, I took a deep breath and looked around, taking some comfort in knowing that the vampire community still had more allies than enemies in Crimson.

Decent people who were willing to go to bat for others. But I was also disheartened by the animosity that was running deep in the veins of this town. Neighbors secretly harboring hatred for each other.

I started to cross the street to the next block, seeing Candy's shop at the other end. There was something odd-looking about the front window, but I couldn't make out what it was from a distance. As I started to walk faster, someone grabbed me and pulled me around the corner of the building. I slammed against the brick wall. When my head cleared, I saw a tall figure standing in front of me.

Ian.

I listened for the sound of wolves coming at us, but it was suddenly dead quiet.

He got in my face. "We still haven't finished our conversation."

And he thought cracking my head open was going to facilitate discussion?

I held out my dinner, which miraculously was still gripped in my hand. "Want a sandwich?"

He stepped even closer until he was looming over me. A shiver ran down my spine when he pressed his cold lips to my forehead, his gold sigil swinging and grazing the hollow of my neck. "Enjoy it," he whispered. "It might be your last."

TWENTY-FOUR

Needless to say, my appetite had vanished. I fought to steady my shaking limbs so Ian wouldn't see my fear, although he could certainly smell it. He was probably feeding off it. The only thing keeping my legs from folding under me was knowing I was more valuable to him alive than dead.

"I guess we're back at square one," I said. "You might as well go ahead and do whatever it is you're planning to do to me because I can't pay you thirty-five percent. Or even twenty-five percent."

He finally gave me some breathing room and cocked his head. "I'm not here to kill you, if that's what you're thinking. I'm here to teach you a lesson."

That would probably be worse. My adrenaline was starting to flow, but as hard as I willed Ian to disappear, he just kept standing there leering at me, with his entourage of vampires looming behind him. And where were all the people? When I left the Stag, it was fairly crowded outside. But suddenly the streets were empty.

He held his hand out. "Shall we?"

"Shall we what?" I glanced at it and recoiled until my back hit the wall.

"Start the lesson."

A shadow caught my eye. I almost sighed with relief.

Samuel stepped out from the dark recess of a doorway. "What lesson might that be?" He looked at the vampires surrounding him but didn't seem the slightest bit concerned that he was outnumbered by a small army.

Ian gave him a smug smile. "You're really starting to annoy me, vampire."

I brought my eyes to Samuel's, praying he had a plan. He seemed confident, but I wasn't convinced he fully comprehended the gravity of the situation.

In a flash, Ian was standing in the spot where Samuel had just been, grasping at air. His eyes darted back and forth, and then he looked up. Samuel had performed his jumping trick again and was standing on the roof of the building.

He peered down at Ian. "Not very fast for a vampire, are you?" A moment later, he was back on the street, standing behind Ian and his band of thugs. "I'm right here."

A collective of fangs clicked into place. Ian gave a signal and they closed in on Samuel, backing him up toward a wall.

They parted as Ian stepped closer to look Samuel in the eye, grinning triumphantly as he snapped his fingers at them. "*Eat him.*"

Samuel threw his hand up. "Wait. You know what happens when a vampire feeds off another vampire."

He had me curious.

Ian mulled it over. "You're right." Then he backed up and snapped his fingers again. "Just kill him."

Swiftly, Samuel pulled a rather large revolver from his jacket, stopping the vampires dead in their tracks when he aimed it at Ian's face. "Which eye would you prefer I take out first?" His brows cocked. "*Then* you can take your best shot at *me*."

Ian froze. "You know you can't kill me with a gun."

"Ah... but it isn't loaded with your average bullet. There's a nice little surprise at the core of it, and I can assure you it'll put a nasty damper on your night."

I was even more curious now.

The sudden sound of growls coming from the shadows was music to my ears. Lux rounded the corner and slammed into the vampires, taking one of them down. More wolves appeared, and within seconds there was a riot taking place in the street.

Wisely, I backed up to the wall and started to slide down its length toward the other end. When I looked back at the chaos, Ian was coming toward me. He grabbed a handful of my hair and yanked me with him as he headed toward an alley between the buildings. I lost my footing trying to keep up with him and fell.

"Get up!" He grabbed my wrist and yanked me harder, triggering a surge of energy that shot from my head to my toes. A blue light raced up my arm and continued into his, catapulting him against the brick wall. He slid to the ground but quickly found his footing to come at me again. This time he lit up like a flare when he grabbed me.

I ducked when a wolf sailed over my head and landed on top of the vampire, rolling him into the street. It was Dog. They went at it, spinning at such speed I couldn't make out fur from flesh. Ian slid out from under the wolf and came to a stop several yards away, jumping to his feet before disappearing down the alley. The rest of the vampires scattered like rats around the building.

Dog shifted and headed toward me, his braid swaying across his back from the force of his stride.

A vein popped from his forehead as he stuck his finger in my face. "*That* was stupid."

I thought about stepping out of the line of fire but opted to lean away from his rigid finger instead. "You're right. It was stupid."

He pumped his fists, releasing his adrenaline before continuing. "Don't ever do that again. Understood?"

"Got it." I felt like an idiot. But jeez. It was only two blocks, and I didn't expect the pack to lollygag when Ian came out of the woodwork.

Max, the wolf who'd been attacked by crows the night we went down to Reaperstown, shifted and walked over. He patted Dog on the back and grinned at me. "Is Daddy giving you a good tongue lashing?"

"What gave it away? His finger in my face or the vein popping out of his head?"

Dog practically growled at Max. "And you. I ought to chew off your ears for letting her get past you. Now get out of here."

Max dropped down on all fours and disappeared into the night with the rest of the pack.

"Simmer down, Dog. Everyone makes a mistake now and then." I wiggled my fingers at him. "I still have all ten of these. How'd you know to come looking for me?"

Dog nodded to Samuel who was leaning against the building across the street. "Your friend over there stopped by again. He had a word with Lucy and left in a hurry. A few minutes later when I asked her where you were, she let me in on your little stunt."

"I wouldn't call it a stunt. Candy called and sounded kind of strange, so I decided to run down to the Cauldron to check on her. I needed you in the kitchen and figured the pack would be watching me, so I didn't make a big deal out of it."

Dog looked over my shoulder. "Speaking of which."

Candy crossed the street to where we were standing. "What in Hades is going on out here?" She glanced down at Dog's naked body and smiled. Then she noticed all the fur and blood on the street. "Did I miss something?"

Thank God she did. "Just a little scuffle with a vampire."

Her eyes shifted to Samuel, who was still leaning against the wall. "Samuel?"

"Not him. Ian."

"I don't think Samuel's going anywhere," Dog said. "You might want to go over there and talk to the man." A slight grin slid up his face but quickly disappeared. "Show him a little gratitude."

Candy was giving me the same look.

"Do I look like I need help from you two?"

Dog lifted his brows. "Apparently."

"Who's manning the kitchen?" I said to him, trying to get him out of my hair. "Quit worrying about me and go do your job."

He turned to leave but did a double take over Candy's shoulder. "What happened to your window?"

Before she could explain, I headed for the shop to see for myself. Her front window was shattered, and there was a thick plastic sheet taped over it.

She caught up to me and stared at the plastic. "Well, you were right. The crazies in this town don't like witches either, only I got a bag of horse shit thrown through it instead of chicken guts." She groaned. "It's too bad. I could have used the guts to cast a spell on the idiots, but I'm not touching horse shit."

"We need to board it up," Dog said. "That plastic won't keep them out if they come back tonight. Or if those vampires show up again."

"It'll hold. I threw a spell up that'll stop an elephant from getting inside. At least until morning." She wrapped her arm around my shoulders and pulled me closer. "You need to be extra careful, honey. Everyone in this town knows your mama was the baddest witch within a hundred miles of here. That makes you a prime target too."

"They already sent me a message."

"Contrary to what some people think, lightning can strike twice." She let go of me. "I'm heading inside, and Dog is going back to the bar so you can talk to that handsome vampire waiting on you across the street."

I did want to talk to Samuel.

"Have him walk you back," Dog said as he was leaving.

"Don't worry, I will. And make sure Beau puts that blood in the refrigerator when he gets back."

After he dropped down on all fours and ran toward the bar, I walked across the street. Samuel's eyes seemed to pull me in as I approached, which I attributed to typical vampire lure. You never knew which sensations were real and which were manufactured when dealing with one. I found myself tongue-tied. Lost for the simplest words. But I managed to say something stupid when I did find my voice. "Are you stalking me?"

He pushed away from the wall. "Do I look like I need to stalk a woman?"

Hardly. "I was joking."

"I came back to collect my cat who seems to find his way back to you every chance he gets. What are you feeding him? Bluefin tuna?"

I shrugged and leaned back against the wall. "Canned, but just once. I think he's gotten used to the place, but I'll stop letting him in if it makes you feel better."

"But then I won't have a reason to show up at the Stag."

I didn't expect that to come out of his mouth, and then the faint smell of musk or something... earthy filled my nose. Once again, I was lost for words and my heart started to beat a little faster. I tried to avert my eyes so I didn't flush right in front of him, but I couldn't pull them away. When he pressed his hand to the wall and leaned in, I thought he was going to try to kiss me. But he suddenly stepped back.

"Come on. I'll walk you back to the Cauldron."

"That's probably a good idea. I have an early morning." Which was true.

We walked across the street with a strange tension filling the space between us, our fingers brushing once or twice.

"By the way," I said when we reached the door. "What's in those bullets?"

He inhaled sharply. "One of the few things that will bring a vampire to his knees, if only temporarily—liquid sunlight."

I gave him a skeptical look. "You're kidding me?"

"Not at all. I was the guinea pig who tested them. Believe me, I know how effective they are at incapacitating a vampire."

Those could come in handy with Masterson lurking around. "Where do you get them?"

"It," he corrected. "There's only one left in my gun, and the witch who invented them is long dead. I won't waste it on a bottom feeder like Ian Masterson, but he didn't know that tonight."

It begged another question. Why would a vampire possess a magic bullet that would do serious damage to his own kind? "What did you say you do for a living?"

"I fix things."

"Things that require sunlight bullets?"

He smiled faintly. "Good night, Charley."

So he wasn't going to tell me.

"Thanks for saving my neck tonight. Literally," I said as he was leaving.

He trapped me in his gaze. "You're very welcome."

As I watched him disappear around the corner, I found myself thinking of ways to lure a cat. If I could just keep Sebastian coming back, so would Samuel.

"Everything okay?" Candy asked with a grin when I walked inside. She was sweeping up some glass on the floor.

"Sure. Everything's fine."

My best friend was missing, civil war was breaking out all over town, and the co-op was teetering on the verge of shutting down. And now I was hopelessly drawn to a vampire I knew nothing about. No problem. Everything was just fine.

TWENTY-FIVE

Sebastian wasn't in the back room when I got to the Stag before dawn. I was hoping Samuel hadn't picked him up last night after walking me back to the Cauldron, but I guess he had.

Dog came into the room with Lux as I was looking through the mail on the desk. "The pack is here. I just wanted to let you know."

He'd brought them in just in case Ian pulled another stunt while the members were lined up outside. With Patrick out of commission, I'd considered rescheduling the deliveries for high noon when it would be too dangerous for those vampires to show their faces. But calling everyone would have been more work than it was worth, considering I didn't even know if there would be another delivery. We were taking things day by day.

Lux yawned. "We've got your back, Charley, but I'm going to need some coffee before I'm useful to you."

"I'll make a pot," Dog said.

As they were heading for the kitchen, Beau walked into the room carrying an ice cube bin in one hand and Patrick's brief-case in the other. He set the bin on the desk. "This is all I could find to put them in before sticking them in the refrigerator." Then he set the case down and opened it. "Now what?"

I grabbed the notepad from inside. "We go through the orders and make sure we have enough blood to fill them." Patrick was meticulous about making sure everything was exact, and it usually was. But just looking at the number of vials in that bin made me nervous. Maybe it was because they weren't strapped to the inside of the briefcase in neat little rows.

After matching the orders to the vials, we came up short by almost half.

"Are you sure you didn't overfill them?"

Beau shot me an irritated look. "No, I didn't overfill them. I went right up to the mark."

I held one up to the light and verified that they'd been filled precisely to the line. "Then I guess everyone is getting only half their order today."

I noticed an envelope in the briefcase. "What's that?"

"Oh, yeah." Beau grabbed it and handed it to me. "I found it on the table next to the blood bags."

After opening it and reading the note inside, I set it on the desk and rubbed my eyes. "Looks like my worst fears are coming true. One of our donors is leaving town."

"For how long?"

"For... ever. All this violence toward vampires is too much for him, so we're down another donor. The co-op can't survive this, so it's official. We're closing up shop." I prayed it was temporary until this storm blew over Crimson, but I'd be lying if I said I was optimistic about the future of the enterprise.

Beau and I stood there in silence for a few minutes, waiting for the members to arrive. At exactly seven o'clock, there was a knock on the back door. I was only giving this speech once, so instead of having them line up in the alley, I motioned for everyone to come inside. The wary looks on their faces as they squeezed into the room told me they sensed bad news was coming.

"Is there a problem?" Mabel asked.

I took a deep breath. "I hate to tell y'all this, but the co-op is shutting down."

A collective gasp filled the room.

Mr. Russell stepped forward. "You can't do that to us, Charley."

"I'm sorry. It's out of my hands. We don't have the supply." He didn't seem sympathetic to what I was saying so I laid it out for him. "You've seen what's happening in town. Vampires are being targeted left and right, and they're scared. They're keeping their heads low, and no one wants to donate."

Mabel started to whimper, which was the last thing I needed. If she didn't stop, I'd start sniffling myself. "We're hoping this is temporary until things settle down."

"What are we supposed to do until then?" another one asked.

Beau took a firmer approach. "You need to go see your doctors. Get your regular prescriptions filled."

Mr. Russell shook his head. "It ain't right."

"No, it isn't, but there's nothing we can do about it. As soon as things settle down around here, I'm hoping we'll be back in business." It was the best response I could give them. "Just hold on tight and wait to hear from us." It was time for the other bad news. "Unfortunately, we only have enough blood to fill half your orders today, so you need to make it last."

Another collective gasp filled the room.

Before everyone could start complaining again, I told them to line up at the desk. We spent the next hour filling partial orders and giving bad news to latecomers as they arrived. Though unhappy about it, most of them were cordial as they took their vials and left, knowing as soon as they consumed the last drop, their lives would be upended again. Either we reopened for business in the near future, or opioids were about to make a comeback in this town. Come hell or high water, I'd never let that happen.

Never.

* * *

After finishing up co-op business, I went back to worrying about Patrick. There was no official waiting period to report a missing person in the state of Georgia, but after what happened with Mutt, I doubted the Crimson police would bother looking for him anyway. I was more afraid of what Patrick might do to them if they found him.

I heard Murphy's voice. He was talking to Dog when I went up front. Both of their expressions looked grave. "Now what?"

Murphy had his official face on. "Was Keith Barnes in here last night?"

"I don't recall seeing him, but I left the bar early." I glanced at Dog and then back at Murphy. "Why? What did he do?" I'd known Keith for a long time, and I couldn't recall him ever getting in trouble with the police.

"We just need to pinpoint his whereabouts last night."

"Come on, Tom. Since when is police business around here a secret?" He'd never had a problem divulging information before. "I'm not saying another word until you tell me why you're asking."

"Jesus, Charley." After staring at me sternly for a moment, he relented. "The whole damn town probably knows by now anyway."

"Knows what?" Dog asked.

"There was another attack. The guy who works over at the pharmacy. He got jumped on his way home last night and was beaten up pretty bad. To a pulp, to be exact. He's in critical condition over at the hospital, but he managed to give us a name."

"You mean Dave?" I said.

"Yeah. Nearly killed him."

I didn't like where this was going. "What does this have to do with Keith?"

"He's the prime suspect. We have him locked up over at the jail right now."

I snorted. "You're not serious?"

Murphy didn't flinch.

Dog eyed him closely. "I think he is."

I'd never seen Keith be the slightest bit aggressive. "Keith can be annoying at times, but he's harmless. The man wouldn't hurt a fly."

Murphy pulled a small pad of paper and a pen from his pocket. "Was he here or not?"

I didn't remember seeing Keith in the bar before I left to check on Candy last night, so I looked at Dog. "Was he?"

"I didn't see him."

Murphy jotted it down. "That's all I need."

"What's going to happen to him now?" I asked.

Murphy stuck the pad back in his pocket. "He stays in jail. We're thinking he might be the same guy who attacked Patrice Henderson."

At least they weren't trying to pin it on Mutt, but this was crazy. Keith Barnes was no more a killer than I was. "Can I see him?"

Murphy looked at me like I had a screw loose. "No, you can't see him."

"Why not?"

"Because you're not family for one. Or his attorney."

"Does he even have an attorney?"

Murphy pulled his authority face. "This is none of your business, Charley. Why would you want to see him anyway?"

Instead of answering, I stared back at him in silence hoping he'd get the message and leave. He finally turned around and walked toward the door.

As soon as he left, I asked Dog, "Was Keith really not in here last night?"

"Nope. Unless he stopped in for a quick beer while I was saving your ass from a bunch of vampires."

I could count on one hand the number of Friday nights that Keith hadn't sat at the bar drinking until closing. Maybe this was one of them, but I doubted it.

"I'm getting into that jail to see Keith if I have to bribe the clerk at the desk." I didn't think that would be necessary, though. The Crimson jail was nothing more than a small building with two cells, and I doubted the second one had ever been used. The clerk who manned the front desk was a high school classmate of mine, and it wouldn't take much for me to get in there. It wasn't like I was breaking the law. Murphy was just pulling his usual stunts.

Dog groaned. "Charley, stay out of it."

Did I hear him right? "Why would you even say that to me? If it was you, I'd be breaking down the door. Besides, the man doesn't have any family left. He'll sit in that jail and rot."

"Because Murphy's right. Keith might be dangerous."

"Then I'm going to find out what made him so dangerous."

Seeing the look in Dog's eyes made me second-guess my own logic, but I needed to follow my gut. The only way to confirm my suspicion that people in town were getting hopped up on dragon's tears was to strike while the iron was hot. Look Keith in the eye while he was still under the influence and ask him straight out. Then we could hunt down whoever was dealing the stuff and put an end to it. God knew, Crimson PD wasn't doing anything about it.

Dog rubbed his forehead. "Charley..."

"Look. I'm not planning to step inside Keith's cell. I won't even get within arm's length of it, but I'm going over there to talk to him."

He set a firm gaze on me. "Do whatever you want, but if you're not back here in a couple of hours, I'm coming down to that jail."

* * *

Making sure neither of the patrol cars were parked in front of the station, I went inside and walked up to the desk.

"Charley Underwood! Girl, I haven't seen you in... How long has it been?"

"Hey, Jen." I plastered a smile on my face. "Months. You should stop by the Stag sometime."

She shrugged. "I don't drink anymore."

"That's okay. I'll buy you lunch, and we can catch up." We never did like each other very much, and if I recall, she wasn't the sharpest tack in the box. She was a cheerleader in high school. Turned her nose up to me because her mother never liked mine. That animosity trickled down a generation.

She got a funny look on her face as she stroked a strand of her long blond hair. "Well, that's awfully nice of you."

"We're adults now, Jen. I can forget about high school if you can."

"I'd like that." She eyed me for a moment. "So, what can I do for you?"

I leaned over the desk and lowered my voice. "I heard Keith Barnes is in one of the cells."

"I know." She lost her smile. "I was shocked when they brought him in. He didn't even look like himself."

"I was hoping to talk to him."

She leaned back, putting some distance between us. "Oh, I don't know about that. I was told to stay away from him. Tom and Rick said he's dangerous."

"I'm not planning to get close to him. I just want to talk to him through the cell bars. And he does have a right to an attorney. I'm going to act as his advocate to set that up for him." When she stared at me suspiciously, I upped the pressure. "You wouldn't want him to be deprived of his rights, would you?"

"No, but—"

"Because not allowing his advocate to speak with him could be construed as a violation of those rights."

Her brows pulled together. "I wish you would wait until Tom or Rick gets back to the station."

I didn't say a word. I just let her squirm and question herself. It didn't take very long.

She smiled again. "You know what? You're right. I don't know what I was thinking. Just don't get too close to the cell."

"I won't. Just a few minutes and I'll be out of here."

She got up and walked around the desk. "Follow me."

We went down a hallway that led to the back of the building that housed the cells. Keith was in the one on the left. The other cell was empty. He was sitting on the floor staring straight ahead at the wall, and there was dried blood all over his hands, face, and shirt. They hadn't allowed him to wash up, but I guess it was evidence.

Jen pointed to a chair against the wall several feet away from the cell. "You can sit there." Then she glanced at Keith with an uncomfortable look and just stood next to me with her arms crossed.

"Can we have some privacy, please?"

She seemed hesitant to leave but finally got the message. "You have fifteen minutes, and don't get too close."

After she left, I walked up to the cell but stopped short of touching the bars. "Is it true?"

As if suddenly realizing someone was in the room with him, Keith pulled his eyes away from the wall but still wouldn't look at me. "Is that you, Charley?"

The hell with it. I stepped closer, feeling sick to my stomach when I got a good look at all the blood. "Tell me what happened last night." He turned his face away from me and clammed up tight. "I can't help you if you won't talk to me, Keith."

"Help me? How the hell are you going to help me?" When he finally turned to look at me, his eyes seemed strange. There was a darkness in them I'd never seen before, and his hands were shaking. "You need to leave, Charley. You can't fix this."

"I can see about getting you a lawyer. Maybe Bob Flanders can help." Bob Flanders was the only attorney in town, but he was a retired ambulance chaser who probably didn't even have an active license to practice anymore.

A low laugh filled the room. A second later, Keith was on his feet gripping the bars. I stumbled out of reach, unable to recognize the man standing in the cell in front of me.

"What made you do it?" I cautiously stepped closer. "You might as well tell me. What do you have to lose?"

He let go of the bars and walked to the center of the cell. With his back to me, he finally started to talk. "You see, that's the problem. I don't remember any of it."

"Then how do you know you did it?"

A nervous burst of laughter came from his mouth as he held out his bloodstained hands. "This, Charley! I'm covered in the man's blood, and he identified me."

How do you beat a man senseless and not remember any of it?

"I need to ask you something, Keith, and you need to tell me the truth. Did you take any drugs last night?"

He let out a weak laugh. "I wish I did. It might explain everything. But I don't mess with drugs."

"Where were you last night?"

He took a seat on the floor again and propped his arms up on his bent knees. "I got me a free dinner." He shrugged. "One minute I was eating something I couldn't even pronounce, and the next I was waking up outside the hardware store at six a.m. covered in blood. The cops were waiting for me when I got home."

"You ate at Morceau last night?"

He turned his head away again. "Forget about me. I'm a monster."

"I can't do that, Keith. Something's wrong with this town, but I'm going to find out what it is."

His head slowly turned back to me, but the Keith I'd just been talking to was gone. He climbed to his feet and stared at me blankly. "You want to know what's wrong with this town?" He stepped toward me, his eyes growing wider. It was the same look I'd seen in Mutt's eyes just before he attacked me. He was standing at the bars a second later, gripping them so tightly his fingers were starting to turn white underneath the bloodstains. "You want to know what's wrong with this town?" he repeated louder through clenched teeth. "What's wrong with this town?" His voice continued to escalate, his eyes feral.

"Calm down, Keith."

He pressed his face to the bars, his eyes bulging as his mouth spread into a grin.

Jen came running down the hallway. "You need to go, Charley."

"Look out your window!" He shook the bars, his voice escalating into a growl. "You want to know what's wrong with this town, look out your damn window!"

The only thing keeping him from trying to rip my head off was the set of bars between us.

Jen pulled out her phone. "I'm calling Tom."

"Don't bother. I'm leaving."

Hurrying down the hallway, I pushed the door open to get some fresh air. I could barely breathe in there. Keith had just convinced me that he was innocent. He may have committed the crime, but something else had taken the wheel when he did it.

I climbed into my truck and drove the four blocks back to the Stag. When I got out, my eyes immediately went across the street to Morceau. Atticus was standing outside looking back at me.

Look out your damn window!

Crimson was never perfect, but it wasn't until Devereaux came to town that people around here started to do strange things, and most of them had stopped at Morceau before climbing on the crazy train. I'd been so blinded by Ian Masterson's attacks that I'd missed the giant red flag right in front of me. It was time to find out if Keith's message had any merit to it, or if I was just being paranoid.

"Let's go see what you're hiding, Atticus," I muttered as I headed for him. Halfway across the street, a queasy feeling rolled through my stomach. The closer I got to him, the more I thought I was going to be sick. But as soon as my foot hit the sidewalk in front of the restaurant, the feeling vanished.

"Charley." Atticus puffed at a cigar. "Your timing is perfect."

I caught a glimpse of something around his neck. A pendant partially concealed by his shirt. "What is that pendant you're wearing?"

"Pendant?" He frowned. "I'm not wearing one."

I looked again, and it was gone. "But I—"

"Is something wrong?" He took another puff.

"It's nothing."

What are you, Atticus Devereaux?

His smile returned. "You're just in time. My chef has prepared something new. You can help me decide if it's worthy of tonight's menu."

He wove his arm around mine and tried to lead me inside,

but my entire body started to vibrate the moment he touched me. It was like a heavy current racing over my skin.

I pulled my arm away. "Sorry. I was just on my way home to check on something."

"Of course."

I went back to my truck and got in, allowing the excess energy to dissipate before starting the engine. "Dragon's tears, my ass." I watched him through my rearview mirror for a second and then I drove toward the house to find out what I was dealing with.

TWENTY-SIX

Rex flew across the yard and landed on my shoulder when I got out of the truck. As soon as I walked inside the house, he sailed through the living room toward the kitchen. By the time I followed him in there, he'd spilled a box of cereal on the counter and was devouring it.

"You're not a baby anymore." I picked him up and set him on the edge of a chair. "You need to eat crow food." I felt a little guilty for leaving him alone out here, but he was a wild bird whether he liked it or not.

He cawed at me a couple of times when I continued down the hallway to my mother's bedroom. If anyone had known how to spot something through smoke and mirrors, it was Delia Underwood.

I opened the door to a small adjoining room and scanned a bookshelf containing my mother's books and journals. They'd gone unopened since she died, but I had a feeling they'd be getting more use now that my gifts were starting to manifest.

Several books caught my eye, including one on demonology. After pulling them from the shelf and dusting them off, I took the stack of books back to the kitchen and set them down. Rex jumped on the table and hopped over to them, cocking his head like he was reading the titles.

"Let's dive in, shall we?"

I went straight for the book on demonology and flipped it open. The table of contents listed everything from Lucifer to fallen angels, and I could tell by the first few paragraphs that I was about to go down a rabbit hole of Christian mythology. But that wasn't what I was looking for. I shut it and pushed it away, surprised my mother would even have it in her collection.

After briefly flipping through a few more and finding nothing remotely relevant to what I was dealing with, I came to the last book in the stack. It was titled *Malevolent Beings*.

Rex pecked at the cover, digging his beak into the edge like he was trying to open it. "Okay. I've got it." I flipped to the table of contents, having no idea what I was looking for, but the list of things in front of me was a good starting point. The word *incubus* made the hair on the back of my neck stand on end. But so far, Atticus hadn't tried anything that perverse, although some of his customers were questionable. He didn't fit the bill of a banshee either. However, a jinn wasn't far off. Something had possessed Patrick, and a jinn was certainly capable of it.

I was starting to get a headache, so I pushed the book away and closed my eyes. They popped back open when I heard Rex pecking forcefully at the page. He'd nearly drilled a hole in the table of contents next to a chapter titled "Incarnates." When I flipped to the section and started to read, the first paragraph got my attention immediately.

An incarnation of a god or a spirit in the form of a human, but it can also embody the essence of evil or the devil. Such entities are known to possess humans and compel them to do unspeakable deeds, often by luring them with arcane symbols or human sustenance.

I sat straight up in my chair and looked at Rex. "Sustenance?"

In other words, food and drink. Not to mention those symbols above the door at Morceau. The ones Dog had called *chalking*.

It was entirely possible I was wrong, but I knew one thing with absolute certainty—Atticus Devereaux wasn't human. No one could have pulled off that restaurant in a week. No one.

I scanned the rest of the chapter and didn't find anything else notable. "Well, that was about as helpful as a bonfire without a match," I said to Rex.

It would be dusk soon, and the bar was already open. I needed to get out of here before Ian came lurking around or Dog sent out the cavalry to look for me.

After watching Rex fly up into the tree, I climbed into my truck and drove back to town, thinking about all that had happened over the past week. The more I thought about it, the more I believed Atticus was responsible. By the time I drove around the square, I'd convinced myself I needed to get inside that restaurant. If for nothing else, to prove myself wrong.

The Stag was already crowded when I got there, and someone had parked in my spot out front. The nerve. I pulled into a space at the end of the block. As I walked inside, Beau waved me over to the bar.

"Where have you been?" he asked.

"I had to go by the house for something. Is that okay with you?" I looked around the packed room. "It's barely six o'clock." By the look of the crowd, it was going to be a record night.

He had a funny look on his face. "It's been like this since we opened the door an hour ago. You'd think it was Oktoberfest."

We usually took advantage of the traffic headed up to Helen, Georgia, where they held a huge Oktoberfest, but it was nowhere near that time of year.

Most of the people were regulars, and Lucy and Tucker

were running up and down the bar trying to keep up with orders. I would have jumped in to help, but four people behind the bar would have been a calamity. More hindrance than help. Instead, I decided to see if Dog needed me in the kitchen.

He looked wary. "Where have you been?"

"Why does everyone keep asking me that? I went out to the house."

"What happened at the jail?"

I grabbed an apron and tied it around my waist. "Keith said he's guilty. The kicker is he doesn't remember actually doing it. He said he ate at Morceau and doesn't remember a thing after that until he woke up covered in blood." I couldn't shake the look in Keith's eyes. "He went crazy in his cell. He kept repeating something about looking right outside my window if I wanted to know what was wrong with this town. And you know what's outside that window out there?"

Dog stopped what he was doing and looked at me. "Atticus Devereaux and that restaurant of his. Are you seeing a pattern here?"

"I am now."

He hacked his cleaver through an onion on the cutting board. "That man ain't right."

"How long have you suspected him?"

"Since he sent Masterson running out of here like a bat out of hell the other night. That vampire was scared." He gripped the cleaver tighter. "I don't like being played for a fool, and that's exactly what Devereaux's been doing."

I put my theory out there and hoped he didn't think I was crazy. "I think he's poisoning people. There's something in his food. Maybe dark magic. I'm going to get inside that restaurant and find out what it is." That got his attention, and I regretted telling him immediately. "Don't look at me like that, Dog."

"Like what? Like you're out of your mind?" He shook his

head and continued to chop. "You're not doing it, Charley. If anyone's going in there, it'll be the pack."

Like a bunch of wolves breaking in there would go unnoticed. Dog was already on Crimson PD's shit list for nothing more than being a wolf. If I got caught, Murphy would call in a favor to get me off, but Dog would rot in jail for God knew how long.

"No one's going in there, so forget about it." My lie had good intentions. "We'll find another way to ferret him out."

With the discussion ended, I looked around the kitchen for something to do. I was about to dive in and start washing dishes when I heard a ruckus. It sounded like a Super Bowl party taking place out front.

"What the hell?" Dog pulled his eyes away from the order window and strode toward the kitchen door.

I looked out and saw a crowd circling around someone. Lucy and Beau were pouring drinks like their lives depended on it, but Tucker was pressed against the wall near the order window, staring at the spectacle. She looked terrified.

Tossing my apron on the counter, I ran out and nearly collided with Dog as he stood there glaring at someone. In the center of the crowd was the devil himself.

"What the hell's going on?" I said.

Dog slowly shook his head. "I don't know, but it ain't good."

"Another round!" Atticus declared. The crowd erupted again, raising their empty glasses in the air. "Drinks are on me tonight!"

A third eruption.

I motioned Tucker over and took her into the kitchen.

She stopped just inside the door. "Are you firing me?"

"Firing you? For what?"

On her first attempt to answer, nothing came out. "I froze when I saw him," she finally managed to say.

My eyes darted to the order window. "Who? Atticus?"

She nodded.

I was even more curious about her background now. "Why? Do you know the man?" Wouldn't that be a stroke of luck.

"No!" She hesitated as she opened her mouth to continue.

"It's okay. You can speak freely. I don't like him either."

"I can see things," she muttered, her eyes glued to the floor.

"Oh yeah? What kind of things?"

"Things I shouldn't be seeing!" she blurted out. "That man out there isn't what he seems to be." She lowered her voice to a whisper. "And he saw me looking at him."

This was getting interesting. "It's okay. It's kind of hard not to notice him." Whether I liked Atticus or not, I couldn't deny he was a handsome man.

She shook her head briskly. "You don't understand, Charley. He saw me *looking* at him. I saw right through his facade, and I think he noticed."

I was starting to catch on. "You mean like... otherworldly things?" She just stared back at me, and I realized Tucker had some secrets of her own.

I grabbed her wrist and took her to the back room and sat her down. "Have you ever heard of something called an Incarnate?"

She clamped her hand over her mouth as a sharp gasp escaped it. Then she pulled it away and leaned closer to whisper. "You know what he is?"

"I wasn't a hundred percent sure, but I think you just confirmed it." Which got me wondering what *she* was. "What are you? Psychic?"

"Something like that. It's gotten me in trouble a few times, that's for sure." She shrank like a mouse again. "It's why I had to leave Atlanta."

Dog came into the room, interrupting the conversation that was just getting interesting. "We've got a problem."

"No kidding. What's going on out there?"

He motioned toward the hallway. "You need to see for yourself."

I walked back out but didn't get very far. The place was packed with way more people than it was zoned for. It could get me fined or shut down if the fire chief got a bug up his ass. I could barely see the bar, let alone what Atticus was up to, but I could hear his deep laugh coming from somewhere.

Dog pushed through the crowd, cutting a path for me behind him. When we finally made it within six feet of the bar, the crowd parted and left me with a clear view of Mary Ellen's long legs draped over the side. She was sprawled out on top of it, propped up by her elbows with her skirt hiked up to her hips. At least she had panties on this time, but her skimpy tank top was pulled down below her breasts. If the overcapacity didn't get me shut down, the indecency charge would.

Beau and Lucy were standing behind the bar gawking at her.

"What the hell are you doing?" I said to her. It was a rhetorical question.

She spread her thighs wider. "Having fun. You should try it sometime."

I did a double take when her eyes suddenly went black. Then I grabbed her by her tank top and yanked her off the bar. After dragging her to the front door and throwing her out, I turned back to the crowd. "Get out! All of you! Now!"

When no one budged, Dog came up beside me and let out a high-pitched whistle. A few seconds later, the pack appeared on the sidewalk in front of the bar. They lined up and stared through the window, prepared to drop down on all fours to facilitate an evacuation if necessary.

Loki walked inside. "You called?"

"The place was just clearing out," I said, but instead of everyone funneling toward the door, they parted like the Red Sea.

Atticus emerged from the crowd and came toward me, but Dog stepped in his path. "That's close enough."

"Have we outstayed our welcome?" His eyes flashed a bright shade of orange. A shade of fire. "I do apologize for such bad behavior."

"I'm on to you," I said, regretting it immediately. Stupid to lay my cards on the table so early.

His grin spread wider. "Figured me out, have you?"

"What do you want, Atticus?"

He took a deep breath through his nose, letting it escape slowly. "I think you know what I want."

I genuinely didn't have a clue, but instead of playing his game, I nodded to the door. "You can leave now. And take your new friends with you."

After staring at me for a few seconds, he let out a boisterous laugh and turned around. "Who's hungry?"

The crowd, including many of my patrons, followed him out the door. The pack waited until the last person was across the street and inside Morceau. Then they disappeared as quickly as they'd shown up.

I locked the front door and gave Dog a questioning look. "Is the pack surrounding the place twenty-four seven now?"

"After what happened last night? You bet your sweet ass."

The backup was appreciated, but it was going to be tricky getting past them tonight. I also needed to make sure Devereaux stayed put in that big house he'd bought over on Davenport Street while I broke into Morceau. What I needed was an accomplice. Someone who didn't have a personal stake in stopping me, and I knew just the person.

TWENTY-SEVEN

Dog was going to kill me when he found out I'd slipped past the pack, but it was either me or him going into that restaurant, and my position on Dog staying out of jail was firm.

After closing, Dog had walked me down to Hecate's Cauldron. I said good night to Candy on the way up to my room and slipped right out the window and down the fire escape to meet Tucker a few blocks over.

"I don't know, Charley." Tucker bit her lower lip, looking like she wanted to bolt. "You sure you want to do this?"

"I'm not sure about anything right now, but I don't have a choice." My hands were getting clammy as I spoke. "If you're not up for it, now would be the time to tell me."

My gut instinct was telling me that Atticus was poisoning people with something, and it was somewhere in that restaurant. If I didn't find anything tonight—or end up in the back of Murphy's patrol car—I'd hit that big house across the street next. Tucker was here to keep an eye on the place to make sure Atticus didn't leave. If he did, she was to call me so I could get out of the restaurant fast.

She pulled herself together and gave me a thumbs-up. "I'll be on the phone in a heartbeat if he leaves."

I patted her on the shoulder. "Easy as pie. Just stay out of sight, and I'll come and get you as soon as I'm out of there."

She took a deep breath and nodded. "You better get going before I change my mind."

"If I don't come back within an hour, call Dog." I figured that was plenty of time, but after thinking about it... "Make it two."

Just in case Ian and his thugs were out there, I stuffed my blond hair under a baseball cap and kept to the bushes as I headed for Morceau. I didn't want the pack to spot me either, so I took the long way around the buildings across from the Stag, hoping I didn't run into a wolf or a vampire.

The restaurant was dark inside. I'd seen Atticus leave and then watched his staff lock the place up shortly before the Stag closed. Then I talked Tucker into helping me. Bribed her with the promise of a full-time job. Beau would have gone straight to Dog, and Lucy would have told me to eat shit if I'd asked her to hide in the bushes and watch Atticus's house for me.

I slipped around to the back of the restaurant and questioned my sanity for the tenth time. If I didn't find an easy way to get inside, my trespassing charges would be upgraded to breaking and entering.

Unlike the first time I was here with Dog, the back door was locked. I tried the window near the kitchen, but it wouldn't budge either. I spotted a pile of bricks left over from the renovation and realized I'd have to break the glass to get in. Although I doubted Atticus had bothered to install an alarm system, it would be messy, and I really didn't want to leave a calling card.

I grabbed a brick and thought about Patrick to ramp up my courage. If I found him in Atticus's walk-in freezer, it was over. The whole town would hear me.

As I was about to smash my way in, I caught a glimpse of

something on the ground. It was a well around a basement window.

I stepped down into the hole, thankful that it wasn't one of those tiny windows barely big enough for a cat to fit through. Relief washed over me when it slid open, but my elation ended quickly when I saw the pitch-black void in front of me and something sulfur-like filled my nose. I was starting to regret not bringing some kind of weapon with me.

"This is a bad idea," I mumbled as I twisted around and stuck my leg through the opening. My foot hit something immediately. A shelf or a table. I lowered myself backward, planting my feet firmly on the surface before ducking inside. I could barely see a few feet in front of me, the moonlight shining into the well doing little to brighten the darkness. Hopping off the table onto the floor, I pulled my phone out to use the flashlight app.

Particles of dust filled the light beam as I aimed it at a worktable pushed against the wall. There was a tall cabinet in the corner, and on the other side of the room was a metal contraption that looked like a remnant from the old machine shop that had once occupied the building. Everything was covered in soot, and it appeared no one had used the basement in years.

After getting an eyeful of nothing but relics, I spotted the stairs across the room. Halfway up, I caught a glimpse of something in the beam of light pointed at my feet. A metal hatch under the steps. A door in the floor. I debated whether to go back down, but the thought of climbing into a dark hole under the basement was enough to make me second-guess what I was doing there. If I didn't find anything in the restaurant above, *maybe* I'd get the nerve to open it.

Letting my nerves settle for a moment, I continued up. It occurred to me that the door at the top might be locked. That would be my luck. But it opened, and I stepped into the quiet restaurant with the lingering smell of food in the air. It felt eerie to walk through the place. Maybe it was my conscience telling me I was breaking the law.

I turned the flashlight off. There was enough light coming through the windows, and I didn't want to announce myself to anyone passing by, including Crimson PD during their nightly patrols. I looked at the Stag across the street. Atticus had a perfect view of the bar. It kind of creeped me out, thinking of him watching me from over here.

The room looked the same as I remembered from the other night. There was nothing out of the ordinary. But I hadn't explored the kitchen yet.

When I walked through the doorway into the large kitchen, I couldn't believe how spotless it was. There wasn't a drop of grease anywhere, not even on the stovetop. When I pulled the doors open on the two ovens, I was convinced food had never graced the racks of either one of them. But that was impossible.

I ran my finger along the stainless steel countertop on my way across the room to the refrigerator. It wasn't big enough to hold a body, which eased my mind as I pulled the door open. It was empty. Not what you'd expect to find in a working restaurant.

There was a much larger door on the other side of the room. Probably the walk-in freezer. Now *that* was big enough to hold a body.

My heart started to race as I crossed the kitchen and reached for the handle. "Please don't be in there," I whispered. I pulled the door open and saw something hanging from a hook in the center of the freezer. Stumbling, I grabbed the doorframe to steady myself. After looking back at the deer carcass, I bent over to rest my hands on my thighs while the pounding of my heart settled. Then I straightened back up and went inside. There were several whole birds on one of the shelves, and some rabbits on another. All wild game animals.

After walking out, I started opening cabinets and drawers

but found nothing but a roll of duct tape and a few cooking utensils inside. "Where is it, Atticus?" My eyes landed on a door at the other end of the kitchen, but it turned out to be a broom closet. He'd hidden his secrets well.

Sucking up my fear, I went to check out that latch door in the basement. I grabbed a knife from a block on the counter as I walked out of the kitchen and back through the dining room.

The obnoxious smell of rotten eggs hit me the moment I started to descend the stairs. It got stronger with each step, causing a knot to form in my stomach from a sudden sense of dread.

I shook it off, gripping the knife tighter as I walked under the stairs. There was a hook on the latch. I set the phone and knife on the filthy floor to pull the heavy door open. Then I flashed the light into the opening. A rickety set of wooden steps descended into dark oblivion below the basement.

"Hell no," I muttered, taking a step back. I had my limits, and that hole was one of them.

While I debated the sanity of ignoring my instincts by going down there, I heard a sound coming from below. A faint clinking noise.

"Hello?" I heard it again. "Patrick?"

Before I lost my nerve, I shined the light on the steps and went down. My feet hit a dirt floor at the bottom. The flashlight revealed nothing but dust particles in the beam, and then the light went out. My phone was completely dead.

"Are you kidding me?" I started back up the steps but remembered the tiny flashlight on my keychain. The one that was only good for about a foot or two. After fumbling for it, I unclipped it from the chain and turned it on.

"Patrick?"

I swung the flashlight to my left when I heard the noise again, illuminating the edge of a bookcase that went from floor to ceiling. Stepping closer, the beam revealed rows of bottles lining the shelves. They looked like perfume bottles with glass stoppers. That must have been the sound I kept hearing. Glass clinking together.

But who was moving them?

Panicking, I tripped and dropped the flashlight, kicking up a thick layer of dirt when I hit the floor. I rolled on my stomach, spitting dirt from my mouth and using my sleeve to wipe it from my face. I grabbed the tiny flashlight that had bounced a few feet away and saw something on the floor in front of me. One of the bottles had fallen. The dirt floor had cushioned it and kept it from breaking.

After climbing to my feet, I picked it up to set it back on the shelf. I thought it was empty, but when I shined the light on it, I saw something move inside. I flinched, and stepped back, feeling the hair on the back of my neck stand on end. When I approached it again, I noticed a mist moving around inside. I nearly dropped the flashlight when I turned the bottle around and saw the name BILL MEADOWS written on a white label.

I shined the light across the row of bottles. Most were empty, but others had that same mist moving around inside, including one with Maggie Ferguson's name written on it. They were the names of Crimson's missing.

My eyes frantically scanned another row, stopping on one in particular. An empty one with my name labeled across the front.

A bottle at the end of the shelf started to vibrate. The mist whirled like a mini tornado trapped inside, and then it tipped over and rolled toward the edge. I grabbed it just before it could fall, gasping when I read the label.

PATRICK ALDEAN.

The bottle slipped through my fingers when I heard a noise coming from above. A door opening and closing. It was faint, but I had good ears. Someone was in the restaurant.

I grabbed the bottle from the floor and ran back to the steps, watching the basement stairs directly above me as I climbed out of the hidden room. I was just closing the hatch when light flooded in through the basement door. My back hit the wall when I heard a foot hit the top step, and then a figure started to descend the stairs. It was Atticus.

With the knife gripped in one hand and the bottle in the other, I slid down the wall toward the tall cabinet I'd seen on my way in. My eyes adjusted to the darkness with the help of the dim light coming through the window and the door at the top of the stairs, and I could see a space between the edge of the cabinet and the corner wall. I squeezed into the gap, barely fitting, focusing on the window I'd left open and wondering how fast I could get to it and climb out.

The footsteps stopped when Atticus reached the bottom. After a few seconds, he continued into the basement, taking his time as he crossed the room. My adrenaline raced faster when his footsteps came to a halt near the cabinet and he started to whistle. I pressed deeper into the gap and held my breath when I heard one of the drawers open.

The whistling abruptly stopped, and the basement went eerily quiet. The outline of his shoulder broke through the darkness when he stepped a few inches to his right, clearing the edge of the cabinet. And then half of his face appeared. His right eye focused on me briefly, but then he stepped to his left and walked away, taking the stairs back up to the restaurant.

I sagged against the wall, feeling like I was about to be sick.

"Fly, little birdie. Fly," I heard him say as he continued up the steps.

I bolted, dropping the knife when I jumped on the table and scrambled through the window, praying I didn't feel a hand wrap around my leg as I escaped. I made it through but lost my grip on the bottle as I was climbing out. Dropping down on my stomach to reach into the well, I grabbed it and saw a set of glowing red eyes staring back at me from the darkness of the basement.

Climbing to my feet, I ran, glancing over my shoulder several times. The bar was right there, but I kept going toward Davenport Street where Tucker was supposed to be watching Atticus's house. When I got there, she was crouching behind the bush staring at her phone.

"What the hell, Tucker!"

She looked up at me with a blank stare. "What?"

I glanced across the street. "You didn't see him leave?"

Obviously confused, she looked at the house. "No one has gone in or out since I got here." I must have had a crazy look in my eyes because she stood up abruptly and put some distance between us. "Did you get caught?"

"Do you think I'd be standing here if I did?" Atticus had practically opened the door for me on my way out. I couldn't even fathom why. "Let's just get out of here before he shows up." Or before Ian did. There were any number of reasons.

She looked at the bottle in my hand. "What's that?"

"My best friend." I held it up and looked at the mist to make sure it was still moving around inside, especially after what I'd just put that bottle through. "Come on. We need to find a way to get him out."

TWENTY-EIGHT

Hecate's Cauldron was lit up when we came around the corner, and Candy was standing at the door with her hands on her hips. "Where the hell have you been?" She looked at Tucker and threw a hand up when I tried to explain. "Forget it. I don't think I want to know."

I walked inside and set the bottle down on the display case. Gently.

She took one look at it and her eyes grew wider. After stepping closer, she read the label. "Sweet baby Jesus."

"Actually, it's Patrick."

"Smart-ass. Where'd you find him?"

I prepared myself for a tongue lashing. "In a hidden room under the basement at Morceau."

She pulled her eyes away from the bottle to look at me. "You really are just like your mother."

"I'll take that as a compliment."

"I didn't mean it as one. Delia didn't always use her common sense." She grumbled a few choice words and went over to the bookcase against the wall. "Where did I see that thing?"

"What are you looking for?"

She stopped perusing the books and looked over her shoulder at me. "Something that's going to tell us how to get him out of there."

"Good. Keep looking."

Tucker walked over to the bottle and picked it up. "Why don't you just open it?"

Before I could tell her to put it back down, she pulled the stopper out and set it on the case with the bottle. The mist started to expand and seep out of the top.

Candy pulled a book out. "Here it is."

"What did you do, Tucker!" I wanted to wring her neck. But the deed was done, and something was happening.

The three of us watched as the mist floated over the sides of the glass and continued down the display case, pooling into a pillow of fog a few inches above the floor.

Candy slid the book back on the shelf. "I guess that's as good a way as any to let the genie out of the bottle. Let's just hope it is in fact Patrick in there."

I watched as the mist started to take on a shape. "Who else would it be?"

She shrugged. "A demon?"

Tucker obviously didn't scare easily, or she would have packed her bags by now and left town. But this would be the real test of her fortitude and determine if she'd fit in at the Stag for the long haul.

The mist started to move clockwise, spinning up toward the ceiling until it formed a tall cone, the outline of a figure appearing in the center.

"You might want to step back," Candy said, grabbing my arm.

I shrugged her off. "That's my best friend in there. I can feel him."

When the mist finally started to fade, Patrick was left standing there, naked as a jaybird.

I took a step toward him. "Patrick?"

He slowly turned and opened his mouth, but before he could speak, he collapsed.

Candy unlocked the mystery door and pushed it open. Then she came back over and grabbed Patrick under his arms. "You two grab his legs so we can get him in the back room."

I was finally going to get a glimpse of it. I just wished it was under better circumstances.

The three of us managed to get him off the floor and through the door. Tucker didn't seem fazed at all about hauling a naked stranger across the room.

The door opened to a hallway that led to the back of the building, similar to the layout of the Stag. We took a right into a small room furnished with a double bed and a chair. There was a full-length mirror on the wall and a table with various items on it that made me once again question that side business of hers.

"Good Lord, Candy. What is this room?"

"None of your business. Let's just get him on the bed."

She threw a blanket over Patrick and smiled at Tucker. "Would you mind checking the front door to make sure it's locked?"

After Tucker left, she pulled out her keys and opened a door in the room. I assumed it was a closet. "I'll be right back."

"What's in there?"

"Danger." She slipped inside and shut the door behind her.

A minute later, she came back out with something in her hand. A dim light was on inside, and I caught a glimpse of shelves against the wall. The way she locked the door again so quickly made me even more curious.

She went back to the bed and bent down over Patrick. "Don't you freak out on me, Charley. I know what I'm doing."

There was a small jar in her hand, and I knew what it was the second she opened it. "Are you crazy? You're not injecting him with zombie blood again." I don't know what came over me, but I slapped her hand away when she dipped her finger into the black goo.

She straightened up and narrowed her eyes at me. "Don't you know better than to slap someone holding something this volatile?"

"I'm sorry, Candy, but look at him. Do you see a demon in there? That stuff will probably kill him this time."

She scraped the excess blood from her finger on the edge of the jar and bent over him again. "I'm not planning to inject him with it. I'm just going to dab a little on his tongue to see how he reacts."

Before she could stick her finger in his mouth, his eyes flew open. He sucked in a lungful of air and sat straight up, gasping like a baby taking its first breath. His eyes shot to Candy and then to me. "Charley?"

"How are you feeling?" It was a stupid question, but what else was I supposed to say?

He glanced down at his body. "Like I've been tag-teamed and ridden hard. Where the hell am I?"

It was Patrick all right.

Candy stuck the jar under his nose. "Take a whiff of this."

He inhaled sharply and began to cough, his fangs descending. "What the hell?"

"I told you to take a whiff, not suck it up through your nose." She put the lid back on and set it on the table.

"Are you trying to kill me, woman? That shit just about burned a hole through my nostrils."

She glanced at me with a grin. "He's officially unpossessed."

A strange look suddenly rolled over his face. Like a switch had been flipped.

"What's wrong?" I asked him.

He slowly looked at me. "We're in trouble. All of us. The whole damn town."

"You mean because of Atticus Devereaux?" I said, glancing at Candy.

"Atticus *Devil*. That man didn't come here to open a restaurant. He's here to take souls, and he's using that fancy food of his to do it." His upper lip curled into a snarl. "I'm gonna kill that son of a bitch."

"So I was right. Atticus is poisoning people with his food."

Candy huffed. "More like poisoning them with black magic. That's a dirty way to take souls."

"Is there an ethical way?"

Patrick got a distant look in his eyes as a memory seemed to stir. "It was bizarre. One minute I was walking through the woods, and the next, I was standing in front of Devereaux. I couldn't figure out why my legs wouldn't move when I tried to get away from him. And then I was staring at the world from inside a glass cage and feeling real small. But I didn't make it easy for the bastard. I fought like hell." A grin appeared on his face. "Gave him a taste of his own medicine and started to pull him inside that bottle with me." His smile vanished. "Guess who won?"

"Well, you're safe now." I shook my head. "And here I thought it was dragon's tears making everyone lose their minds around town." Until Keith Barnes opened my eyes. "My dishwasher almost killed me in the alley the other night."

Patrick gave me a funny look. "Mutt?"

"Yeah, Mutt. And Keith Barnes beat a man senseless behind the pharmacy."

Patrick snorted a laugh. "DT will make you horny as hell, but it won't turn you into a killer."

"I realize that now." It had been Atticus all along. "I get the part about people acting strange after falling under the influence of his dark magic, but why possess people? You, Mutt, Keith?"

"Like I said, that man's the devil. He likes to play with his prey. Wreak as much havoc as possible along the way." He shuddered. "I don't even want to think about what I might have done to you if that bastard hadn't sucked me into that bottle."

"You wouldn't have hurt me," I said. "You're not capable of it."

"That's what you said about Mutt." Candy got up and walked toward the door. "Enough talk. We need to eradicate that rat."

"Where are you going?" I asked.

"To call in the exterminators."

Patrick threw the blanket off and swung his legs over the side of the bed. "I'm in."

"Uh... no you're not." I tried to stop him from standing up, but he wasn't having it.

"Out of my way, woman. I need to get me some revenge."

He needed to get some clothes on first.

Candy went back into her super-secret room and threw a robe at him when she came back out. "You can wear this, Superman."

He stood up and tried it on, inspecting himself in the mirror as he smoothed his hair into place. "I believe I can rock this." The fluffy pink robe only came halfway down his thighs and barely covered his privates.

When we followed Candy back into the shop, I looked around for Tucker, who'd been gone for a while. She was in the corner running her hands up and down the stripper pole.

"You can hop on it if you want," Candy said to her.

Tucker gave her a curious look. "Are you a dancer?"

Candy smiled unabashedly. "Baby, I was a stripper and proud of it. But back in the day, you could look but not touch, if you know what I mean."

Tucker nodded. "I know exactly what you mean. You can't even serve drinks in a stripper bar anymore without the clientele thinking they can put their hands all over you."

"Not at one of my shows. Touching earned you a broken jaw, if you were lucky." A playful grin slid up her face. "Ever heard of Candy Cane?"

Tucker turned around and put her hands on her hips. "Shut up! You were Candy Cane?"

"One of the best in Atlanta. But I'm retired now."

Tucker snorted. "*The* best. You were a legend."

"I believe I still am."

Tucker dropped her arms to her sides and shook her head. "I can't believe I'm standing in the same room with Candy *freaking* Cane." She looked down at her hands. "And I just rubbed your pole."

Patrick leaned into me. "Is that girl right in the head?"

I motioned her over to us. "Tucker, this is my friend Patrick." It was only right to introduce them, since she'd just seen him buck naked.

"*Best* friend," he corrected. "It's nice to meet you."

Now that we had that taken care of, I needed to rein in the conversation before it veered off again. "About these exterminators you mentioned," I said to Candy.

She pulled out her phone and dialed a number. Without a greeting, she listened to someone on the other end for a minute, throwing in a *mm-hmm* every now and then. "We can talk about your man troubles later," she eventually said. "Right now, we have a problem. An emergency. How fast can you get here?"

TWENTY-NINE

Within the hour, there was a knock at the back door. The one to the alley. The lights in the shop flickered and nearly went out as Candy went down the hallway to answer it. A minute later, she returned with four women.

The Squad.

The moment they entered the room, I could feel the pressure drop. The oxygen grew thinner. Everything about the witches was dark, from their clothing to their mere presence. There wasn't a hint of color on any of them, except for Desiree Dubois's cherry-red hair and brightly painted mouth. Her lipstick bled into the vertical lines of her lips, giving them a feathered look.

I forced a smile when Mia Winston locked eyes with me.

A grin slowly spread across her face, revealing a set of horsey teeth. "Charley Underwood!"

She offered me the back of her hand, but when I reached out awkwardly to shake it, she pulled it away, grimacing.

Her sister, Fay, gazed at me with a weak smile. "I'm so sorry to hear about your mother. Such a tragic loss for the witches of Crimson."

Candy leveled her eyes on the witch. "You're a little late with your condolences, you old fool. It's been two years."

"Who are you calling old?"

Candy ignored her and got on with it. "Like I said on the phone, we have a problem."

Desiree sized up Patrick in his pink robe. "We certainly do. And he's a vampire to boot."

Patrick lowered his chin. "I beg your pardon?" After inspecting her conservative black dress that ran from her chin to her feet, he wagged his finger up and down. "*That* should be a felony."

Katherine Belltower, the voice of reason in the bunch, reined in the conversation—and probably saved Patrick from getting his ass handed to him. "What is this problem?"

Candy grabbed a couple of folding chairs and set them in the middle of the room. "Anyone want to take a seat?"

Patrick glanced down at the skimpy robe. "I'm good."

"There's an intruder in Crimson," Candy announced. None of them seemed remotely concerned. "A demon, or maybe even the devil himself. We don't know what the hell he is."

That got them buzzing.

Mia glanced at her fellow witches and let out a curt chuckle. "I don't like to say I told you so, but I told you so."

"What are you talking about?" I asked.

"The obvious," the witch said. "Something came through the hills like a hurricane a week ago. I felt it in my bones. Something dangerous." Her teeth clenched. "Something that reeked of sulfur."

"With a bit of rot mixed in," Fay added. "All the lilies in the garden died within hours."

"That's exactly what I smelled in Atticus's basement." Rotten eggs. The unmistakable smell of sulfur.

Candy gave me a look. "You didn't mention that."

"I didn't know I had to. I just thought it was the stinky basement." I looked back at Mia. "A week ago, you say?"

She shrugged. "Thereabouts. Maybe two. What does it matter? He's here, isn't he?"

"How do you know it's a *he*?"

Without answering my question, she lifted her nose into the air and sniffed. She came closer to me and sniffed again, her eyes growing wider as a grimace crossed her face. "You've been with this devil?"

Candy stepped between us before the witch could do something unpredictable. "Charley broke into the man's basement tonight to rescue *him*." She nodded to Patrick. "That's why you're smelling sulfur."

Mia eyed Patrick. "Him? Why?"

"What difference does it make?" I jumped ahead to move the conversation along. "His name is Atticus Devereaux, and he's come to Crimson to steal souls. Patrick was one of his victims, but I managed to get us both out of that basement alive." I suddenly felt a twinge of guilt for not grabbing the rest of the bottles, but I had enough trouble climbing through that window holding onto just one.

The sisters stared at each other for a moment, having some sort of silent conversation. Then Mia turned a questioning gaze on me. "And you know this how?"

I grabbed the bottle from the display case. "Because he sucked Patrick into this. People have been disappearing left and right around town, and every one of them is sitting on a shelf in a hidden room under Morceau's basement."

"Morceau? The new restaurant in town?"

Fay's eyes lit up. "I've been meaning to dine there."

"I wouldn't advise it," Candy said, chuckling.

"Why not?"

"Atticus Devereaux is the proprietor of Morceau," I said.

"He's poisoning people with the food over there. All the chaos around town is his doing."

Katherine's eyes narrowed. "Why bother? Why not just collect what he came for and move on?"

"Because that son of a bitch is twisted," Patrick said. "He gets off on it. Not to mention the fact that he's pure evil." His face suddenly took on an ashen look as he nodded to the hallway. "You got anything to drink in that playroom back there? I could use a stiff one."

"You need to hush about that room," Candy muttered to him.

The witches all sported knowing grins.

I snapped my fingers to salvage the conversation before it took another detour. It was costing us time. "Can we get back to business? Devereaux is probably going to speed up his grand finale now that he's been exposed. I don't know what he has planned, but I can guarantee you it involves more violence."

"Violence?" Patrick huffed. "That man's gonna unleash mayhem on this town."

"Then let's figure out how to stop him."

Tucker backed up toward the front door. "Well, it's been an exhausting night. I think I'll leave and let you guys discuss your plan in private."

Desiree slid her eyes sideways to the girl.

"Where do you think you're going?"

"Um... home?"

The witch let out a strange laugh that made the hair on the back of my neck stand on end. "It's too late for that, dear. You're invested now."

Tucker shook her head. "No. I don't think I am."

"Sit! And will you stop looking at me like I'm planning to eat you." Desiree's lips quirked. "I only eat children."

She flinched at the witch's bark.

I wanted to tell Desiree to shut her piehole, but it would only aggravate the situation and put a target on my back.

Candy took care of it for me. "Will you stop terrifying the girl. If she wants to leave, she can leave."

When Tucker walked toward one of the chairs, I gave her an out. "I don't think you should walk home alone, but you can wait upstairs until we're done down here if you'd prefer."

"It's okay. I'll stay." She sat down and smiled awkwardly, looking about as comfortable as a puppy getting caught piddling on the floor.

Candy gave her a commiserative smile. "That's fine, sugar, but just keep in mind that what happens at the Cauldron stays at the Cauldron. Got it?"

Tucker just stared at her and nodded.

"Good. Now, let's figure out how to kill this thing."

"Kill?" I'd thought about it, but hearing the words uttered out loud made it feel awfully real.

"What did you think we were going to do?" Candy said. "Pat him on the ass and shove him across the county line? The only way to get rid of a devil like Atticus Devereaux is to kill him."

Patrick glanced at that bottle on the display case. "You can count me in."

She took my chin in her hand and looked me in the eye. "I hope you've got the stomach for this, honey, because you're the one who's going to do it."

"Me?" I wasn't a killer. I couldn't even kill a bug. Not even one of those nasty Palmetto bugs that were nothing but giant flying cockroaches. "How am I supposed to do that?"

Candy let out a heavy sigh. "You really don't have a clue, do you?" She walked around the display case and reached inside. As she straightened back up, she threw something. I caught the glint of a steel blade as it flew across the room straight toward me.

Gasping from a painful surge of adrenaline, I darted out of the way like it was second nature. My hand flew up as the blade whizzed past my ear, stopping it in midair with a blue light shooting from my fingertips.

Tucker nearly knocked her chair over when she abruptly stood up, and Patrick just stood there gawking at me.

The grin on Candy's face vanished when the blade began to spin, reversed, and flew back toward her. It sailed over her head as she ducked, embedding itself into the wall behind her. She straightened back up and stared at it for a moment before looking back at me. "Touché."

The Squad clapped, beaming with pride.

"Well done, dear," Katherine said.

Candy's brows lifted in question. "Me or Charley?"

I gaped at her, wondering if she'd finally lost her mind. "Are you insane?"

"It's time for you to wake up, Charley. No more training wheels."

"You could have killed me!"

She waved me off. "I knew that knife wouldn't have touched a hair on your head." Then she glanced at the blade embedded in the wall behind her. "I didn't expect that, though."

Now I knew she'd lost her mind. "And if it did?"

"Then I guess we'd be cleaning up a mess." A brief laugh escaped her lips, but after seeing the hurt look in my eyes, she came over to me. "Now, you listen to me. You've got just as much magic in you as your mama had, and it's time you learned how to use it properly."

I shook my head. "She told me I wasn't like her."

"Your mama was wrong."

"She was never wrong." My mother discouraged me from exploring any gifts I might have gotten from her. She said I didn't have enough to brag about. "If I had a trace of her power, she would have warned me and taught me how to use it."

"Honey, Delia was trying to protect you. She was afraid for you."

I took a step away from her. "Afraid of what?"

"Afraid you'd do more damage than good. She wanted you to mature a little. Grow into it gradually before finding out."

My brow furrowed. "Mature? What did she think I would do? Panic?"

"You mean like you are now?" She glanced down at my hands. "Look at you."

They were vibrating, and a glow was spreading from my fingers all the way up to my elbows. "Jesus!"

"That ain't Jesus, honey. You've got napalm in those hands." She glanced at the clock on the wall. "If we get started now, we might be able to get you ready for tonight."

Everyone was staring at me when I looked around the room. "Ready for what?"

"Ready to take down Atticus Devereaux."

I laughed nervously. "I barely made it out of that basement. Devereaux let me walk out of there, so I doubt he sees me as a threat."

"That's exactly why it has to be you," she said. "The smug bastard will have his guard down."

"But I'm not a threat." I held my shaking hands out. "I don't have a clue how to use any of this."

Candy got a wicked smile on her face. "Give us a few hours, and not only will you be a bona fide threat, you'll have him begging for mercy. But you need to get close to him to work your magic."

"I still say we go in there together. Seven against one are much better odds."

Candy's gaze grew more sympathetic. "I don't think you understand, Charley. I just figured it out myself when you showed up here tonight and told me what happened."

"Figured out what?" My heart was starting to pound from the ominous feeling I was getting.

"Now that we know what he's up to, he'll never let me or the other witches near him." She nodded to the Squad. "But he'll let you in because it's you he wants. I bet he's over there right now waiting for you to show up again. It's all part of his power play." Seeing the confused look on my face, she continued with her theory. "Why do you think he set up shop in that dump across the street from the Stag? There are plenty of better spots he could have chosen. The man's been practically stalking you since he came to town, but his dark magic is useless on a witch." She shrugged. "We both ate his food, didn't we? He needs to find another way to control you. Get you into one of those bottles."

"You're the daughter of Delia Underwood," Katherine said.

Candy brushed my hair off my shoulder. "Now, that's a real prize. The perfect soul to steal. But you're going over there tonight to turn the tables. To show him how special you really are. You're going to catch that devil with his own trap."

THIRTY

I was so nervous I wanted to puke. As I stood behind the bar looking across the street, all I could think about was how I was going to keep Atticus distracted long enough for the witches to build an incantation to force him into one of his own bottles. Ironically, the one with my name on it.

"Charley!"

Beau was staring at me when I turned around. "What?"

"I called your name three times. What's so interesting out there?"

Glancing back at the restaurant, I resisted the urge to say goodbye to Beau. I was about to become a sacrificial lamb to save Crimson, so I'd probably never get another chance. But I was being pessimistic, and negative thinking was dangerous when mixed with magic. If this was going to work, I needed to snap out of it and have some faith.

I let go of the rag I was twisting in my hands and got back to work. "Nothing."

"Nothing, huh?" He glanced at Tucker at the other end of the bar. "What the hell is wrong with you women tonight?

Tucker's been screwing up orders since she got here. How do you mess up a beer?"

Tucker and I were both nervous. Her job was to stay quiet and act like it was just another Sunday night, and I was trying to do the same. But Dog kept glancing at me through the order window like he sensed something was up.

I looked at the time. In twenty minutes, I was supposed to be across the street chatting up Devereaux so he didn't sense it coming. Sense the spell that was supposed to trap him so he could be disposed of properly. Like hazardous waste material.

"I'll be back in a few minutes." I said it loud enough for Dog to hear. "I want to see if Sebastian decided to show up again so I can feed him."

"I thought you said you weren't going to feed him anymore?"

"Well, I'm not letting him go hungry."

Before he could start a debate about why I should or shouldn't feed someone else's cat, I disappeared down the hallway. I had a few minutes to kill, but it was now or never. I took a few calming breaths and slipped out the back door, thankful that Sebastian wasn't actually out there so I didn't have to go back in and fill his bowl.

It was quiet enough in the alley to hear the blood rushing through my ears and a little too dark for my liking. I still had a vampire gunning for me.

Halfway to the corner of the building, a figure stepped out in front of me. I startled, and my back hit the wall. "Are you trying to give me a heart attack?"

Samuel flashed a million-dollar smile and leaned into me with his hand pressed against the wall. "Sorry. Scaring you wasn't the reaction I was going for."

I found myself caught in his gaze. Clearing my throat, I pulled a serious face. "Is there something I can help you with?"

Is there something I can help you with?

Dog was right. I was getting rusty at this.

His gaze grew more intense. "I thought I'd stop by and we could have a drink together."

Although I was thoroughly enjoying his intoxicating scent and mesmerizing eyes, I was also acutely aware of where I had to be in a few minutes. "I'd love to, but I'll have to take a raincheck."

His brows pulled tightly together as he stepped back. "A raincheck? Really?"

I don't think he was used to working this hard at his game. "Yeah. I'm down a bartender, so I'm working tonight. In fact, I need to get back in there."

He pointed to the corner of the building. "But you were walking that way."

"I just needed some fresh air." He wasn't making this easy, and I was on a strict clock. I slipped past him and headed back toward the door. Sniffing deeply, I reached for the handle. "Now I have some. I'm going back to work now, if that's okay with you."

He cocked his head. "Have I misread what's going on here?"

Well, that was a little presumptuous, but there was definitely something going on between us. I just didn't have time to pursue it at the moment because I had to kill my neighbor in a few minutes.

"Look. I like you, but I have a bar to run. Why don't you stop by tomorrow night for that drink?"

He stared at me for a moment before disappearing around the corner of the building without another word. I had a feeling my best chance of seeing him again involved luring a cat, but right now, time was ticking.

After going back inside, I waited a minute and cracked the door to make sure he was gone. Convinced it was all clear, I got out of there before Dog came looking for me. Then I took the long way around the block to the restaurant so no one saw me crossing the street.

It was ten o'clock on the nose when I walked into Morceau, the chimes on the door announcing me. The lights were dim, and I could sense someone was watching me. The place was also empty, like Atticus had cleared it out knowing a big showdown was to come.

The chimes on the door sounded again, but when I turned around, no one was there. My eyes traveled up to the symbols above the entrance. The chalking marks, as Dog had called them. They suddenly seemed familiar.

"Hello?"

No one answered.

I could smell something cooking, so I walked toward the kitchen, noting the strange vibrations in the room. Either the witches were hard at work on their incantation, or Atticus was cooking up more than just food back there. Either way, something otherworldly was in the air.

He was standing at the huge butcher block with his back to me when I walked inside, whistling that same tune I'd heard in the hidden room last night. He raised his arm, a meat cleaver gripped tightly in his hand. The blade came down with force, spattering blood on the wall.

I flinched, and the whistling stopped.

With his back still turned to me, he set the knife down and wiped his hands with a towel. "Hungry?"

Ignoring his attempt to distract me, I came right out with it. "I know why you're here." I had to suppress my morbid curiosity to try to see what he was chopping.

"I imagine you do. Your friend Patrick must have been quite talkative."

Stepping to the side to give me a clear view of a pile of organ meat and hooves, he turned around and followed my gaze. "Americans tend to waste the best parts. The heart is particularly good for persuasion magic. But not with you, little birdie. My magic can't seem to get past your lips."

"A bite or two got past them. I just didn't care for it."

The vibrations picked up, and I noticed a slight twitch in his right eye.

I shrugged, attempting my own distraction. "Looks like your magic doesn't work on me. Better luck next time."

His pupils contracted and then expanded almost as wide as his irises. I thought he was going to burst into a rage. Instead, he nodded thoughtfully and walked over to the counter, leaving me to stare at the bloody parts until he returned with a bottle and set it down on the butcher block. It was the one with my name on it.

"Why did you let me walk out of the basement last night?"

"Because it will be much more satisfying if you surrender to me. Surrender your will." He glanced at the bottle. "I'll leave town tonight, restaurant and all. The fine citizens of Crimson will be free." He removed the stopper and set it down next to the heart. "All you have to do is choose to come with me."

The room suddenly felt smaller. Like the walls were closing in. The spell was getting stronger, and that bottle was about to have his name on it instead of mine.

"Why me?" More distractions. "I'm sure there were plenty of witches along the Eastern Seaboard you could have picked up on your way down here."

His lips rose into a grin as he wagged his finger. "Ah, but you're wrong. None of them were quite like you. You're special, Charley."

"I know. I've been told I'm a real catch."

I heard footsteps behind me. When I turned around, I had to stifle a gasp. Ian Masterson strolled past me toward Atticus, the gold pendant around his neck shining like a beacon. Suddenly that same sigil was around Atticus's neck. It matched one of the symbols above the front door. The one in the center. Ian had been working with Atticus the whole time.

"Yes, you are a catch. A witch from a powerful bloodline with untapped magic." Atticus snapped his fingers, and the rest of Ian's vampires appeared in the kitchen. "You're also the only one who comes with a gold mine. A blood co-op."

"The co-op?" I glanced around the elaborate kitchen. "It's petty cash to someone like you."

"You think small, Charley. Great empires have been built on less. Of course, I'll have to expand the business outside of Crimson and multiply it by a thousand."

"*We'll* have to expand it," Ian corrected.

The look on Atticus's face shut him up. It was clear who was in charge here. Ian must have been quaking in his boots when his boss caught him stirring up trouble at the Stag the other night.

"So, you two are planning to take vampire blood to the masses." Something told me Ian was working both ends just in case Atticus's plan failed. "Did your partner tell you he's been trying to extort me?"

Atticus shot Ian a lethal look but said nothing.

"I didn't think so." I was also wondering about all those bottles in that room under the basement. "I don't get it. Why take all the others if I'm the one you really want?"

His smile returned. "I feed the good citizens of Crimson, and in return they feed me."

He was awfully forthcoming with information, but I guess I was right about him not thinking I was a threat. In his mind I was a foregone conclusion.

"But I have no intention of eating you, Charley."

I chortled. "What a relief."

He glanced at the bottle again. "Not the daughter of Delia Underwood. I'm going to savor you slowly."

More footsteps came from behind me, and Samuel walked

into the kitchen. "That's a vile image I won't get out of my head anytime soon."

"One of yours?" Atticus asked Ian.

Samuel's face turned to stone. "You insult me, sir."

"You followed me?" I muttered.

"You think I bought it when you asked me for a raincheck? Please. That's not what the rest of you was saying." He nodded to Ian and his vampires. "Besides, I saw that motley crew creeping around the square and decided to see what they were up to."

"Watch your mouth," Ian growled. "Your wolves aren't here to save you."

Samuel sneered and reached for his pocket. For that magic bullet. "And you'll be speaking through your ass when I blow your mouth to smithereens."

It was probably another bluff, but he was throwing a wrench into the plan. "This is my fight," I said to Samuel. "Back off."

He took a deep breath with his eyes still glued to Masterson's. "Fine." Leaning his shoulder against the wall, he crossed his arms. "Have at it, but I'm staying."

The energy in the room picked up again, tightening around the kitchen like a rubber band, forcing the pots and pans hanging from the ceiling rack to sway inward at an unnatural angle ever so slightly. It was just enough to tip off Atticus to the spell. *If* he noticed it.

Don't look up.

No luck. He glanced up at them, his face filling with rage. Or was it fear? He grabbed the bottle and shoved it toward me. "I'll destroy every man, woman, and child in this town. Make your choice!"

I closed my eyes and focused, just as Candy and the Squad had trained me to do. A brilliant blue light filled my mind, connecting me to the ring of power they were building back at the Cauldron. When I reopened them, the light was still there, circling the perimeter of the kitchen, giving me hope that I wasn't about to be sucked into that bottle.

Atticus signaled to Ian. The vampire lunged at me, but Samuel stepped in his path and wrapped his hand around Ian's throat, squeezing so tightly I thought he'd sever the vampire's head.

The other vampires charged, and Samuel found himself pinned against the wall.

I focused harder, directing the energy clockwise, moving it faster. It sped up until the walls became a blur and a sphere had formed around us. It cocooned us in blue light, trapping me in the eye of the storm with Atticus.

His eyes darkened with rage as he looked up at the spinning hurricane. "What are you doing? You'll destroy us both!"

Sticking to the plan, I closed my eyes and blocked out my fear, continuing to build the energy field. In the distance, I could hear the howl of wolves. The pack. But nothing would get past the sphere. It was just me and Atticus now. Only one of us would walk away.

My eyes flew open when I felt Atticus's hands around my neck. His dark eyes bored into mine as he cut off my ability to breathe, shaking me so hard I nearly lost consciousness. With a mental thrust, I released the energy, gasping as it blasted outward and took half the kitchen walls and roof with it. Atticus flew backward, and I could breathe again.

The energy suddenly reversed, circling back around us, keeping the wolves and vampires at bay. When I climbed to my feet, Atticus was still very much alive.

He came toward me, surveying the destruction. "I can always build another restaurant, Charley." A wicked grin edged up his face. "Give me a week, tops."

It was time for plan B.

I glanced at the bottle that was still miraculously gripped in his hand. "If you honor your agreement to leave Crimson, you can have me. That's the deal, or we can do this all over again until one of us doesn't get back up."

"You have my word." He set the bottle on the floor between us. "Whenever you're ready."

I nodded, saying a silent Hail Mary as I closed my eyes and tapped into the astral mind of the Squad.

Now!

I took an involuntary step forward, like someone had shoved me. Then I felt a powerful pull. Suddenly I was flying, seeing the world slip away as my essence started to vacuum into the bottle. The plan was failing.

Or the witches couldn't hear me.

Panicking, I screamed, "*Now!*"

A voice suddenly filled my head. A voice I knew as well as my own.

Grab hold of him, Charley!

It was my mother.

Pull him with you!

I reached for Atticus, remembering what Patrick had said about fighting back. But my lifeline slipped away as he stepped out of reach. Then I heard my mother's voice come roaring back.

Don't you dare give up!

Mustering every ounce of strength I had, I broke away from the force pulling me for a mere second and managed to grab Atticus's wrist, clamping my fingers around it like a vise. And then it was over. A second ago, I could hear the world around me, but now all I had was a distorted view of it from the inside of a glass bubble.

Get out!

I closed my eyes and pictured myself floating toward the sky. I kept moving until sound returned and dust filled my lungs. When I got the nerve to reopen my eyes, I was standing in the destroyed kitchen, looking down at a plume of smoke starting to emerge from the bottle near my feet. Atticus was escaping.

"No, you don't." Snatching it off the floor, I pressed my palm over the top. A painful burning sensation spread through my hand as I frantically searched for the stopper. I spotted it on the floor a few feet away and stuffed it into the bottle as far as it would go, careful not to drop the damn thing when Atticus decided to have a meltdown inside.

For good measure, I grabbed that tape I'd seen in the drawer and used it to secure the stopper to the neck. Then I set the bottle on the counter and bent down to glare through the glass. "Let's see you get through duct tape, asshole."

I leaned against the counter as the last bit of energy dissipated around me, and Dog came running in. "Better late than never," I said.

He raised a brow. "How were we supposed to get past that storm you created?"

Samuel was right behind him. "I guess you didn't need our help after all." He grinned. "You're a beast, Charley."

A weak laugh slipped from my mouth as I looked at the bottle, barely believing I'd actually pulled it off. Trying to comprehend that the mist whirling around inside was the cause of all the misery in this town. "It's over. I don't think Atticus will be a problem anymore."

The three of us looked up at where the back wall used to stand when Ian came around the corner with his crew. He halted when he saw me and then locked eyes with Samuel. But instead of starting trouble again, he spit out a few choice words. Then he spotted the bottle quivering on the counter. "Is that Devereaux?"

"Well, it isn't me in there."

He groaned and ripped the sigil from his neck, tossing it on the counter where it came to a stop next to the bottle. "Fuck this." Then he trained his eyes on me again. "I'd suggest you stay on your side of the fence." After snapping his fingers for his vampires to fall in line, he threw me a final glance over his shoulder. "Have a nice life, Charley."

Dog growled back at him. "You too, bloodsucker. No offense," he said to Samuel.

"None taken, mongrel," Samuel replied.

While their bromance bloomed, I grabbed the bottle and held it up to the light to examine the tumultuous black mist swirling inside. "I just made a citizen's arrest, so I better go hand him over to the authorities before he finds a way out of there. I'll see you guys back at the Stag later."

They looked at each other but didn't try to stop me. Ian Masterson had just called a truce—I thought—so I was free to go wherever I wanted without an escort. But after what I'd just done, I had a feeling that truce was just a way for those vampires to save face. The playing field had been leveled.

"Hey," I said to Ian before he disappeared around the corner.

He stopped but didn't turn around. "What is it now?"

"Just to clear the record, did you attack Patrice Henderson? The girl they found tied to a tree in the woods?"

He turned around to face me. "I hear she liked to spend time at the Beast, but it wasn't me, darlin'.'"

I guess we'd never know for sure. It could have been one of Devereaux's victims who tore her neck open. Look what Mutt did. It could have also been a rogue vampire, which meant we had another problem on our hands. But I'd worry about that later. Right now, I needed to get that bottle to the Cauldron. Then we'd take care of Atticus Devereaux once and for all.

THIRTY-ONE

Candy was lounging in one of the chairs in front of the shop when I walked down the sidewalk. She was smoking a cigarette, but this time I didn't bother to rag her about it.

"Did you get an eyeful?" I asked.

She took a steady drag. "Sure did. I was just out here enjoying the fireworks."

"By the way, thanks for the backup." I shouldn't have said it, but they did fail me tonight.

"You didn't need it. You did just fine with a little help from your mama."

"How'd you know?"

She just smiled, snuffing the cigarette out in the ashtray on the table. "I'll give them up again in the morning."

I held up the bottle. "What do we do with this? Burn it?"

Her eyes lit up. "Well, would you look at that. We got us a genie in a bottle." She took it from me and examined my handiwork. "Good old duct tape. One of man's brilliant inventions."

Actually, it was invented by a woman.

"I didn't trust him not to blow the stopper out." I gave the bottle a curious look. "What do you think Atticus is?"

She squinted at the glass. "Who knows. I can tell you this much, though. He'll make a nice addition to my collection."

"Your collection? Do I dare ask?"

"Come on. Let's get inside before those vampires show up."

I chuckled. "They won't be bothering us anymore. I'll tell you about it after we take care of that bottle."

The place was empty when we walked inside. "Where is everyone?"

"Patrick's upstairs in your bed. I gave him a little something to knock him out because he kept trying to *help*. That man's got some stupid energy when he's nervous, and that was the last thing we needed tonight. He'll be out until morning. I made sure of that," she added. "You can either sleep with him or climb in bed with me."

That was Patrick. He could suck the air right out of the room at times.

"Where's the Squad?" I wanted to thank them.

"They left as soon as the building blew. I think holding up all that energy wore them out." She winked at me. "But it was when your mama showed up that they decided to leave."

So, Candy did know what had happened.

She crossed her fingers. "Your mama and I were like this, and I could feel her tonight. It was like she was standing right next to both of us."

When she saw tears welling up in my eyes, she grabbed my hand and pulled me toward the hallway. "Let's get this nonsense over with before the dam bursts."

She pulled her keys out and unlocked the mystery door inside the small bedroom. It wasn't exactly a closet. It was more like a tiny room, dimly lit even with the light on.

"Why is it so dark in here?"

She nodded to the shelves I'd gotten a glimpse of last night. "Because of all this." There were boxes, cloth bags, and bottles arranged evenly along the shelves. Some of the vessels had symbols painted on them, but others were unmarked. There were also several mason jars with objects inside. "It's best to keep them in the dark. Disoriented. The light gets them all stirred up."

"Them?"

Without answering my question, she set the bottle on the middle shelf, positioning it between a jar with something black floating inside and a box sealed with red wax. "He'll be in good company right there."

"That's it? I thought you said we were going to kill him?"

She looked at me sideways. "Oh, honey. This is much worse than death."

"What exactly is this room?"

She lit another cigarette and took a drag, exhaling the smoke over the bottle. "Let's just say it's where bad things go to serve their time." She leaned closer to it and grinned. "The devil came down to Georgia to play a dangerous game." Then she snuffed the cigarette out against the glass, sending the mist inside into a chaotic whirl. "But the bastard lost."

* * *

Beau leaned over the bar and stared out the window. "I wonder how long it'll take for them to clean up that mess over there."

I looked at what remained of Morceau across the street. "Technically Atticus still owns the property, so he's got thirty days to comply before the town can do anything." Which would be difficult from that shelf in Candy's back room. If he didn't have it demolished and cleaned up himself, the taxpayers of Crimson would get stuck with the bill. But I didn't feel an ounce of guilt. The alternative would have been much more costly.

As soon as Atticus disappeared, most of the people in town came to their senses and stopped being major assholes to one another. Of course, there'd been bigots in town long before Devereaux arrived. But for now, most of them had toned it down. Crimson was basically back to normal. Even the co-op was back up and running, with vampires feeling safe to donate again. And the rest of Atticus's victims? It took a little digging through the rubble, but we managed to retrieve the bottles from that room under the basement and set them all free. Most of them were coping, but a few were iffy, having been sucked nearly dry by Atticus. Only time would tell.

Tucker was smiling at something when I looked over at her. When I followed her gaze, I saw Samuel approaching the door.

He walked in and took a seat at the bar. "Charley."

"Samuel."

His blue eyes locked on mine. "How about that raincheck?"

We'd been trying to resume that conversation for a while now, but something always got in the way, and tonight was no different. "It's kind of busy tonight."

He frowned. "Please."

I poured him a glass of the most expensive scotch we had and set it down in front of him. "It's on the house." Then I leaned my elbows on the bar to get a little closer. "Some of us have to work for a living." Which reminded me to find out how he paid his bills. I didn't really know anything about him, which was why I needed to make time for that raincheck.

I straightened back up and walked down the bar. "I'm off tomorrow night," I said without turning around. When I did finally glance over my shoulder, his glass was empty and he was gone.

Beau grinned at me when I nearly collided with him. "What are you smiling at?"

Before he could answer, we both looked down and saw Tucker crouched on the floor. She was pressed against the bar, and her eyes were fixed up at the mirror behind it.

There was a slight shake of her head as the front door

opened and two men walked in. Two very large men with fancy suits that didn't come from a store around here. I'd certainly never seen either of them before.

Beau was about to say something to her, but I elbowed him.

"What did you do that for?"

"Shut up." I went over to them when they walked up to the bar. "What can I get you?"

The one with jet-black hair pulled a picture out of his pocket. "We're looking for someone." There was a young woman with short red hair in the photo. Maroon red from a bottle. But her blue eyes gave her away. "We think she may have recently shown up around here. Have you seen her?"

I gently stepped on Beau's foot when he looked over my shoulder at the picture. He got the message quickly. "Nope."

"I haven't seen her either," I said. "Why are you looking for her? Is she wanted for something?"

He put it back in his pocket, keeping his eyes on mine for a few seconds before handing me a business card. "Call me if you see her. I'll make it worth your while."

The card had a glossy black finish with KITTY CAT LOUNGE printed in gold letters across the front.

The other guy wandered down to the end of the bar, dangerously close to the edge. He was only about four feet away from where Tucker was hiding on the other side.

He started to walk around, but Dog had come from the kitchen and stepped in front of him. "Employees only back here." The guy was big, but Dog was bigger and had the advantage of being a wolf. He could have easily taken them both down.

The guy smirked, stepping back with his palms up. "Sorry. My mistake."

"If you're not going to order a drink," I said, praying they didn't sit down and decide to have one, "I'll have to ask you to leave." I smiled pleasantly. "Nothing personal. It's just bar policy."

The men glanced at each other before heading toward the door, but something told me it wasn't the last time we'd be seeing them. They climbed into a black SUV and drove off, slowing down as they circled the square and passed the half-standing restaurant across the street on their way back out of town.

When the coast was clear, I motioned for Tucker to follow me into the kitchen. Dog joined us. "That was you in the picture," I said to her. "Who were those men?"

Tucker lowered her eyes. "They're from Atlanta."

"Yeah, I know." I showed her the business card. "It's on the back. Tucker, why were those men sent to find you?"

She slowly raised her eyes up to mine. "They weren't sent to find me, Charley. They were sent to kill me."

Dear reader,

Thank you for reading Bloodlust Blues. I hope you enjoyed meeting Charley and crew as much as I enjoyed writing about them. But this is just the beginning. I can't wait to share more of the Crimson world with you! You can stay up to date with my latest releases by signing up at the link below. Your email address will never be shared and you can unsubscribe at any time.

www.secondskybooks.com/luanne_bennett

The best way to support an author is to spread the word and leave a brief review. It really does make a difference, and I appreciate every one of them. Just a sentence or two is all it takes.

I love hearing from readers. Get in touch on my social media or website. And don't forget to follow me!

www.luannebennett.com

facebook.com/LuanneBennettBooks

instagram.com/luannebennettbooks

bookbub.com/authors/luanne-bennett

goodreads.com/lbennett14

ACKNOWLEDGMENTS

I wanted to take a moment to thank the team at Second Sky and Bookouture. Everyone has been gracious, and it's been a pleasure. And a special thanks to my patient editor, Jack Renninson, for pushing me to make the story even better, especially during structural edits. They can be brutal for even the best writer.

As always, thanks to all my friends and family for listening to me go on and on about deadlines and edits. All the gripes of having one of the best jobs in the world. I promise I'll quit doing that someday.

And of course, to my readers, many of which have stuck with me from day one. Never leave, because without you the books would be pointless.

PUBLISHING TEAM

Turning a manuscript into a book requires the efforts of many people. The publishing team at Bookouture would like to acknowledge everyone who contributed to this publication.

Audio
Alba Proko
Sinead O'Connor
Melissa Tran

Commercial
Lauren Morrissette
Jil Thielen
Imogen Allport

Cover design
Damonza.com

Data and analysis
Mark Alder
Mohamed Bussuri

Editorial
Jack Renninson
Melissa Tran

Copyeditor

Rhian McKay

Proofreader

Maddy Newquist

Marketing

Alex Crow
Melanie Price
Occy Carr
Cíara Rosney

Operations and distribution

Marina Valles
Stephanie Straub

Production

Hannah Snetsinger
Mandy Kullar
Jen Shannon

Publicity

Kim Nash
Noelle Holten
Myrto Kalavrezou
Jess Readett
Sarah Hardy

Rights and contracts

Peta Nightingale
Richard King
Saidah Graham

9 781835 252413